Maureen Lipman was [...] drama at LAMDA. Her work on TV and film have earned her BAFTA nominations for AGONY, OUTSIDE EDGE, ROLLING HOME, ABSURD PERSON SINGULAR and EDUCATING RITA. Her stage work in MESSIAH, OUTSIDE EDGE and the musical WONDERFUL TOWN won her nominations for the Laurence Olivier Award and the Award itself for SEE HOW THEY RUN, for which she also won the Variety Club Award in 1985. In 1987 she received the same Award for WONDERFUL TOWN.

Her most recent TV appearances were in SHIFT-WORK, THE LITTLE PRINCESS and EXCLUSIVE YARNS, and she is currently working on RE: JOYCE, a one-woman show about Joyce Grenfell, and a second series of ALL AT NO. 20 for Thames TV.

She also writes a monthly column in OPTIONS magazine. She is married to the playwright, Jack Rosenthal; their continuing association has produced Amy, 13, and Adam, 11, who are open to offers from shabby tabloids to reveal the dross behind the schloss.

Also by Maureen Lipman and available from Futura:

HOW WAS IT FOR YOU?

MAUREEN LIPMAN

Something To Fall Back On

Futura

A Futura Book

Copyright © 1987 Mistlodge Ltd

First published in Great Britain in 1987 by
Robson Books Ltd

This edition published in 1988 by
Futura Publications
A Division of
Macdonald & Co (Publishers) Ltd
Reprinted 1988

ISBN 0 7088 3931 2

Typeset in Palatino by Fleet Graphics, Enfield, Middx.

Printed in Great Britain by
Hazell Watson & Viney Limited
Member of BPCC plc
Aylesbury, Bucks, England

Futura Publications
A Division of
Macdonald & Co (Publishers) Ltd
66–73 Shoe Lane
London EC4P 4AB
A member of Maxwell Pergamon Publishing Corporation plc

Contents

4 MUSICAL CHORES

5 HOME, HOME AND DERANGED

DEDICATION

I'd like to dedicate this book to the memory of my uncle Louis Pearlman – ex-Lord Mayor of Hull, city councillor, lover of life, laughter and the Labour party – and to Rita, David and Michael, who will miss him even more than I do.

My thanks go to:

JOANNE KYDD: For typing up during Braxton-Hicks contractions.

NAOMI APPLE: For finishing off. Without them.

CLINT EASTWOOD: For leaving me alone for long enough to write this book.

ROBSON BOOKS: For the studied casualness with which they rang me only once a week. And much else.

EDITOR LIZ ROSE: For deadheading my excesses of floribunda.

PRINCESS MICHAEL OF KENT: For offering to proof-read – and good luck with her next book of *How Was It For One?*

ADAM AND AMY ROSENTHAL: For saying 'How's the book coming on?' when they meant 'Is there any chance of a meal?'

OPTIONS MAGAZINE: For holding the presses, twelve times a year.

MARGARET THATCHER and EDWINA CURRIE: For teaching me that some women's place is in a home.

LIBERTY'S OF LONDON: For furnishing the fabric for falling back on.

MY FRIENDS LIZZIE AND ASTRID: Without whom I wouldn't have my friends Lizzie and Astrid.

JACK ROSENTHAL: For being the tower behind the prone.

1

House and Garden,
Slightly Overlooked

Deflowered but not For-Lawn

ARE YOU SITTING comfortably? Then get up. This is no time for sloth. Against all possible odds, my lobelias are up. Red where I planted blue, blue where I planted red and puce where they've been strangled by the busy lizzies, but to a first-time gardener they represent Wisley, Kew Gardens and Capability Lipman rolled into one. London pride isn't in it!

It all started with the purchase of two halves of a wooden ale keg and four antique Salford chimney pots. You know, the sort of things that once you couldn't get the Salford rag and bone man to take away for less than ten bob and a pair of nylons, and which now sell upwards of £60 a pot with extra for original soot.

They looked very cute on the patio, but lacked the necessary sprouting foliage to give them that rustic look so beloved by your average Salford roof. I bought a trowel from Woolies and put in some soil. It fell straight through to the patio. I kept adding until the pot was full and the garden was virtually empty. I then added my fuchsias and lobelias and a spiky looking creature, name of Potentilla, and waited with breath that can only be described as bated.

Each morning, I've taken my Morning-Starter tea on to the patio and, in dressing-gown and cucumbers,

surveyed my domain. Gentle reader, the little buggers
have grown! Albeit not above the tops of the pots, but
on a clear day were one to be standing on a medium-
sized stool or step-ladder one would have seen a
display which would have had Bill Sowerbutts at his
most underwhelmed. 'Now for the big stuff,' I told my
husband Jack. 'I'm off to the Ally Pally Garden Centre
for to buy a watering can and some slug pellets.' And
it's highly unnecessary to point out that slugs can't
climb chimney pots because it was the front lawn I
now had in mind – total transformation of same. Sixty-
three pounds later I returned home in a car which
resembled the camouflaged truck driven by Radar in
M.A.S.H. Lilac, wisteria, begonias by the boxful,
honeysuckle, pansies and enough lobelias to border
the Borders of Scotland. I had to leave Simone, my
Mother's Help, there. Not as a deposit, but it was her
or a bay tree, and I reckoned she'd be lousy in a lamb
casserole (even though she was a wonderful girl who
came from Hull, two qualifications which are totally
synonymous).

Before I left, I asked the cashier for some soil. 'Soil?'
she gawped, 'Oh, we don't sell *soil* here.' Her
amazement was such that it was like asking for a Spam
sandwich in Bloom's. 'But . . . but . . . it's a garden
centre,' I spluttered. 'I mean, what am I to do with all
these plants and no soil?' Patiently, and with more
than a little of the air of a midwife, she gave me some
leaflets on home deliveries. I thanked her and, while
writing out two cheques and considering a home loan,
I asked her in what other substance people planted
plants.

'Potting compost and peat.'

My ears went up like elevators. Hadn't I been
growing my own compost for three years from
Pushkin Rosenthal's cat litter? A short discussion

followed about the acid nature of cat poo as opposed to dog poo and within minutes a third cheque was written out and the boot of my car written off with the weight of three bags full of non-feline compost.

I won't go into the business of the actual planting – fascinating though it is to us of the 'Gang Green-Fingers'. I will say, however, that had I realised that each lobelia strip contained twelve plants and that there were eight rows of strips, I might very well have jacked in the whole procedure and got a little man in. I will also say that when Stan, our weekly, arrived to plant the tiny bay tree, he took great pleasure in pointing out to me that the nine-foot-high tree growing profusely by my front gate for the last ten years was none other than *Laura nobilis*. Yes, you've guessed it, a bay tree.

But are we downhearted? Does it bother me that every plant entering our portals appears to see a sign reading, 'Abandon Hope All Ye Who Enter Here'? Do I care that the two £20 rhododendron bushes both suffer from premature ejaculation and spring into glorious flower on April 28th – and drop clean dead by the 29th. Leap Year or not? Do I give a damn that the apricot tree was struck by forked lightning and now bears beige prunes? Or that one side of the lawn is so completely waterlogged in all seasons that the only suggestion the lawn expert offered was that we might keep ducks?

Am I for-lawn? Fingers off the buzzer and no conferring. Quite frankly, I don't give a sod. When that first passion flower opens its glorious face for one glorious day, I shall bloom. When the first little bunch of tiny black grapes starts dropping all over the car, tasting of stoat pee, I shall feel divine, and as for the miracle of my seven yuccas – let him who is without yuccas cast the first yuck! My dears, they have flowered – all seven of them. First came the pokers, looming, Cleese-like, out of the leaves, then suddenly, one day last week, they burst into bells – the palest, greenest, whitest bells – hanging in majestic clusters all over the show. I mean, I've got the message, man. As old Rambling Syd Rumpo used to say, 'The answer lies in the soil.' If you can get it, of course.

My mother wouldn't agree. 'She cares more about those plants than she does about anything,' she audibly whispered as I Baby Bio'd my spiders. For this, read 'The kids' drawers look like they've been burgled, there are stains in the toilet, and she's busy with her mist spray.' Mother's idea of a perfect lawn is all-over concrete with two squares of soil full of ever-lastings and a sheet of Astroturf for the deckchairs.

My late mother-in-law, however, was a genius, and I think it's her genes I'm feeling the vibes from. 'Lakey' sang opera to her plants, and they never let her down. Her idea of a really good aria was 'Collect the labels the gifts are free/With Black and Greens, the family tea'. Verdi it wasn't, but verdant was her patch and her cucumbers were legendary. She used to mate them, serenading the while. An early form of sex therapy, I guess.

However, there is one snake in my grass: the hose. _Hoses_! They make me so permanently angry that I'd like nothing better than to line 'em up and circumcise 'em en masse. Without a blessing.

All right, my garden is fairly large – what? – 150ft-ish? – but there ought to be a way of watering it without emerging at the end of an hour wringing wet, covered in compost and with your inner-soles stuck to your feet in damp corrugated waves. Here's the scenario: woman gingerly turns on outside tap in hope that water emission will indicate location of nozzle amidst several yards of hosepipe. Nothing happens.

Woman goes to investigate, finds nozzle, but no water coming through it. She picks up and examines nozzle. Nothing apparently wrong. She shakes part of hose-pipe, releasing kink, and water gushes frantically through nozzle and up woman's nose, sending glasses aquaplaning on to concrete surface. Woman curses nozzles throughout the land and moves down towards bottom of garden, pulling hoseline behind her as she sprays.

Half-way down garden hoseline yanks her back, having wound its way round bike abandoned on patio. Woman drops nozzle on to flower-bed and runs back to release pipe from under wheel-guard. Races back to find antirrhinums flattened by force of jet from nozzle. Proceeding down towards rose-bed (i.e. shady patch covered by apple tree, soil like tarmac, won't grow anything except self-seeded mint), woman sprays roses for couple of minutes before spattering starts and water slows down to dribble. Woman walks back, in search of kinks. No kinks, but second connection point has unconnected and water is gushing on to lawn. Woman can't be bothered to turn off water at tap before attempting to reconnect junction. As she pushes plastic hose into joining device, water pressure causes fan-shaped waterfall to hit woman's crutch and inside leg of trousers, causing her to dance backwards like circus horse. Defeated, woman walks back to turn off tap, then returns to junction, unscrews cap, replaces hose in threaded bit, realises cap now on upside down, removes hose, realigns cap and reseals join. Wet and weary she trudges back, turns on tap, walks back to nozzle, which spits into life and weakly sprays two and a half miniature rose bushes before junction connecting hosepipe to tap falls off wall.

Woman slowly and menacingly walks back in new, light pink sandals she forgot to change out of before assault course began, and, cursing and swearing like a merchant seaman denied leave, jams hose back on to tap. Half an hour has passed and three quarters of one garden bed has been watered. Woman falls to knees and prays for rain.

Then there's the garden furniture schism. During the four days of brilliant sunshine we had in May I became obsessed with the need to buy lounging chairs. Considering that I never sit down for long enough to know the meaning of the word 'lounge' and that if I do I'm covered in prickly heat within minutes, this was, you'll agree, an unnecessary necessity.

Anyway, my mother was staying at the time and it gave us something to do other than re-arranging each other's re-arrangements. So, off we went to Fenwick's, John Lewis, several garden centres and a huge Sainsbury's Home Base off the North Circular. I should point out that my idea of buying anything means going to one shop and ordering it, while my mother's idea is to ring every shop in the 'G' for garden section of the Yellow Pages to compare prices, make a list, ring them all back to check they've understood her original enquiry, then visit each one to look at the goods, and finally decide to leave the purchase until next year's January sales. Several boiling hours later we'd lounged in every adjustable lounger this side of Hatch End and encountered a whole new set of dilemmas. For example, some plastic chairs can be left out all summer so long as you remove the covers. These look *exactly* like the ones which can't be left out in so much as a light drizzle except they have a little label secreted under the seating. Then there are the wrought iron ones, some of which are £16 and others £65 per chair for no discernible reason, except to make the buyer over-wrought. Then there's the incredibly posh-looking German ones which only sell with matching table, parasol, table napkins, coasters, candle holders and probably Bratwurst slicer, and for which you need a second mortgage. Not to mention the rustic wooden ones which look golden the first year, then, after being left out all year as recommended, turn a curious sort of elephant grey and take chunks out of your Gotex'd bum.

Finally, at Sainsbury's, I found them. Four green-and-white cushioned, all-weather plastic adjustable loungers plus one on wheels for chasing sunshine, plus matching table-cloth for existing table. Reasonable and rugged. Thank the Lord, we'd done it! The assistant placed two huge flat packs (with instructions – hah!) in my trolley, then went to the storeroom to bring down the other four boxes. During the wait my mother said, 'You know what you *do* need?' (thereby implying that what I've just ordered is a frivolous extra, which I'm sort of suspecting anyway). I indicated I didn't know what I did need, so she told me. 'Tiles.' 'Tiles?' 'Yes, tiles. Around that little wash basin in the guest-room toilet. There's absolutely no splash-back. At all!' This latter she made sound as unthinkable a deficiency as having no door on your oven. 'You should get a double row of nice matching tiles on each side. It would *make* that toilet.'

I was fortunately stopped from making the cynical response which would have sprung from my lips in spite of the resolution I'd made three times that day not to make any such cynical remarks, by the arrival of the four extra flat packs, and we duly loaded the trolley and got in line at the check-out. Whilst I waited, Mother disappeared. Not a good sign. She would undoubtedly be asking somebody something. She was.

Red-faced with anxiety she rushed up to me. 'Don't buy them, Maureen. I've just spoken to the man. You won't believe it! What a good job I thought to mention it. What do you think – the covers won't come off!'

'So, I'll wash the whole thing in the machine.'

'Are you mad? They're all foam-lined. They'll bunch up! It's nothing to me, I mean, it's no skin off my nose, but if you do buy them you'll be sorry! You'll have to buy new again next year. It'll be a complete dead loss. They have to have removable covers. You ask anybody – excuse me asking' (this to the woman ahead of us in the queue) 'but are you buying chairs with removable covers or are they all in one? There, you see. My daughter says it doesn't matter but they get filthy, don't they, when you can't take them off? There you are, Maureen, this lady agrees with me. Yes, she is on television. I'm her mother – where are you going, Maureen – ?'

I pushed the trolley back to the shelves, unloaded five huge boxes back into place, hurled the matching tablecloth across two aisles, and was heading back through the superstore in search of the super sodding exit. Mother followed.

'Well, don't say it's my fault – I don't mind what you do. It's not my money, but I'm right. You'll see.'

I branched off at the tile section, intending to buy a pack of twelve tiles for over the wretched sink, as a way of diverting my mind. After a couple of minutes' contemplation of colours I felt a tap on my shoulder.

'What are you *doing*?' asked Mother incredulously.

'I'm choosing the tiles for the toilet,' I said in measured tones.

She gawped at me, aghast. 'What? NOW?'

'Well, as I'm in the tile section I thought I'd choose them here.'

'But – but – you haven't measured the space! What if you haven't got enough? What if you've got too many? What if – No, you've got to get it measured properly by a man . . .'

I replaced the tiles, abandoned my trolley and all thoughts of either chairs or an amicable journey home. It's July as I write this and outside the rain pours down on four ancient canvas director's chairs, two torn deck chairs and a parasol that used to be green and white, but is now white and grey, courtesy of every pigeon in town.

The fact is that my garden is full of earthly delights, mostly bought at vast expense from every beckoning garden centre. Mother stands purse-lipped as I lash out another thirty or forty quid on plants and says, 'Do you know, I've never had to buy a single thing for my garden. Ever. They just come up every year. Doesn't that happen in London?' I've got a monkey puzzle tree, an ancient gazebo, gooseberries, purple clematis, and I'm training a wisteria to throw itself up the side of the house. Meanwhile, my passion flower *is* in flower, three or four fantastic flowers a day. They make the most beautiful buttonholes.

My garden gives me grubby nails, backache and total pleasure. The three taciturn, shirtless men who spend an hour crimping the lawn each week and grunt monosyllabically every time I speak to them, have no idea that they are bringing up my baby. I don't expect them to love it as I do, but I expect them to be equally interested in its development. It may be a bit short of floribunda, but it's full of the green stuff in more ways than one. Or, as Andrew Marvell used to say, 'Annihilating all that's made/To a green thought in a green shade.' 'E was a marvel, that Andrew. Also a Hull lad. Need I say more?

My Pound in Their Pockets

RECENTLY MR ROSENTHAL, my co-director and joint mortgagee, and I were called to an urgent, financial board meeting in the very dining-room of this very house. Five sets of elbows, some grubbier than others, rested on the polished (once) table top, and the Chairman, whose feet didn't quite reach the carpet, proceeded to open the proceedings by sombrely inverting an egg-timer.

'We have called this meeting to discuss the *appalling* pocket money situation in this house.'

'Hear, hear,' said his sister severely from the other end of the table. 'And it's not fair.'

From the centre of the table, Simone – Mother's Help and sometime secretary to the revolutionaries – sniggered as she committed these remarks to the minutes.

The Chairman continued. 'It has come to our notice that every child we know gets regular pocket money and has done for years! *We* never get *any*!'

'Hear, hear,' came the cry from his relentless second. 'And if you do give us any, you take it away the minute we accidentally do anything wrong.'

'Tell them about Melanie's brother,' prompted the Chairman, now inverting his egg-timer every time anyone spoke.

'Yes! Melanie's brother gets 50p and he's only four.'

'And Melanie gets £3.50!'

I cleared the management's throat and spoke for the first time. My voice, I noticed, was slightly higher in pitch – like an octave. '£3.50? Well, you've had _that_! Does she do any jobs for it?'

'No. It's just for buying things with.'

Their father spoke through the chair (and clenched teeth): 'Name two things that you two want that Mod and I have denied you.'

'We want money for Holly Lodge.' (A corner of the garden they've chosen as their own which, unfortunately, doesn't enjoy the benefit of one single ray of sunshine at any given moment of any day of the year.) 'We're going to plant fruit trees and carrots.'

Faced with the facts, what could I and my co-director do, other than get on our knees and thank God that Woolworth doesn't sell marijuana plants? Settlement was reached and the minutes recorded that £2.50 per child would be allowed on condition that the payees kept their side of the agreement, that being, the washing of ears, elbows and parts so private that water apparently changes direction when confronted with them, the practising of a certain stringed instrument on a nightly rather than three-monthly basis, and the undertaking of small, helpful household tasks such as clearing the odd table or washing the odd car.

This last was received with massive enthusiasm to the extent that buckets were filled with half a large container of Fairy Liquid and 14 drops of water, last year's good T-shirts were torn up into cleaning cloths, and our muck-grey mottled vehicle was assembled for attack. Roughly four minutes later, the sound of tinkling laughter came from outside the door. Roughly three minutes after that, the laughter had changed to the sort of noises you only hear on _Disap-_

pearing World when two musk boars are charging each other in the cause of a life-and-death struggle for territorial rights.

A glance through the window showed us, as if we didn't know, that the bodies of both protagonists had just received more soapy water than they'd received in the last ten years of their lives. Which could, I suppose, be said to be them keeping to their side of the bargain. Meanwhile, the uniformly grey car was now a fetching grey and white stripe and so were the workers. They were also wet. And bored. The management put its feet down. The job had to be done again, with elbow grease. The workers were now wet, bored and livid. Unfairness was mentioned.

Three-and-a-half minutes later, they rang the door-bell and demanded £4 for doing the job twice! The management refused. The workers became emotional and accused the management of lying, collusion, misrepresentation of facts and worst of all, chronic lack of fairness. Finally, the management clipped the work-force round the ears and, in an amazing display of conciliatory behaviour, stopped all pocket money until the year 2000, including wedding presents.

To be fair, I always got ten bob. Every Saturday. A nice, russety-brown, crinkly note you could fold beautifully into the old 'Have you seen the Queen's bum?' joke. It was lovely, the old money.

There's a pub in Islington called The King's Head where they resolutely stick to the old currency over the bar. It's quite a culture shock, I can tell you, to pay seven shillings for a Coke, eighteen shillings for a pint of beer and – wait for it – a guinea for a pint of cider. The Americans, I understand, find it 'just darling', but it depresses the hell out of me. I'm the person who's still prowling round Mothercare with a ruler, trying to convert 146cm into the length of a daughter from neck to knee. And why, when you drop in for £15 worth of petrol, does the serve-yourself pump jump straight from £14.97 to £15.20 before clicking off and dripping 23p worth on your new suede loafers? I suppose you get the nice, thick sherry glass at the end of it all by way of compensation.

And now, ladies and gentlemen – at enormous expense – a monetary joke. It was the milkman's last day at work, and at the final house on his round, the lady invites him to come in. 'I've made you a special breakfast,' she purrs. Inside, he finds the table groaning with home-baked bread, scrambled eggs, kippers and freshly-ground coffee.

He delightedly enjoys the fine fare and thanks her profusely. 'Right, then,' she coos. 'Shall we go upstairs?' Unable to believe his luck, he follows her to the bedroom, where she proceeds to give him the sexual equivalent of the cream off the top of the milk. Afterwards, and to his amazement, she presses a pound coin into his hand and shows him the door. On his way out, he says, 'Well, thank you for a truly memorable morning, but there's just one thing I don't understand. Why did you give me the pound?'

'Oh, well,' she says, 'I said to my husband last night, "It's the milkman's last day tomorrow – what shall I give him?" And my husband said, "Oh, screw the milkman! Give him a pound!" The breakfast was *my* idea!'

My Husbandry and I

I'M ABOUT TO be profound for posterity and I expect you to have at hand a sheet of 2-ply, a square of card, a pair of pinking shears and an adhesive of your choice. For herewith I give you 'The Lipman guide to domestic tips, folklore superstitions and husbandry' – possibly the thinnest and most useless tract in the non-Esperanto speaking world.

I'll start with tips – since I only know five it won't take long. The first two concern the cooking of a duck, which I personally do once or twice a summer solstice, if at all, as anyone knows one large duck feeds roughly two under-fives and an anorexic vegan before it's reduced to soup bones. Nevertheless, if you *are* roasting one, do it over a shallow pan of water to draw off the fat, thus making it crispy. If you wish your duck to be wind-dried, then use the method favoured by Julia McKenzie, who hangs it over the shower head whilst blow drying it with a fan heater on an upturned wastepaper bin. Yes – you knew she was talented, you knew she was gorgeous, but you never knew she was mad as a snake! Stick with me, kids, I promise you revelations that would drive a *Sun* reader to Jane Austen.

Now. If you want a flesh-coloured bra, soak a white one in cold tea. Alternatively if you go bra-less you could soak your breasts in cold tea. PG Tits, I suppose. And for really shiny brass knobs, soak 'em in Brown Sauce. This is a little known fact which actually works. I don't know why they don't brag about it in their advertising. 'If our product can bring a shine to your knobs, just think what it can do to your stomach!'

Then there's carnations. I'm not going too fast for you, am I? Carnations, and how to keep them fresh in a vase for up to four weeks. You've heard of Carnation Milk, haven't you? Well, get ready for Carnation Lemonade. Yes, you stand your blooms in a vaseful of 7-Up and 'up' they'll stay, as fresh as a bloomin' daisy for a whole month. No, I *don't* know if it will have the same effect on other limp things. And no postal queries, please, as to whether Diet Pepsi or Root Beer will work as well – just take Derek the wig-dresser's word for it, as I did, and your pinks will be in the pink. He also recommends a drop of bleach in the chrysanths, but I drawn the line at bullying. I could happily peroxide a germ, a shirt collar or an unwanted facial hair, but not something that's fought its way through fertiliser and lived.

On the medical front I cannot advise you too strongly to try the Bach Flower Rescue Remedy. It comes in a small bottle from most homeopathic chemists, and I find it cures me of whatever I think I've got, i.e. everything in the Pears Medical Encyclopaedia. In the odd moments of stress, shock and general hysteria which make up 93% of my life, I find it invaluably calming. (During the run of *Wonderful Town*, the stage musical, my little bottle ministered to a migrainous musical director, a fainting co-star and any number of cases of chorus throat and hoofer's ligament.) I *used* also to have a bottle of homeopathic pills which were labelled 'For Fear of Oncoming Events'. I carried them everywhere but never used them since my fear of not having enough left for tomorrow was greater than my fear of any event that might 'come on'.

Much of the soundest, if more unorthodox, medical advice came from a sturdy Irish lady who once 'did for me', in more ways than one. Amongst her 'pearls' was a sure-fire cure for removing verrucas which involved the burying of a piece of raw meat at a cross-roads. Presumably this folklore stemmed from the days before tarmac. I have this picture of myself in the dead of night limping through N10 with a plateful of steak tartare and a pneumatic drill . . .

Her other gem concerned nits and went somethin' like this: 'Der was eleven of us at home, and at noight me mother used to make us all rinse our heads in a bottle of our wee-wee. And I tell you dis, Mareeen, not one of us was *ever lousy*!' Nor popular, I fear.

As far as superstitions go, I don't believe in *one* of them! Touch wood. God, I wish I had a Beauty Flash ampoule for every time my mother made me sit down and count to ten because I'd left my plimsolls under the bed and had to come back for them. ('Mother, I'm ten minutes late' – 'It won't take a second' – 'It'll take ten' – 'It's bad luck' – 'Oh, for heaven's sake! Onetwothffssnenten! There!' The resulting good luck earned you trapped fingers and a detention for un-punctuality.) Not to mention the mounds of salt I've thrown over my left shoulder into the eyes of passing au pairs, who think their employer is a pervert, nor the screams that ensue when shoes go on the table, knives get crossed or you happen unavoidably to cross on the stairs. Arguments and bad luck will follow – particu-larly if the stairwell is narrow and there's a black cat approaching from the left. Sally, my dresser at the theatre, got the shock of her life when she tried to sew up the hem of my dress just as I was going on. 'Bite me!

Bite me!' I yelled. 'Why?' she asked, justifiably enough. 'I don't bloody know – just bite me, or I'll forget my lines!' Bless her, she did it – rather heartily, I thought.

If I were to tell you the elaborate ritual I go through before going on stage, to ensure I never 'dry' – you'd smirk. Suffice to say it takes me at least three quarters of an hour and involves standing on my head, deep breathing, repetitions of mindless phrases and the putting on of clothes, make-up and jewellery in a precise order – left ear-ring before right, etc., muttering all the while.

The other day a pleasantly shy young man from Hospital Radio came to interview me in my dressing-room, bearing tape recorder and carefully researched questions. He began nervously, 'Miss Lipman, you have played many varied roles in your career, from Lucy in *Dracula* to the Third Witch in *Macbeth* . . .'

'Stop right there, please!' came my peremptory voice. 'And go out of the room – close the door – go *on* – I'll explain later – turn round three times, knock on the door and ask to come in – off you go!'

Poor soul, I thought he was going to be sick, but how else could I avoid the appalling curse which descends as sure as a politician on a baby, on him who utters the name of the Scottish play within theatre walls.

And gloves. How many times have I dropped one in the street and had to wait till a complete stranger walks past to say, 'Excuse me, but would you mind picking up my glove for me? Er – no, I'm not paralysed, I'm superstitious. Oh – and I'm afraid I won't be able to say "thank you" afterwards – it's unlucky – but I will be very grateful – oh, thank you – oh shit! I've said it! Oh, I'm sorry I said shit . . . ' etc?

Who was it, I want to know, who first decreed that neither lilac nor hawthorn should be brought into the house until the geese's eggs have hatched? And will I have to buy a bloody goose to find out? Will a dropped spoon forever mean a disappointment rather than dented lino, and does it bother me that if I dry my hands on the towel at the same time as someone else we'll never speak again? Must I forever wait for a second magpie, be delighted when I step in a 'lucky' dog poo (for whom?) and say 'Kenen Ahorah' every time I mention something is going *well* in the company of elderly Jewish relatives, for fear of the evil eye?

In Mel Brookes' and Carl Reiner's record *The 2000-year-old man*, Reiner asks the 2000-year old man what is the secret of his amazing longevity. Brookes replies: 'I never run for a bus. There'll always be another. I never touch fried food. I stay out of any small Italian car and I eat a nectarine a day. I love that fruit! Half a peach, half a plum. Even a rotten one is good. I'd rather have a rotten nectarine than a fine plum.'

You think he's wrong? I suppose you think you're safe if you avoid ladders and cholesterol and keep a stone with a hole through it under your bed to ward off arthritis? You should be so lucky!

Doggerel or Worse

I HAVE BEEN thinking dogged thoughts lately. A pal of mine bought his mum a King Charles Cavalier puppy to take her mind off things. Now what do the words 'nine inches of silky, tumescent fun' mean to you? Yes, I thought so. What if I were to add 'with draped ears and ebony eyes'? Well, at least you know what it isn't.

Maggie, as she's called, was utterly enchanting – and still is now she's a few inches longer. She sleeps on Mum's lap (except that since Mum doesn't have much of a lap and what she does have slopes precariously towards the hearthrug, Maggie spends a good deal of time dangling paw from pinny, fast asleep and no doubt dreaming she's the slalom champion of Southgate).

We never had a dog at home. Correction. We had a dog at home. A dachshund puppy. We had him for exactly one hour thirty-five minutes during which he committed the most anti-Semitic crime known to canines since the days of the Canaanites. He wee'd on the uncut moquette. My father had accepted him in to his tailor's shop in lieu of payment for a tie and two pairs of Y-fronts. He was instructed by my Domestos-clutching mother to return him forthwith to the owner who was by now halfway to Greenland on a trawler.

For once in his life he did what she said.

Inspired by the unfairness of such domestic dogma, I plotted my revenge. It took the form of the purchase of a 'Mucky Pup' from Hull's only Magic Shop. (Not a lot of magic anywhere in Hull in those days.) I popped the plastic poo into a plastic bag, filled a cigar container with water for verisimilitude and headed for town and my father's shop.

It was a bustling Saturday on Monument Bridge, and Jennifer and Susan, my trusty cohorts, employed diversionary tactics whilst I slipped the offensive item on the doorstep and poured the water haphazardly down the wall. Then all three of us sauntered breezily into the shop.

'Hello, sweethearts.' Dad was in an expansive Saturday afternoon mood. 'Don't you look smart!' We were all three wearing suits and dog's dinner hats, having spent two hours in the synagogue that morning purifying ourselves – that is, ogling the boys from the balcony above. 'Here's ten bob, go and buy yourself a Vienna slice.' We swapped glances and I faltered. But only for a minute. 'Oh, thanks, Dad . . . see you.' (Studied casualness here.) 'By the way, that's a pretty grotty thing to have on your doorstep, isn't it? No wonder the shop's empty . . . Byee.'

From the corner of Monument Bridge we could see my father peering down at his doorstep, uttering loud and distinctly unsabbatical profanities and calling for the shop boy – the 'gofor' – to gofor a bucket of hot soapy water and a flagon of disinfectant . . . '*Now and gerra move on,*' chunter, chunter, rumble, rumble, 'bloody people with their bloody dogs should be bloody strung up; dia-bloody-bolical I call it . . . ' Only after the first sweep of the broom sent the foul facsimile clattering down the steps in most unturdlike fashion, did he glance in the direction of his doubled-up daughter, and an expression seen on the face of every self-respecting King Lear as he leaves his thankless daughters (Act II, ScI,) crossed his plebeian countenance.

Flushed with success, we tried the same trick on my Auntie Bella's doorstep. Auntie Bella was a reclusive aunt who wore a bicycle seat cover on her head (and still does), and was much given to biting criticism of her niece's personal appearance (and still is, bless her). When we pointed out what was gracing her doorstep, she had not a moment's hesitation. Grabbing three pages of the *Hull Daily Mail* she advanced on the sham poo like a cat on a mesmerised mouse. 'Aha!' she cried, triumphantly, 'Got you! And all in one piece!' At that moment, I truly believe we peaked.

In the fullness of time my own children became 'Mucky Pup' owners. Before one wet and dreary Thursday matinée of *See How They Run* they handed me the offensive article to cheer me up as I left for the theatre. Once there, I decided to plant it on the tea tray for Ida, the maid – played by my good friend, Carol Hawkins, a pro if ever there was one. Her reaction would have been one small scream, a lightning coverup and some brief retaliation during the course of Act 3. Unfortunately, the actor who was playing the Bishop saw it first and names were demanded and heads were to roll. George Washington-like I sheepishly owned up. 'Please, sir, I cannot tell a lie, 'twas I who put the Mucky Pup in the tea strainer. *But*, in my own defence, it *was* on a doily.' I won't repeat what the Bishop said to the actress.

While I'm on the subject, and I rather wish I wasn't, and I'm sure you do too, I must tell you what happened in episode four of the television series *All at No. 20*. The script called for me to leave a building society, in dire financial straits. With fingers crossed, I had to walk along the pavement, avoiding the cracks for good luck. So intent was I on looking down that I was halfway under a ladder before I realised it and had to duck out from under it to avoid further misfortunes. Breathing a sigh of relief I was then to walk straight into a pile of what I've spent the previous lines trying to find euphemisms for. So far, so tasteless. No, doggone it – why should I apologise for a mere variation on the theme that won Alan Bennett a clutch of awards and a wallet of readies, in the British Year of the Pig and its private functions? Point of Ordure, M'Lud.

Meanwhile, back at the building society, the prop men laid down two large frankfurters and squashed them into a horribly realistic mound into which, as the cameras rolled, I duly squelched. Then, as I rolled my eyes to heaven and scraped my shoe on the rungs of a ladder, Fate – in the shape of a large bull terrier taking its large bull mistress for a walk – stepped in. So to speak. In full view of the cameras, it took one sniff at the meaty mess, strained for several seconds at its leash, then gobbled the lot down in one. We couldn't use the shot, of course. It was funnier than anything else in the episode.

In future I shall confine myself to writing about crocheting lace collars, manicuring your herb garden and perfuming your pot pourri. However, I must just tell you about a fellow I once knew who had a talking dog – or so he claimed. He took it into a pub and began to brag about its ability. A large crowd gathered round and money was offered if the dog could indeed speak. There was a hushed silence as his owner said, 'How are you feeling today, Fido?' To which the dog replied, 'Rough!'

The crowd regarded him cynically. 'Ask him another,' someone called.

'What do you find on the top of a house?' To which the dog replies, 'Roof!'

A groan goes up from the crowd. 'Wait, wait,' says his owner. 'Fido – there was a famous American baseball player called Babe – ?' Straightway the dog goes 'Ruth!' The crowd hiss and boo, turn away to a man and leave the pub. The dog looks up at the man and says, 'Should I have said Joe DiMaggio?'

He had a cousin, this chap, who was an Israeli – he was a big dog lover, too. Strangely enough he was having a terrible argument one day with an Arab about politics – they were going at it hammer and tongs. It was just about to end in blows when the Israeli said, 'Look, why should we fight – let our dogs fight it out to the death and whoever's dog wins wins the argument.' The Arab had an enormous wolfhound, and seeing the Israeli's tiny, squat-legged, long-tailed mongrel, he agreed.

The dogs circled each other in the dusty street, then with a croaking bark the little one leaped for the wolf-hound's throat and tore him to shreds within seconds.

The Arab had to admit defeat. 'You win. You win!' he cried. 'But tell me – that little dog is one hell of a fighter for such a small dog – what do you call that breed?'

'Well,' replies the Israeli, 'until he had his nose job we called him a crocodile.'

Finally and without further ado, two horses were discussing the next day's race. Said one, 'I'm terrified about tomorrow, I overheard my owner saying that if I don't win he'll have me put down.'

'That's funny,' said the other horse, 'I heard *my* owner saying he'd have *me* put down if I don't win tomorrow's race.'

'Oh God, what shall we do?' said the first.

A small dog had been listening to their conversation

and piped up, 'Excuse me, horses, but it seems to me that what you should do is gallop at exactly the same pace and go through the tape at precisely the same moment, in a neck and neck finish.'

The horses stared at each other, then at the dog, then at each other again. 'Stone me,' said the first horse, 'a talking dog!'

And that, folks, is a shaggy horse story.

From Cabby to Flabby in 21 Days

SUDDENLY I BECAME a minicab driver. Working nights and driving a beat-up Toyota Estate, canary yellow with one ochre door which looked like the result of a collision with a Colman's Mustard lorry. I had three children under 12, no noticeable husband, and I wore glasses, an anorak, one glove and an elderly perm. If this is not the dashing sophisticate you've come to associate with my good self, then you'd probably like to know what the hell I'm talking about. And I'm just in the mood to tell you.

It was a TV play ('actually, Darlings') and for three weeks my erstwhile family and I were living it for real, i.e. I left for work at two in the afternoon when the kids were at the blackboard, deep into the sex life of the hermaphrodite worm, and the husband was at the chopping board, deep into deep-frying the salmon patties without which the whole house would starve. 'You don't have to do all that, love,' I lied. 'I'll make some in the morning.'

Thirteen hours later I returned to the still pungent homestead, wide awake and ready to eat a broiled antelope and devoured the entire fruits of my husband's toil. At 4 a.m., having read with enormous interest both sides of the Rice Krispies packet and a brochure on a machine which wanted to replace the negative ions in my air, I made positive moves to go to bed.

The kids were irresistibly asleep. I rearranged their bedclothes with a heartiness which could only mean I wanted them to wake up and recognise me as their long-lost mother. They smiled in their sleep to humour me, teeth braces gleaming in the nightlight's glare, and turned away. I crept into the marital bedroom, stumbled over the marital chaise-longue and, almost comatose, removed BBC make-up from the marital mug. Four 'Quiet Life' tablets for alternative sleep, then I hit the frozen side of the marital duvet – and by dawn's early light I finally flaked out.

All right, put the violins down. I know there are thousands of you out there who work nights and wake up as fresh as a vat of Vim to fill your kids full of that stuff which gives them a bright red halo around their gaberdine macs, then wave them off at your front door with a ring of confidence on your face and pink cheeks. Like a Mum. Please forget the stringed instruments and send instructions only: 'How I do It', by A. Mum.

Mind you, it wasn't easy, this filming lark. First of all, I had to *get to* the location. This entailed a drive in a real minicab – which was good material in itself. First off, there are no happy minicab drivers (well, there's one and I'll come to him later). They have all just left the car spraying business and are awaiting a job in the ladies' lingerie business. When did you ever hear a child say, 'When I grow up I want to be a minicab driver?' Exactly. Mostly, they have a bag of chips on their shoulders and are more than willing to cry a little on mine.

My favourite was John, who hadn't had a night's sleep since the birth of his hyperactive daughter some five years ago. Faint with fatigue and rosy of eyeball, he catalogued the various sleep-inducing techniques he and his wife had tried on their peppy progeny. As usual, the latent agony aunt in me let rip: 'Soak her Marmite soldiers in Benalyn!' Childsplay! This child could outdrink W.C. Fields and still stay on her feet. I left him forlornly contemplating the prospect of yet another night spent hiding behind the spare room futon. Should you ever read this, John, I hereby submit my latest sleep cure, told to me by Remi, the cameraman, a prince among mortals. You take a wet sock, no, I don't mean the Young Conservatives, wring it out and place it on the insomniac foot, cover it with a dry one and, before you can say, 'Zzzzz' – and, let's face it, who can? – the brain sends blood rushing to the cold area, leaving an empty brain, which is so bored that it drops off. This gives a whole new meaning to the expression, 'My foot's gone to sleep.'

Another driver, the happy one, happily took me to the eastbound Granada Service Station on the M4, to begin filming. No one but me showed up. After a decent interval (i.e. when the palpitations began to get out of hand), I asked the waitress, in what I think was called 'The Jolly Sizzler', if the BBC were filming there that day. She looked askance, and brought her friend over to look askance with her. Soon, there was a whole circle of askance-looking people around me. Giggling. Finally, someone rang the Granada Service Station on the *westbound* carriageway of the motorway, where all the 30-odd members of the crew had been waiting for me for some time. Winning prizes for looking askance.

I won't try to describe the temperature during those February nights, nor the sight of my body in neck-to-ankle thermal underwear, because I want you to feel well enough to finish this and read on to the end of the book. I will just point out that if you ever see this play (*Shiftwork*) with me driving contentedly along the M4, just bear in mind that it's a *manual* car I'm driving (for the first time in years), that it's driving rain I'm driving through, that Tony, the actor I'm addressing is, in fact, back at the catering bus having his supper, since there isn't enough room in the back seat for him, the director and the cameraman, and that the sound man is doubled up in the rear luggage compartment. And nobody knows the way . . .

Out at Heathrow, Tony was waiting to walk into shot, wearing full Arab dress, when he was approached by a passing young lady (not part of the film) who told him, meaningfully, that she had nowhere to sleep. I suggested he told her she could sleep at his place. In Dubai. Later, in the car park, we were filming getting into the minicab. In an extremely complicated sequence, I removed babyseat and toys, loaded six pieces of luggage, seated the Arab in the back, ran round to the front seat, only to find that the same persistent young lady had just got in there before me – and into the film. Cut! Unload. Retake. Action.

Once it was over, I was back on days. Well, attempting to be. Mostly, I was wide awake at two in the morning, looking for action, and totally clapped out at noon, looking for my eyes. Another side-effect was the condition of my hips after three weeks of location catering. Nothing in life was more comforting in the dead of night than steak pie, three veg, jam roly-poly and custard and a couple of plates of Bourbon biscuits. I went from cabby to flabby in twenty-one days. There was nothing much to look forward to except a waddle in the woods, a Ryvita and half an hour's 'Beginner's Buttocks' on my return. There's no business like show . . .

The Jewel and the Clown

NOW TAKE MY jewellery collection – please! Listen, if you can find it, you can have it. Over the years, my heirlooms have been moved from a wooden tool-box to a cardboard egg box and finally, for increased security, into an elderly plant pot under the dressing-table. Here they rest in a curious system known only to me and best described as a 'wodge', which would drive any self-respecting burglar to phone 999 for assistance.

The system works perfectly well for me. Should I require a second ear-ring to go with the one I've dug out of the pocket of my jacket, I merely turn the wodge upside down on the carpet, scrabble around for eight to ten minutes, find the missing link and scoop everything back into the pot. Then all that's required is a couple of butterflies to hold the ear-rings in place. This necessitates tipping the whole shebang on to the carpet again, and extracting the little bleeders by the use of a plastic straw and a fair amount of suction.

Once found, the tiny gilt stick at the back of the ear-ring is forced through the hole in the butterfly which is deliberately made smaller than the stick in order to propel the butterfly, frisking through the air, into the clothes basket, giving it its pretty name and the washing machine a breakdown in its filter pipe. This is no problem either, as your repair man will be glad to pop round Wednesday morning or afternoon (can't say which) four months hence for a coming-out and going-home fee, *if* you have a set of wheels, a jack and long-nosed pliers.

Where was I? Jewellery. Yes, I used to have a wedding ring. Well, five, actually. A very classy Wendy Ramshaw set, purchased by me in the absence of my then fiancé, from the Electrum Gallery. Two flat gold bands and three silver, with moonstones of various shapes set at angles to make a sculpted whole. Very modern, very chic. 'Ooooh,' said my mother as I flashed a very un-Fergie-like finger at her. 'Isn't it . . . unusual?' Many bliss-filled years later, I was down to two moonstones and no wedding ring. I last saw it at the TV Centre during a play in which I decided it was too upmarket for the down-trodden character I was playing. After wrenching it off by dogged and persistent use of an entire bar of Palmolive, I swapped it for a conventional band of gilt-veneered brass and spent the next few hours twisting it round my finger to indicate some emotion since forgotten.

Fellow sentimentalists, I never saw my wedding ring again. Went home in the fake and by the time I'd rung up in hysterics, it had disappeared into the 7,000 shoe-boxes of the Prop Jewellery department with a polite but firm 'This company disclaims any responsibility for articles lost within its radii, so yah, boo, sucks, tough titty, get a new one!'

For a few weeks, I wandered around single again, hoping that Jack would notice (he didn't). Then, one day, my attention was caught by one of those Russian wedding rings which twist round each other in tastefully differing hues. My finger was measured through a card with a hole in it, and the ring slipped on – well, shoved, 'cos I've these largish knuckles to my fingers;

knuck-fingered as well as knock-kneed – and, to my embarrassment, once on, it refused to come off. After several minutes of jocular twisting and wrenching, you will not be surprised to hear that the jeweller and I decided unanimously that the Bolshevik band was absolutely perfect, and I duly paid up and wore it until I played my next single girl and out came the Palmolive. However, this time, the finger that does dishes just grew as raw as my face and the day before opening night I had it sawn off. The ring, not the finger. So next time you see me, don't say 'I'll give you a ring', 'cos I'm likely to give you a knuckle sandwich.

One wedding anniversary – I think it was our eleventh; the tin foil one, isn't it? – Jack bought me a truly sensational present. Normally, a few weeks before a birthday or a Christmas, he starts wearing the look of a beagle who can't remember where he's buried his bone and starts sniffing around for clues with overwhelming subtlety. None of that happened, however, that February. Just Gerald Harper-like smoothness, the occasional smirk, and even one or two 'Everything's perfectly under control, m'dear'. Having nothing brilliant lined up myself, I panicked and ordered him a stained glass window for his birthday.

I was presented with a silver ring in the shape of a dressing-room door (featuring my name, a gold star and a tiny door knob) which opened. Inside was a room with a tiny gold chair in front of a mirror circled by light bulbs, shoes on the floor, dressing-gown on the back of the door, flowers on the shelf. I can't tell you how beautiful it was. Is. I've actually hung on to it; I still have it. Mind you, I had to have it changed into a pendant as the door kept opening every time I changed gear and while wearing it under a glove, it looked as if I had a ganglion. (For those of you without a medical bent, a ganglion is a lump of tissue which suddenly appears on hand, foot or head, or in a tendon sheath. When my mother gets one, she asks me to hit it with a copy of *Chambers Twentieth Century Dictionary*, after which it apparently sulks and goes away. Who wouldn't?)

Bobby Cartlidge, who'd made the ring, carefully donned her eyeglass and smelting kit and adapted it for the neck. She's a gem of a jeweller, a Freeman of the City of London. Her own ring is a Victorian parlour which opens to reveal a roaring fire, a cat asleep on the mat, a rocking chair and a round table with long fringed cloth. Unique and marvellous.

En passant, she told me a wonderful story about when she and her husband Derek were young and struggling to make a crust. It was in the days before the invention of tape. The only way of recording sound was on a 78 rpm disc, four minutes each side – a bit like breast feeding. Derek had his own disc cutters and HMV gave out his number for special recordings. One day someone rang and said, 'Can you get down to Ramsgate today to record a talking dog?' 'Can I ever!' said Derek, one foot out of the door and his ball and biscuit in his hand. (Now steady on, 'ball and biscuit' was the vernacular for disc and microphone.)

It was, he says, the oldest dog he'd ever seen, and it refused to bark a single syllable. The disc only lasted four minutes, and since the disc and the petrol were just about all his worldly goods, the situation grew desperate.

Finally the owner said, 'Come along, Fido, what's 19/11d from a pound?' To which the dog said wearily, 'Woof.' And the dog and its owner practically expired with excitement.

Bobby and Derek returned to London with a short but meaningful dog recording. Over the next few weeks they recorded a talking parrot, a Siamese cat that made baby noises, and they were feeling pretty well pleased with their new little niche.

One day the phone rang and a voice said, 'Do you do Barmitzvahs?' 'All the time, madam,' said Derek, who'd never heard the word. This was, after all, *years* before Mr Rosenthal's play *Bar Mitzvah Boy*. He took down the details and agreed to be there on the day. Then he put down the phone and said to Bobby, 'What kind of dog is a Barmitzvah?'

Bobby came originally from Germany and had never heard of the species. They tried to look it up in the Ganglion Basher. Curiously enough, it wasn't there.

'Perhaps it's not a dog,' said Bobby. 'It could be some other sort of animal.'

Derek nodded. 'Well, she said we've to be at the Porchester Hall on Saturday morning. That's where the baths are, isn't it? Maybe it's a reptile . . . '

In desperation they rang London Zoo. (Honestly, I promise you this is true.) They spoke to the admin office and asked if they had such a thing as a Barmitzvah in their Zoo.

'What kind of animal is that?' asked the administrator, who obviously numbered very few Jews amongst his immediate circle. On being told it might possibly be amphibious he added, 'Right, I'll put you through to the Reptile House.'

'Do you happen to have such a thing as a Barmitzvah amongst your inhabitants?' enquired Derek. 'Er, I'm not sure what species of reptile it is. We're going to record it in the Porchester Baths so it could be some sort of porpoise or – oh, you haven't – no, well, we've not heard of it either. I just thought with your knowledge of – yes, I see. Well, thank you, anyway.'

The following Saturday Bobby and Derek, wearing

sou'westers, waterproof capes and wellington boots,
with their recording equipment encased in plastic,
arrived at the Porchester Hall to see five hundred
elegantly-dressed Jewish people milling round the
thirteen-year-old boy in whose honour the celebration
was. The only fish worth recording had been dead for
some time and was sitting nicely fried on five hundred
plates.

So there you have it. My jewellery collection further
consists of two batty old brooches bought for me by
my friend Jerry, because, as he said, 'No one else but
you would wear them,' a cameo ring given me by Mrs
Niven, my landlady in Fog Lane, Manchester, and a
pair of marcasite dress clips with several missing
stones which I once wore for a photo for *The Sunday
Times* colour magazine. The following week I received
a letter from a delightful fellow in the Chelsea Antique
Market, offering to replace the stones for me and clean
them up – which he duly did. They nestle contentedly
next to the plastic bucket and spade ear-rings and the
quartz watch which packed up after taking an instan-
taneous dislike to my pulse rate.

Now, the Duchess of Windsor's baubles I wouldn't
mind. That little floppy cheetah bracelet and a couple
of those chokers would do me nicely, thank you. I
would have given my eyes and my teeth, were they
functional or my own, to have been at that auction in
the South of France. All that naked greed in one room!
As it was I had to suffice with seeing the TV
programme, once at home and once on a plane on my
way to New York.

Such a sad programme. Such a strange, sad
romance. I can't entirely help but feel that each jewel
was for something more than an anniversary. They
were as much for him as for her, surely? How desperately he wanted to make her into a queen. How much

he wanted to make her into his remote mother. And there was Prince Charles failing to capture Uncle David's diamond for his own Diamond. It's the Prince of Wales disease, you know: too much pressure, inevitably, on the first-born heir. We all do it. Majestically or otherwise. No one prepares us for parenthood and we're so anxious to get it right that we often err on the side of perfectionism. The Duke, like the Edward before him, went from one strong, dominating woman to the next, till he ended up with the one he couldn't live without and according to the Constitution he couldn't live with. Poor desperate man, ill-suited to the task he was born to and frantic for frivolity. Dining nightly with his Duchess in solitary splendour in their hotel suite, dressed and bejewelled to the tens, must be the strangest act of sublimation this century.

Which brings me inexorably to the Blomberg Diamond. 'Oh no,' you groan, 'not that old joke, she can't have sunk so low.' But I have . . .

A busty blonde at a Las Vegas wedding party was showing off a huge diamond pendant. 'It's the largest in the world,' she purred. 'Ya hoid of the Hope Diamond and the Koh-I-Noor Diamond? Well, this is the Blomberg Diamond.'

'Oh, that is superb; oh, you are lucky,' buzzed the women guests.

'Lucky?' shrieked the blonde. 'Are you kidding? With the Blomberg Diamond you gotta take the Blomberg Curse.'

The women tut-tutted. 'And what's the Blomberg Curse?'

'Blomberg,' groaned the blonde.

So, it's old – but it's still a gem!

Lock, Stock and Barbecue

THE KIDS were depressed. It was their last day at their old school and they were trying to make themselves cry.

'But, darling,' I said to Amy, 'you should be pleased you're leaving.' She had, after all, been miserably bullied by hulking great adolescent eleven-year-olds.

'But it's still my school. I'm used to it.' Her left eye was batting relentlessly, whilst her brother made batting motions of a far more sporting variety with both hands and stared at the wet car window, poetically.

'Tell you what,' I offered, 'shall I take you to Brent Cross for tea and buy you something?'

'An Australian cricket cap?' said Adam immediately, as though this was the first thing that would occur to any mother cheering up a sad son.

'Cindy's fireplace, tongs and scuttle?' added his sister with a small, brave smile.

'Certainly. And what would *you* like, Simone?' I asked the then new Mother's Help. (I find it as well to show my Mother's Helps Brent Cross Shopping Centre early on, since that's where they tend to spend a great deal of time in The Sawn-off Trousers and Elasticated Plimsoll Shop.)

'How about a Cartier watch?' she replied. You can't

mess about with Hull girls. Not for long anyway.

By 6 o'clock we'd done every sports department of every shop in the Centre. Finally we settled for 'Aussies' printed on a baseball cap, and one of us at least was contented and had a warm head.

By 6.15, we were 'waste-deep' in Cindy fixtures, fittings and furnishings, and the lip-chewing dilemma of whether to plump for the fireplace, the hostess trolley or the barbecue. This went on long enough to arouse the staunch denial that someone was angling for all three. Someone got the fireplace. Personally, I wish Cindy in Hades along with her pony and trap, her functional shower and her Tampax holder. Give me the old breastless version with the dimples on the hands and the clicking eye-lids. But then, who wants my opinion? I'm just the wallet round here, whinge, mutter, moan, what thanks do I get . . . ?

On the escalator up – and down again – I made the mistake of catching sight of a real barbecue. Red and gleaming with a round lid and three legs, it resembled something from the blasted heath scene in *Macbeth*. It was love at second sight. Our friends had been hinting heavily for weeks how the quality of our lives would change with just such an acquisition, and once I'd discovered that it was £10 cheaper in black I clearly couldn't afford to miss it.

It was at this point that I recollected Jack's claim that if God had intended us to have barbecues He'd never have given us Neff Circotherm ovens and rain-free kitchens, but by then I'd already opened up my cheque book. The saleslady said, 'Pick it up at the Customer Collection Point – George will be delighted. He's a big fan of yours.' Preening only slightly, I manoeuvred the family past the Picnic Cafeteria with promises of an entirely chocolate tea at home, and we drove round to the Collection Point.

'Hi, George,' I called to the overalled gentleman who approached. 'How are you, George? Barbecue for Mrs Rosenthal, thank you, George.'

'Madam – how do you think I'm gonna get that parcel in your boot if you leave your car half a mile from the Collection Point, Madam?'

Dumbfounded by this excess of hero-worship on his part, I did as I was commanded. Afterwards I slammed the boot, got back in the car and would have driven off at a cool seventy had not the car keys been firmly locked in the boot, with the barbecue . . .

Need I continue? Or would you prefer to watch a re-run of a couple of *I Love Lucy*'s? Suffice to say that we did arrive home. Eventually. That Jack's first words were 'Has anyone bought me a present?' That he spent two and a half sodden hours assembling it to a Javanese instruction pamphlet. And that the following day we had a triumphant barbecue, at which as the last hamburger left the spit, the Great Patio in the Sky sent down twelve tons of acid rain on to nine marinated mixed grills. As Jack was heard to mutter, if he'd wanted his dinner singed on the outside, raw on the inside and tasting of smoked worsted, he could have had it in the comfort of his own kitchen. Like every other night.

It's odd how keys tend to play a high profile role in domestic dramas. A friend of mine, the distracted mother of a grumpy infant, grizzling toddler and yelling baby, was telling me how she arrived home from a stressful shopping trip and after an increasingly frantic search of bag, pockets, doormat, etc., remembered last seeing her key lying on the kitchen dresser. Her husband's key was, like her husband, en route for New York. Faced with a house like Fort Knox and with children now screaming for food, drink and urgent attention, she had a blaze of inspiration – the police –

surely they would have a master key! She rushed to
the police house, where the policeman was just getting
up for the afternoon shift. Between yawns and
scratches he explained that the police no longer have
skeleton keys, and suggested she go back and search
for an open window. Accepting the offer to leave her
kids with his wife (thank God this happened in the
country – can you imagine that suggestion coming out
of Bow Street?), she rushed home and found – joy of
joys – a slit-like crack in the upstairs bathroom
window.

Her elderly neighbour brought a ladder and gallantly
insisted on climbing up to the window. At which point
the policeman (a six-foot seven-inch giant) arrived in a
Panda car to check on the situation. Seeing gallant
elderly neighbour up ladder he heaved a sigh of relief:
'Can't stand heights meself,' and beat a hasty retreat.
Meanwhile the gallant elderly neighbour discovered
that the bathroom window opened upwards like the
flap on a letter box; he climbed down ladder, fetched
tool-box, climbed up ladder, unscrewed latch,
descended ladder in search of stick to wedge flap
open, climbed up ladder, and posted elderly self
through window, scattering a sill full of toiletries,
medicines, pills, etc. (Mother-of-three, heart in mouth,
head in hands, made mental note to purchase
bathroom cabinet on next shopping trip.) Saintly
neighbour then descended through house, opened
front door and was mobbed by effusive mother,
incoherent with relief and gratitude. Fending off wild
woman, he reascended ladder, removed prop,
rescrewed latch, closed window, descended ladder for
last time, and carried it home.

Mother-of-three hurriedly replaced everything on
bathroom window sill, noting with despair the state of
bedrooms, landing, stairs as revealed to neighbour's

unfamiliar eyes. Suddenly mindful of fractious infants and by now demented policeman's wife, she rushed downstairs and out of front door, slamming it behind her. Too late she remembered key still sitting on kitchen dresser.

A silent scream, followed by mad head banging. She briefly considered hurling herself into nearby river, or better still through lounge window. Stoically, though she dismissed these as easy ways out, and with heavy heart and carefully rehearsed speech, returned grimly to gallant elderly neighbour . . .

One of the happiest married couples I know are our friends Bryan and Edith, who first started courting at the age of fourteen and have been together ever since – about thirty-seven years. Edith tells of how she parked her bike outside Bryan's house, dressed in her school uniform and beret, and while waiting for him heard his mother say, 'Bryan, there's that brazen hussy outside!' When we lived in the flat above them we used to race down for the rows, because it was – is – so wonderful to see them both revert to adolescence. They disagree on just about every issue, and do so at the tops of their voices, yet it's forgotten within minutes.

One of the main bones of contention between them is Bryan's supposed super-efficiency. Once, after a spate of burglaries at their flat, he replaced the small window through which the thieves had gained access, and had an alarm fitted. About a week later he arrived home from work without his key. As Edith wasn't due back for some time, he decided to scrape away the putty on his new window and gain access the same way as the burglars had. Finding a sharp object in his pocket, he scraped and pushed and pushed and scraped until finally the new putty began to give. He pressed and scraped a bit more, until at length the window fell in, setting off the ear-splitting sound of the alarm. Only then did he glance down at the sharp object with which he'd been scraping at the putty.

It was, of course, his key.

2

How It Was For Me

Jeffrey Archer,
Pork and Migraine

THE PUBLICATION OF my first book, *How Was It For You?* opened a new chapter in my already over-booked life. To complete the writing of it had taken three months of disciplined avoidance of pen and paper and all telephone calls except those of an urgent nature, such as fifty minutes of the latest on Sandra's sex therapy course or Lesley's discovery of two years' dust behind the guest-room bed. I'd finally push myself through the dining-room door with a loud cry of 'I'll be in here if anyone wants me . . . ' followed immediately by 'So don't disturb me . . . unless anything happens . . . Anything . . . ' This, sitting down at a dining-table covered, as it had been for months, in twelve hundred unco-ordinated sheets of ill-assorted writings. Then and only then, the writer in me took over:

Long sigh. Pick up pen. Push papers round table a bit. Drink tepid tea. Shake head violently hoping for signs of imminent migraine. Draw and carefully shade bunch of drooping flowers on plinth and ponder psychological significance of same. Decide I'm clinically depressed psychopath with lesbian tendencies. Alter doodle to look as though I'm nice well balanced wife and mother in case of passing analyst.

Decide second one is even more revealing and leap up
to answer doorbell, along with four other people in the
house. Conduct long and fascinating conversation
with milkman re virtues of Gold Top over Homo-
genized. Pay up and return to dining-room, noticing
children playing happily in hall. Decide against their
will they need fresh air and drag them unwillingly to
park and then to pictures, thus writing off rest of
day . . .

Don't ask me how it got written but somehow one
grey July day the proofs arrived, which was all the
proof I needed that I'd done it, albeit the day before
going on the family holiday. To somewhere I can't
now remember. With the immaculate sense of timing
for which I'm a legend in my own lunchtime, I thus
had twelve hours, excluding sleep, to inspect and
correct seventy thousand words and pack for four.

The situation called for mettle, method and mind
over matter. What we in the world of authorship call
'the four Ms'. What it didn't call for was the fifth M,
namely Maureen. I took two looks at the respective
piles of words and beachwear, gave a silent scream,
rang my mother two hundred miles away and voca-
lised it, leaving her puzzled and shaken, then
retreated to the back of the walk-in wardrobe for some
really heavy whimpering.

It was there that I was discovered a lifetime later by
Mr Rosenthal, a man who's seen a deadline or two and
lived to tell no tales. (Writing two hundred episodes of
Coronation Street teaches a man a certain stoicism. After
the read-through of his first-ever half-hour script, the
director said, 'I think it's a bit too long' to which the
late Jack Howarth, playing Albert Tatlock, added
encouragingly, 'Yis. About twenty-nine minutes too
long.') I was picked up, dusted down, and, as Magnus
would have it, we started so we finished. *And* went on

holiday, albeit with inky nostrils and inflamed brains. The one lesson I've learnt from all this is that Ernest Hemingway was right. Writing is applying the seat of one's pants to the seat of a chair. And from a writer of his standing that's no bullshit.

The rest was all fun. Like thanks, dedications, choosing photos and captions and what to serve at the book launch other than writs. Then literally (or literaturely) we went down the plug-hole.

Plugging is a draining business. On the night of Monday, November 11, 1985 (and here, if you'll pardon me, I must celebrity drop), Terry Wogan asked me if I'd had a good week. I don't mean he asked me over dinner or in the queue at Waitrose; I mean he asked me 'live', in front of just the x million viewers.

'Oh, fabulous!' I lied with disarming honesty. 'I had my teeth scaled and polished . . . ' (I hadn't and to this day I've no idea why my mouth said I had.) 'I had the launch of my book *How Was It For You?* (Cue laughter and twinkle from Terence into camera one.) 'And . . . ' I was about to continue when the rest of the week flashed before my eyes and shut me up. At which point Terry asked me what TV programmes I'd been watching and the rest is mystery.

At roughly 5.45 the following morning I shot bolt upright – or, in my case, bolt right-angle. My neck was locked sideways with tension, giving me the look of a distressed budgie. Slowly, I went through the events of the previous week.

It had started, as weeks do, on Monday – my day off; I was at the time recording an episode of a new TV sit-com every Sunday night before a live audience. The night before, it had been impossible to tell if the audience was alive or not. The studio was cold, the warm-up man colder and the leading lady (the woman reliving this nightmare) had the coldest feet in town.

To the extent that when she tried to introduce her fellow actors, she forgot every one of their names. This is a phenomenon known in showbusiness as senility.

Monday morning saw the arrival of my secretary, Christine. Accustomed as she is to seeing me with cucumbers under my bags and a face the colour of Alpen, she blanched visibly and made a rapid succession of herb teas to bring the corpse back to life, and the prospect of two newspaper interviews and the Wogan show. (To avoid confusion to my weary reader, I should point out that in this story I appear on his show on two successive Mondays.)

By 11 o'clock, I was answering questions from a charming lady from *The Daily Telegraph* with black-rimmed glasses and a black-rimmed tape recorder. Somehow, my mouth formed words, phrases, even whole sentences. You press the right button and the performance comes out. 'How do you always manage to look so relaxed? Don't you ever have any nerves?' With a hand placed over my palpitations, I denied the very existence of the word.

The second reporter arrived as I was dishing out the Marks and Spencer chilli (he had his with baked potato), and we trod the familiar ground, this time in a Manchester accent – him at first, then very quickly both of us. Sheila from down the road had arrived with Max, her youngest. She washed my hair and told me how well I looked. Bless her kind heart. Then Naomi, Simone and Astrid, my friends and minders, stood round while I modelled three dresses – one purple, one black and one pink and borrowed.

Unanimously, they chose the black, so I slipped into the purple, then headed for the BBC. Jeremy, my publisher (I love saying that), was waiting and the show went well. Except I didn't quite manage to mention the title of my book. It's a bit embarrassing, this plugging business. Halfway through the interview, Terry asked if I'd like to come back next week to review TV programmes. Amazed, but with an eye to the main chance and an ear to the plug, I agreed.

Tuesday was okay. I drove the one and a half hour journey to rehearsals in Teddington at 8.45 a.m. as usual. I've no words to describe my feelings about the North Circular Road without recourse to pornography. In the afternoon, I recorded an interview on the book at the BBC. Back home, my parents had arrived from Hull. My mother had already pulled out the beds and found ancient and seemingly deadly fluff underneath.

On Wednesday I awoke with a migraine. This is not unusual. My mother had a migraine every Wednesday for years and I've inherited the complaint. I drove to Teddington pretending I hadn't got one, gave in during rehearsals and took the solubles. By the time I reached the BBC and _Woman's Hour_ in the afternoon, I was ga-ga. Victoria Wood and I went on the air to be amusing about our books, me with pounding skull and fur tongue. Not only was I not funny, but I also said 'masturbation' on the air. On _Woman's Hour_!

I crawled home. _Options_ had rung. They wanted an article by Monday. There were six firemen, two of them female, sitting round my kitchen table telling stories to Jack. This would have been bizarre without a migraine! I honed in on the kids and their homework and learned my lines in the bath.

Thursday was the book launch. I dressed (in the black) at 7.30 a.m. The make-up sat on the surface of my skin like scrambled egg. I drove to work, rehearsed until noon, and drove back to the Theatre of Comedy. The foyer was packed with friends, loved ones and others. Astrid, having made fish-balls, bagels and lox for hundreds, plus cakes and cookies, still looked fresher than the newly-cut flowers. My brother turned up from Geneva and I shed a tear. Faint with hunger but unable to eat, I made a speech. Because they loved me, they laughed like drains. (How does a drain laugh?)

The invitation had said, 'This book does not tell you how to: get thin, stay fat, acupuncture your axolotl, programme your orgasms, tighten your friend's inner thigh, frame your own marmalade, make gourmet smorgasbord from soil, marry above yourself or become the perfect executive wife, mother and abseiling rabbi. It does, however, have lots of nice paper with writing on it, and the odd funny bit.' It also said 'Trousers optional'. David Shilling arrived in mink coat and no trousers. I drove home flower-laden and very, very happy. Amy was not pleased; she should have been invited.

Friday was the killer. After work, I had a business meeting. There, three men (two of whom I liked) screamed at me for an hour and a half for something I was supposed to have done with intent to maim. For once in my life, I shouted back, and refused to be brow beaten. Proud of myself, I paused for a moment and a colleague was nice enough to defend me. This, of course, made me weep. I stormed out, furious with myself, dried my eyes on the toilet roll and returned to the fray with renewed vigour. Delighted with my new assertiveness (perhaps I'm growing up at last), I stomped to the car park, blubbed all over the rear-view mirror and drove home.

Saturday's rehearsal was better. We had a show. Amy was with me watching every move, knowing every line. Afterwards we drove into Oxford Street and, much against her will, she had her first grown-up haircut.

On Sunday we rehearsed from 10 a.m. to 6 p.m. At

7.30 the studio audience came in, the warm-up man warmed them, the leading actress remembered the names of her fellow artistes and the show went well. That night I slept like a person.

Monday again. Christine arrived and we did the mail. Then to BBC radio to do *The Gloria Hunniford Show*. Once again, while explaining the title of the book, I said 'masturbates' on the air. It was beginning to be a compulsion (saying it, that is). I went home, played ping-pong with Adam, and headed Woganwards. Calm as a hyperventilating cucumber, I sat in the guest's chair and Terry said, 'Well, Maureen, have you had a good week?'

Most of the radio and TV shows I appeared on wanted one thing only of a girl. That she tell 'the Barbra Streisand story'. By the time *How Was It For You?* was on its way to those Christmas lists, I must have told that story over 150 times and had started re-inventing the dialogue. No, I have no intention of ever telling it again – you'll have to read it for yourselves.

The literary luncheons were easier. You travel to the designated place, meet your fellow authors, try and fail, because of pounding gall bladder, to eat your bland fare, then stand up when announced and do your recitation nicely for the ladies and – well, just ladies mostly. Nice ones in hats who *read*, God bless them. Afterwards you sit at a table mentally begging one of the hats to buy your book and ask you to sign it. I signed beside Sir Geraint Evans in paperback, Suzy Menkes in coffee-table-sized hardback, and Jilly Cooper in jolly hardback. I was very much the new girl, a hybrid figure, but meeting the seasoned pros and their partners was lovely. Rather like doing a charity gala. The sinking feeling beforehand 'Why did I ever agree to do this – they can't possibly want *me*?' – heart banging visibly in your temples and neck followed by a relaxed camaraderie when you've all got through it, and an absolute ravenous hunger and thirst when all that's left is petits fours and brandy.

At one luncheon I was due to speak before Jeffrey Archer, but gladly agreed, at his request, to reverse the order as he had to catch a train to some important engagement. Mr Archer took the floor – what do I mean? Mr Archer took the floor, the walls, the ceiling – even the tables and chairs stood to attention, waiting to be taken. His speech (and remember this was before he 'never met that woman') was un peu grandiose. The word 'I' was occasionally mentioned. Also the word 'One'. We were informed how easy it is for one to start a second career as a best-selling author when one's first one goes wonky. It was a remarkable speech, if only for the molten fluency with which he championed his own cause. Then with a flash of blue and more than a hint of gold he was gone, leaving us all feeling a little humble, a little blessed, and more than a little fragrant.

One rose to one's feet to follow and found oneself saying, 'Mr Archer didn't really have to catch a train, he wanted to go first because he's terribly, terribly shy and nervous in front of strangers.' One would have gone on, but the audience's laughter prevented one.

The Manchester literary lunch was my favourite episode. It started without a minicab – the one which should have taken me to Euston. I tried to ring Jeremy, my publisher, with whom I was travelling, but his phone was out of order. The train was due to leave at 8 a.m., and at 7.10 I was getting nothing but 'Yes – we could have a cab with you in forty-five minutes – how would that be, Madam?'

We don't live near a tube. That's one of the advantages of Muswell Hill. It entitles us to pay Haringey Rates. The highest in London outside The Mall. That and nowhere to buy knickers or hardware. Jack took me to Highgate and I hopped on and off the tube to Euston – where I spied Jeremy looking like the White Rabbit in *Alice*, only whiter. He'd been trying to phone me from every vandalised booth between Hampstead and Euston and almost needed carrying to a Second Class compartment. I might add that he had wanted to book First Class, but I refused on principle to allow anyone to pay an extra twenty quid for turquoise greasy upholstery instead of orange greasy upholstery. More of that later.

We settled down to a nice, uneventful journey to Stockport, where we were being met by another non-existent car to take us to a book-signing. Marginally daunted we hoofed it through the rain to the nearest cab-rank and thus to the signing, distinguished initially by the arrival of a jolly young man whom I'd never met before. He was recently married and asked me point blank if I would come to dinner that night with him and his new wife, as she was a fan of *Agony*. I made a lot of 'Gosh, that's *very* nice of you . . . *What* a shame I'm only here for a few hours . . . *Ah, well,* that's life . . . ' noises, although in reality he was absolutely sweet and dead right to ask. I wish I had his chutzpah. Months later, I used the incident in a radio game called *Hoax*, when asked to tell a so-called True Story. In my story, I did go to their house, was greeted at the door by the young man in his bathrobe, and was shown into the 'Disrobing Room'. I made great play about seeing couples entwined around the jacuzzi surrounded by Marks and Spencer stacking crisps and mounds of goose-pimples all over the shag-pile (tastefully furnished in what my friend, Ruby, calls 'Jewish beige'). Finally, after rebuffing several buffoons in the buff, I escaped by the skin of my underneaths.

Understandably enough in this day and age, the audience believed my story and voted it the truest of the three. I was pleased but felt vaguely guilty about Mr Newly-Wed recognising the beginning of the story, if not the end. But then, that's what you get for your chutzpah – lies made up about you in the media. I did define 'chutzpah' in Book One, but for new and bemused readers here is the second definition from *The Joys of Yiddish*: A boy murders his parents then throws himself on the mercy of the courts on the grounds that he's an orphan.

Back in Stockport, however, the book-signing went as well as you'd expect, and we upped and offed to the literary lunch at which, no doubt, I told the Barbra Streisand story, defined 'chutzpah' and rambled on a bit in the name of humour. Suzy Menkes was talking about her beautiful and lavish book on the Royal Jewels which, since the Windsor Auction, I've kicked myself for failing to buy; and Susan Brooks about her Granada TV cookery book. She bears a striking resemblance to what I can only describe as me. Even I could see it and she asked me to appear on her show as a guest cook. 'But my meat-balls were used as ammunition in the Malvinas,' I hooted, and told her of the last time I cooked a carrot cake. The recipe had said 3/4 teaspoon salt, which I took to mean 3 or 4 teaspoons full. The mixture tasted like a cockle stall, so, to soak up the salt, I added a grated potato. Four guests and the family sat down to a tea of grated potato-carrot-and-salt cake. What was it like. Very nice, actually. 'If you like your latkes lukewarm with cream-cheese frosting. I could send you a slice,' I offered. 'There's still some left. Quite a lot, really.'

'Don't bother yourself,' Susan said hastily. 'Come on and do fishballs.' (I did. We started the programme with me in her place saying 'Good afternoon and welcome to *On the Market.* I'm Susan Brooks and my guest for today is actress Maureen Lipman.' Cut to Susan. Gosh, it was all such fun . . . *and* the fishballs were almost edible, though I says it as shouldn't. After the programme was broadcast a strange woman took me to task in Brent Cross Shopping Centre over the fact that I'd left out the teaspoon of sugar. I thanked her grudgingly, and left, mumbling 'Well, I *never* put sugar in fish (potato in cake, yes – but sugar in fish, no), and neither does my mother nor her mother before her . . . whinge, whinge, mutter, mutter, mind your own business, yes, I do look thinner in real life, don't I? Probably due to the lack of sugar in my minced hake . . . ')

After the lunch, I signed a happily large number of books and Jeremy came hurtling back from the phone, pinker than he'd been since dawn, to say we'd made The Best Seller Lists. Aside from holding a completed book, or a completed baby, in my hands for the first time, it was the proudest moment of my upwardly mobile career.

We headed out towards our next unwaiting car, the one which was supposed to take us to Granada Television. Fortunately some kind gentleman offered us a lift. 'Oh, thank you!' we cried, 'that's so nice of you, we'd hate to be late for the interview.' He said it was no trouble, but that he'd just have to drop his wife off first. 'Fine,' we chorused, not realising that they lived in the Hebrides. We were almost, but not quite, hysterical when we reached Granada, and late enough to be rushed into a piping-hot studio to tell the Barbra Streisand story – oh, my God, pardon the yawning, it's hereditary – and then even hotter-foot to be even later for a BBC radio interview; and so late for a second local radio station that they'd packed up and left before we got there. Heigh-ho.

Back to Piccadilly, Manchester, where we settled gracelessly into a Second Class compartment. The day had been endless – but fun – though little did we know the jest was still to come. Instead of leaving at 6 p.m., the train just sat and sat until even the sanguine Brits were moved to make a fuss (i.e. chunter to each other after the guard had passed through, making no announcement). After fifty minutes, the announcement came. 'This is your guard speaking. British Rail apologises for the delay due to an electrical fault. We regret that we shall be removing the Second Class buffet car. Any passengers bearing a Second Class ticket, therefore, have seven minutes in which to return to the station buffet to purchase sandwiches and coffee for the remainder of the journey. For those passengers with a First Class ticket, dinner will be served in thirty minutes, and the First Class buffet will be open for sandwiches, drinks and coffee throughout the journey. Thank you.'

To say that this announcement made me angry is like saying that Edwina Currie is lacking in tact. I couldn't believe that the whole carriage wasn't on its feet roaring like bulls and rending the upholstery. Why do ordinary people abjectly accept utter snobbery thinly disguised as House Rules? Does it start in school, the army or the doctor's surgery? What about the *older* Second Class ticket-holder who wasn't able to race through the barrier in search of polyester sandwiches, dust-filled apple pies and flat Tizer? What of the passenger who's missed her connection due to BR's arbitrary shunting and won't eat until the wee smalls? And the mother of bairns? She can't just hare back and forth on toddler legs – theirs, not hers – and equally they can't be left unattended while she hares it alone.

In short, it was anti-social behaviour on a vast scale

and it made me see red. When the steward passed, I
asked him if they couldn't waive the rules a bit, since it
was, after all, entirely BR's fault that we were to be
delayed *and* starved for the heinous crime of paying
£20 less per seat than our neighbours in the greasy
turquoise section. Surprisingly enough, he told me
that rules were rules. 'Gosh, really?' I wanted to say,
but said instead, 'Surely you could at least serve
people with a cup of coffee and a biscuit?' This was
apparently a 'jobsworth'*, since, if he gave us all a
centimetre, we'd take a kilometre – hundreds of us
foul-smelling peasant stock would go rushing en
masse to the buffet car, depleting stock and pillaging
staff. He was foreseeing a scene straight out of *Dr
Zhivago*. I'd seen something much more like *Brief
Encounter*. 'Well, can you at least put it to your supervisor?' I bleated to his departing back, which replied,
'I'll see what I can do.' Obviously, he could do
nothing, because half an hour and a ping of a microwave later dinner was announced for First Class
passengers.

I stood it for about as long as I could, then, when I
figured the Cream of Celery à la Mode was blobbing
into the tureen, I decided the moment had come, and
set off on the Long March. After two or three noisy,
bustling Second Class carriages, I picked my way
nervously through two pitch black ones – obviously
First Class and vacant – into the sparsely-populated
buffet car, and finally into the hallowed precincts of
the First Class dining-car.

Twinkling stainless steel and the clunk click of rather
chunky china was the order of the day, alongside
Steak Bordelaise et Pommes Lyonnaise and other such

* ''S'more than me job's worth' = standard reply from
person in public service wishing to incur not one second's
extra work for benefit of customer.

fine British fare. I saw my steward and, to his obvious discomfiture, asked if he'd had a chance to ask his supervisor whether the starving Second Classes could help to fill the yawning ranks of empty tables I saw before me. Exasperated, he told me it would be unfair to those people who'd paid a full First Class fare if he were to allow in the general riff-raff (my words, not his).

'But, sir, with respect, I must point out to you that some of us in Second Class have excellent table manners. We don't swear. We don't fart or dribble, well, no more than your average business executive, and we would in no way attempt to fraternise with those so plainly above our station . . .'

I could feel him sweating a bit with repressed desire to thump me between the eyes. 'Look, Madam. If it were up to me, I don't mind *anyone* who wants to have a meal, having one.' I think my face must have lit up or something, because he added, 'But there's no way I can announce this over the tannoy – it's against company regulations.'

In one sentence I could see Apartheid being reversed. 'But you don't mind letting them in if they should know about it from another source?'

'Well, within reason . . . I mean, I haven't the staff . . .'

This time it was *my* departing back taking the message. 'Thanks, you're a real brick!' I yelled over my shoulder, with extremely careful pronunciation, and, moving in an unleisurely fashion, I made my way back through the darkened carriages, back into Tenko-land, where I proceeded to tell every passenger that, should they require one, a hot meal was awaiting them in First Class, and they should just mention that a lady had informed them, on the steward's behalf, that this would be okay.

Well, I might tell you that from the passengers' point of view this was a rum do. Here they are, chugging along resignedly, minding their own business, when up comes this familiar-looking loony from *Agony*, dressed to kill in her literary luncheon gear – very big shoulders that year – and informs them that dinner is served if they mention her name. Some of them grinned and hastily looked round for Cilla or Eamonn. Some of them found interesting points on their clothing to suddenly concentrate on. Still others said, 'Oh, thank you very much, love', as though I was a Lyons Nippy announcing that tea was imminent, we'd just been waiting on a new batch of baps. And some said, 'Good on you, Doreen, 'ow d'ya manage that, then?' At one point, I passed Brian Glover, the wrestler/actor/writer, sitting reading *The Daily Telegraph*. Perhaps because I'd seen him playing Kruschev so often I assumed he'd share my wrath and join me in spreading the word, perhaps even taking off a shoe and banging the odd table for added emphasis. But, no. Sensibly or otherwise, he said I must be bloody mad, wished me luck and dived straight back into the *Telegraph* crossword.

I have to tell you that it took an age. By the time I was back in my orange upholstery, chaps were coming by the table saying, 'Thanks for the meal, Mo,' and even ''Ere, you know what they're saying in the dining-car? ''Who sent you? THAT WOMAN, was it?'' ' Now that's what I call fame.

But the sweetest moment by far came when the steward and his two assistants came down through the carriage bearing coffee and biscuits for the remaining plebs. I thought that was handsome of them, although, typically enough of BR brainpower, they were burdened with cups, coffee pots and trays on the journey down and one of the young women had to keep returning to base for fresh coffee and hot water. On the way back, however, when they were merely collecting used cups, they had a trolley – Zing, Zing, Zing!

The punch-line, or sum-uppance, of the story came later. Jeremy and I said goodbye at the taxi-rank. We'd had an eventful day, no food ourselves and a bloody awful journey, but somehow a whole trainful of people had been fed and warmed and in my own small way I felt quite Geldofian. A day or so later, that worthy substitute for Bronco Utility Toilet Paper, *The Sun*, printed the following: 'Agony for TV star on Second Class Ticket'. It went on to mis-report that actress, Maureen Lipman, of TV's *Agony*, had made an angry scene because she couldn't get *herself* a meal in the First Class dining-car on a Second Class ticket.

Doesn't it make you want to regurgitate? So when BR say 'We're getting there', it's true. As long as you bear in mind that *where* they're getting is up your nose, in your hair and on your nerves.

The rest of the book-signing tour has paled into insignificance beside that one, but I do recall one wonderfully bizarre literary lunch at which we were served prawn cocktail, roast pork with cauliflower cheese, and chocolate mousse. A menu hand-selected for a Jewish migraine-sufferer. I remember going there, but somehow I can't remember coming back.

I do remember coming back from the Hull book-signing, with Cheryll, who'd organized it. The journey there is etched on my brain. I went Inter-City via Leeds and via Doncaster – and I'll tell you via von't be doing it again. It so happened that Cheryll and I were travelling First Class. No, I know this sounds unlike the sensible Yorkshirewoman you've come to know and tolerate, but that's because Robson Books were paying the fare, not me.

Book-signing can be deeply humbling. I'll tell you about it. You sit at a table bearing your name and book title – and, no doubt, your inside leg measurement – and sign merrily away for about half an hour until the queue totally disappears. Then, for the remaining half an hour, you try to look as though you're just resting before going on to something far more important – and succeed in looking like a tart flogging her wares from an Amsterdam window.

But this is, of course, a diversion, a new train of thought, off the beaten tracks and going right up the sidings. There we were with our First Class tickets in the restaurant car, about to indulge in that Great British institution – the Great BR Breakfast. After a wait of a mere half an hour, the toast (for this read sculptured polystyrene) hit the deck. It was harder and colder than a trowel on a frosty morning, and marginally less tasty. Ten minutes later the butter arrived. My order threw the steward into a trough of despondency. 'Kipper?' he said, as though hard of herring. 'It'll have to be *done*. It'll take a bit.' After another twenty-five minutes in Chez Upchuck, illuminated only by the steward's eyeballs when I wanted tea, not coffee, when he'd already done his pouring into three cups without raising the spout routine, my kippers arrived. And now, let me describe to you a forty-five minute late quartet of BR kippers. Ever eaten wax ear-plugs? Me neither. Until now. And all this a snip at £7.50.

After the signing in Leeds we travelled through to Hull. All the station names had been removed for reasons of security. The night was black, the windows resembled the back of my son's ears, and so Cheryll missed her stop and had to be disembarked at Ferriby, where, naturally enough, there was neither ticket office nor telephone box, and she was reduced to

knocking on the doors of strange Yorkshirewomen
and asking for the use of their British Telecoms.

Hull was in the grip of the coldest day since . . . its
last coldest day, and my mother's chicken soup (yes,
really) went down a real treat – two bowls already. The
book-signing at Browns was grand, with all kinds of
faces from the past facing mine, including the child I'd
last seen enlarging the stomach of one of my English
teachers, accompanied by her husband! Nobody but
me had aged at all, and other people's parents looked
just the same as they did back in the days when they
thoroughly disapproved of me.

At one point, an old schoolfriend marched in and
said, 'I read you were 'ere, so I thought I'd 'ave a look
at you.' Delighted to see her, even more delighted to
be able to open the book and show her a photograph of
herself alongside me in the school play, I beamed in
anticipation of what piece of old school lore I could
inscribe in her frontispiece.

'Well, fancy that,' she murmured, and with a loud,
'Right, I'll be off now,' she was off now – brisk and
bookless.

Now, the whole episode would have made perfect
sense had my mother been present. She was, after all,
last seen at the time of my book launch, leaning across
to a potential buyer and heavily stage-whispering, 'I
wouldn't bother to buy one; it's coming out in
paperback next year.'

Which brings me inexorably to the journey back –
8 a.m. in a totally unheated compartment, wearing
coat, gloves and scarf for 3 hours 5 minutes. Can I
please have a word with Jimmy Savile on the subject of
the Trade Descriptions Act? Mind you, the PR over the
tannoy had me laughing fit to levitate. 'Good mornin'.
This is your guard speakin'. Welcome aboard the
8 o'clock train to London, King's Cross. For your

convenience, we 'ave a buffet-car servin' hot snacks, tasty sandwiches and assorted beverages. We shall be stoppin' at . . . ' This routine occurred before and after every station, and short of singing *My Way*, there was nothing more the guard could have said or done, other than tap dance down the train with an individual fruit pie in his mouth.

My favourite announcement on another such journey was, 'BR wish to apologise profusely for the fact that this train will be three quarters of an hour late arriving at Euston. This is entirely due to the delay. Thank you.'

It's all geared up to work like the airlines, you see, even down to the Inter-City magazines which are stacked inside each compartment door. The first paragraph reads, 'Good customer relations is the reason why this magazine is in your carriage today.' 'As opposed to heating,' I muttered through numb teeth.

This, then, is the organization which is putting up its prices by ten per cent. Higher than inflation warrants. My parents will have to pay £60, with travel passes, to come to London this year, *and* change at draughty Doncaster to boot en route. Small wonder that my mother spends baffling hours cutting coupons off packets of Persil, hoarding fabric softener lids and booking twelve months in advance for the third Wednesday of any month with an R in it, providing you catch any train back which leaves King's Cross before 5.30a.m., carrying pigs.

Which brings me to my most memorable rail journey, and here BR can relax – I take full responsibility for my own brain-drain. Jack was taking the kids to Hull and had a lot of paperwork to do on the journey. I couldn't go as I was in a West End play, but settled the kids in, gave them their books and sandwiches, and was midway through a long lecture on how not to disturb Daddy while he's working, when the train gently pulled out of the station and on its merry way north.

The entire carriage, in particular those closely related to me, thought this was the funniest thing they'd ever lived through. As for me, I had a fabulous day travelling two hours to Peterborough, and two hours back from Peterborough to London, in time to walk straight on stage, engine-lagged.

So don't talk to me about 'getting there'. I'm staying here.

The success of *How Was It For You?* amazed and mystified me. Still does. Unlike a show, there were no notices, either good, bad or indifferent, and no advertising to persuade one that it's any of those things. After the paperback appeared, the mail began to pour in and all kinds of strangers became friends. This time, as I reluctantly sat down to do it all over again – 'If I had to do it all over again, I'd do it all over you' – I all but packed in before writing a word. I'd just read an interview with Debra Winger in *The New Yorker*. In it, when asked about her 'turbulent' relationship with Shirley MacLaine, she told of the time Shirley had given her a copy of her book, *Out On A Limb*, the one about reincarnation. Not one to mince words, Debra had told her, 'Don't give it to me. Unless you really want to hear what I think of it.' Shirley assured her she did. After reading it Debra told her that her *mother* would love it, but *she* thought it was self-indulgent crap and why didn't she (Shirley) just attach a camera to her arm and film herself all day long. That way she could bypass having to write the words to make the book to create a film. The interview didn't print what

Miss MacLaine replied – or maybe it was subbed out.

Anyway, the point of this is that I suddenly felt as though Ms Winger's finger was pointing at me, as well. Wasn't that what I was doing, too? Turning what should have been a personal diary into a public one? Hadn't the kids complained already that they'd been misquoted in *How Was It For You?* – 'It was *me* who said that, NOT ADAM!' Hadn't Jack abandoned all thoughts, not that he'd really had any, of an autobiography? I'd used up his best stories – 'Any funny stories about landladies, love?' I once asked him for a *TV Times* article, and, of course, he had. (The man's got a mind like the British Library – and in his case it's a lending library.) Apparently he and four other boys shared digs in Sheffield under the merry auspices of a certain Mrs Gosling. She was short, round and wheezy and, according to Jack, profoundly amused by everything the lads said and did. She would shake with mirth at their every quip, however puerile, and quiveringly await their return from university each day, as a fresh opportunity to double over with laughter and go scarlet in the face.

It seemed that all the lads had single beds but for Ron, a towering genius of a scientist, who had the double. One night, as Ron was in the bathroom, the others got into his bed and, amidst much stifled hysteria, awaited his return. Ron further convulsed them by getting back into bed, ignoring their presence, but violently bouncing the bed up and down to settle himself. As the hysteria grew, the floor grew weaker and, with a splintering crash, one leg went straight through the ceiling. As they looked sheepishly through the hole, they saw the plaster-covered shape of Mrs G looking up. 'This time,' she wheezed, 'you lads 'ave gone a bit too far' – so saying, she dissolved into helpless, heaving mirth.

No wonder people avoid telling me things now. I feel like a leech. (Did you know they have thirty-four segments and each segment has a brain? What must they all be thinking about? Paranoia, thy name is leech!) People have *always* confided in me, partly because my memory is so unreliable that they knew I'd forget the confidence before I could pass it on. These days there's lots of 'Now, don't you go putting this in one of your books.'

Then there's the fact that everybody knows your business, your politics, your mother's funny habits – and here I go again: I was lying in bed trying to get up the other day when I heard my mother accost my domestic help (or my 'woman' as she insists on calling Chris) with a feather duster and the following dialogue. 'Oooh!' (wafting duster around dado rail) 'Dust! Yum, yum!' Then: 'Do you know, my house never gets dusty. When I get back to Hull, there won't be a layer of dust or anything. I don't know why . . . ' she suddenly sounded sad, 'because I love to dust . . . ' Far be it from me to suggest that no dust speck worth its salt, or even salt speck worth its dust, would have the temerity, let alone the death-wish, to abandon hope and enter that spotless storm-porch. Indeed, it's a known fact that gangs of vagrant dust do mass U-turns at the mere mention of Zelma Lipman. This is a phenomenon known to British meteorologists as 'The Humberside Dust-Sheet', and to Russian meteorologists as 'Dustyoffski'.

Nevertheless, and not with-sitting, I'd agreed on a deadline with Jeremy. I had three months to finish *Something to Fall Back On*.

The dress for the cover was already being made by Ben Frow, the man who's made my fashion fantasies come true this year. One dress: Fifties-style, cinched waist, circular skirt, crisp shirt-collar, Ben can make 'em in a day. I discovered this when he was making costumes for the chorus in *Wonderful Town*, this being a musical which has taken up much of my life since I last put down my pen. There I was with a boring blue skirt and tie-neck blouse, and there was this boy-genius working all night and producing haute couture on a shoestring, a G-string even. The day before we opened, I pleaded (stridently), 'Look, guys, I know my character's brainy not beautiful. I know she never gets near the men her sister has for lunch, but if I go and sing "A Hundred Easy Ways to Lose a Man" in this blue suit, I may end up losing the next General Election instead of winning an award.'

Overnight, Ben created a smart, chic, perfectly-fitting number which I wore every night (but Sundays) and twice Wednesdays and Saturdays for the next year. I know what you're thinking: it did have change-able armpit pads. Mind you, by the time the show closed, you could have picked up the dress with a pair of tongs and frightened off Meatloaf, Sigue Sigue Sputnik and Janet Street-Porter.

So, this year Ben has made 'the dress' in a raffish gentleman's tweed for Buckingham Palace (hang on, and I'll tell you about that one . . .), crisp navy and white for the Variety Club of Great Britain Luncheon – and in Liberty's curtain fabric for the cover of this book. One small problem: the book had still to be written. A piece of strudel! For a proper writer.

Follow the Yellow Beak Road

DEAR DIARY

I am not a proper writer. I'm just filling in time. As we speak, I'm awaiting a delivery of bricks (natural red) for the edges of the borders around my front bays. I've been waiting for them since 9.30a.m., when they were promised. So has Dick the builder. It's now 3p.m., and we've both run out of smiles, nods, shrugs and teabags. Of course, it's probably Dick's last day here for several weeks or years, so I expect I'll be ringing the director of the Tate Gallery this time tomorrow to see if he'd like another large, natural red sculpture at a peppercorn rent.

It's not as though I've anything much else I should be doing. My parents are here, so the house is frighteningly clean, the washing machine is on constantly, and there's a perpetual jelly in the fridge. Simone's gone camping with her boyfriend and more luggage than Moses and the Israelites took out of Egypt, and the kids are at a day camp, heavily name tagged, learning to nature ramble through a north London industrial estate. So what else have I got to do with my time other than wait in for t' bricks? Nothing. Nada. Nowt. Rien.

Jack's out, you see, filming. The physiotherapist came at the crack of dawn, startlingly beautiful, and took him into the bedroom. My father hasn't got over it yet. He thinks this is the sort of thing that goes on in London all the time. Although he looked even more puzzled when I followed suit an hour later and didn't come out.

She did Jack's leg first and my shoulder next. Then Jack limped off to the filming and I stayed 'armlessly at home. 'Course, when he's here the workmen descend on him all day like a ton of . . . Well, he hasn't got a proper job, has he? Just sits at his desk all day, smoking a pen and chewing a fag and gazing into the distance or, in his case, the grubby nets.

Years ago we 'cat-sat' in a rather chic flat for friends who were on a world tour. It had a beautiful view and majored in the 3 H's: Habitat, Heals and Hampstead. Jack used to sit typing at a stark white table surrounded by Casa Pupo rugs and Turkish floor cushions, whilst I was doing my bit for England at the Old Vic.

All the owner's friends were young and hip and occasionally they would show up at the door, after having been for a walk on the Heath or for a cream tea in the village. One night he opened the door to a snake-hipped black guy in cheesecloth shirt, huge gold-clasped leather-belted trousers, shining bald head and gold ear-ring. 'Hi, man. Anyone home?' he growled and grinned at the same time.

'Oh. Hello,' said Jack affably, still mentally halfway through a scene. 'Come in – er – would you like a coffee?' He wouldn't but he came in anyway and Jack explained about the world tour. The guy nodded and smiled and smiled and nodded and said, 'Too much' a few times and seemed patently to be waiting for something. After a while Jack drifted back towards his typewriter, resumed his seat. Finally the guy said 'Well, man, I got some great shit if you can use it.'

My husband probably blinked Eric Morecambe-like and said, 'Pardon?'

'Top shit, man, you wanna try? Gold, man. You wanna roll?'

'Sorry I . . . roll what? Oh, you want a cigarette? I've only got Benson & Hedges but you're welcome to . . .'

'No, man. I got some stuff. For the cats. You want some or not?'

By now Jack was confused. 'Pardon?' he probably said again, if I know Jack. He'd been feeding Nelly diligently on Whiskas Supercat and doubted very much whether she was in need of supplements.

Finally the pound dropped. Jack explained as 'hiply' as he knew how that the only substances that turned him on were fried fish and tea bags. Sam the pusher, for it was he, pushed off, leaving nothing behind but a tiny 'sample' in a tight twist of tinfoil and a promise to call again, for all the world like a door-to-door brush salesman.

A few nights later the doorbell rang again to reveal yet another smiling black guy in colourful embroidered shirt, beads and sneakers, asking for the owners of the flat. Once again Jack gave him a coffee, only this time he was wised up to the situation. He told him they had all the stuff they needed, adding a 'Thanks, man, it was really far out' or two and suggested he called back when our friends returned. The guy smiled and said, 'Well, I probably won't be around this beat any more. I'm being transferred to Special Branch. Anyway, give them my best and I'll see them around. Cheers.'

Time revealed that our friends did indeed have two black friends in their circle of acquaintances. One was a pusher. The other was a young policeman who often dropped in for a cuppa and a chat about show-biz. I am here to tell you that a great deal of hasty toilet flushing was heard to ensue for the rest of the evening and much of the next day.

It was the same flat that played host one night for another odd couple. Once again, we find our hero at work at his ancient typewriter. 'Act III, Scene IV, Mavis enters village hall, sees Mr Beddowes and starts.' Once more the doorbell rings and our hero shuffles, mind full of dramatic interruptus, to open it. There in the harsh overhead light are revealed my old drama school chum, Lesley, wearing a large tatty fur, and her friend Miguel, a Puerto Rican dancer currently wowing the West End in *Show Boat*, wearing a fur vest. What was unusual about this, you may ponder? Nothing but the fact that they were both hysterical with sustained grief. They were leaning on each other, racked with huge gasping sobs, their mutual mascara running in estuaries and tributaries the length and breadth of their faces. 'For God's sake – Lesley, what's the matter?' demanded Jack. 'What's wrong?'

Renewed sobs and howls were their only response. 'Sit down,' said Jack. 'Do you want a coffee? A drink? A cigarette?' They nodded wildly, biting their lips and shuddering with each breath. In a panic Jack made strong coffee, poured whisky and offered cigarettes. The couple continued to whoop and sob between sips and drags. 'Well,' said Jack finally, 'what is it? Are you ill?' They shook their howling heads. 'Have you been hurt? Has someone attacked you? What – I mean – how – ?'

With each successive question the pair grew more immersed in their mutual grief and the information flowed a great deal more slowly than the mascara. It was becoming clear that they were too stricken for anything but tears. Gradually, and after a decent interval, Jack began to drift back towards his table, emerging every now and then to ask if the pair were sure there was nothing he could do or get for them in the way of help. Since every such request drew from them a still more frenetic bout of magnoperatics than the last, he withdrew to his table, his notes and finally his typewriter. Several hours of sobbing later they stumbled from the day-bed into the night with only a passing howl at the door to signal goodbye. Jack sprang to his feet and ran after them saying, *'Please* tell me what it is. Who's done this to you? Please – ' Lesley fixed him with black and scarlet eyes and hiccupped, 'It's nothing – it's the – *sob* – the flat – we've had a – *hic* – a burst! A water-burst, we've got to call the landlord in the morning – *waaah*!' And in another burst they were gone. And were it not for the small black droplets on the Casa Pupo rug, the whole nightmare could have been a dream. Should you wish to know what was the actual reason for their distress – well, so would we.

When we were first married we lived in a ground floor flat in a large house and all the other flat owners thought Jack was the concierge. Mid-sentence, midthought, mid-week or mid-wife, he answered that beleaguered bell: 'Sorry to trouble you, Jack, you're not busy, are you? It's just that our boiler's gone on the blink and the fella said he'd call before nine o'clock but he hasn't and I'm on my way to work now, so here's the key. Would you mind? Oh, thanks. Stick around while he's there in case he's a bit . . . you know. Thanks, Jack. Byee.'

If it wasn't doorbells, it was phone bells. 'Helga, it's for you-hoo again. Spyros from the Green Man pub wants to know if you'll be in as usual tonight.' Plus the wife's callers. 'Hello. *Now.* You must be *Mr* Lipman. This is Betty Kominsky from the Cricklewood and District Jewish Action Group for Recycling Paper for use in Childhood Dyslexia Prevention in a Remote and

Stricken Part of the Negev Desert, or CDJAGRPCD-PRSPND, as we call ourselves. *Now.* May we count on your wife's appearance on Saturday July 19, 1989 at our Meatball and Pastry Brunch?'

And, most insidious of all, the infamous Interrupter Par Excellence, the wife's mother. 'Ja-ack, can you spare a minute? Can you smell a funny smell behind the fridge? You can't? Ooh, it's shocking! It's like cat's whatsit, or is it from that roasting dish? Look, it's encrusted . . . ugh! Don't tell me you can't smell it?'

Then, sotto voice (two decibels less than a bellow), 'This' (shoves produce under nose) 'was in that compartment *last time* I was here. It can't have been cleaned since! Just put your nose inside that flap! Oh, sorry, are you going? Were you doing something? I didn't realize. I thought you were just sitting there.'

Last week it was ducks. He was sitting at his desk at twelve noon, alone and undisturbed in the house when, through the grubby nets, he saw a Wildly Waving Woman on the front drive and went out to find her, and what she was wildly waving at. A duck and eleven ducklings. This is a main road in Muswell Hill, mind!

WWW suggests ringing RSPCA. Disturbed Writer agrees. 'Ignore 'em,' says RSPCA man. 'They're all over London. King's Cross is covered in 'em. Can't move for ducks.' Visions of ducks with tote bags and ducksacks trying to fathom the computerized departure indicator.

'Shall I round them up and take them to the park?' enquires Disturbed Writer, eyeing flapping wings and flapping woman. RSPCA man laughs RSPCA hat off. By now, ducklings are waddling through garage into back garden – where elderly gardener with unfortunate inner ear imbalance is working and occasionally falling into lupins. WWW, DW and FG (as in Falling Gardener) discuss problem and FG suggests DW shuts him, the duck, the ducklings and a large cardboard box inside the garage. DW reluctantly complies.

Garage doors close. Moment of silence, then all hell breaks out. Garage doors resound with the thud of flailing, falling and flying bird. Or is it mammal? Impossible to tell whether sound-track is caused by lurching duck or lurching gardener. Mother duck is by now livid.

Cut to DW (now as in Deranged Writer) phoning police. 'You've got what, sir?'

'Duck; and eleven ducklings. I don't know what to do.'

'Are you aware, sir, that you are speaking to Scotland Yard?'

'Er . . . no . . . I was ringing Muswell Hill police station . . . It's this duck . . . '

'This is the Crime Squad, sir, we don't do ducks.'

'Well, it's just there's this mother duck and . . . er . . . she's getting violent.'

'You're a big, strong man, sir. I'm sure you can manage.'

'Yes, but she's in a right muck sweat. Won't she bite?'

'Ducks don't have teeth, sir. They have beaks. Just a beak. You'll handle it, sir. I have every confidence.'

In the end they all waddled off, woman, gardener and writer. The ducks? Last seen, they were heading for the 134 bus stop – and Swan and Edgar's, no doubt.

It's five o'clock. Bricks haven't arrived. Dick's gone home. Ducks have gone home. Six pages written; no interruptions. As I said, I'm not a proper writer.

*   *   *

I did once try to be a proper travel writer. At *Options'* behest, I went to take a look at Israel. The day before, I took a look at my passport – which read 'M. Rosenthal' – and then at my air ticket – which read 'M. Lipman' – and realised at once I was going to be no Eric Newby. Twickenham Travel graciously lent me Pat – who brought me a new ticket, shepherded me through the cocktails, cashews and Ceefax of the British Caledonian VIP room, and giggled with me all the way to Ben-Gurion Airport. My minder.

For the first time in my life my brand new suitcase was first off the carousel. Avraham Kortzer, my big, avuncular, friendly guide, hauled it into a waiting car, where Nissim, the driver (already suffering from a frozen shoulder before he'd even met me), drove us straight to the Golden City.

For 'golden' read 'looking as though made of gold', nothing more metaphysical. For the moment. Jerusalem nestles between two mountains and is built in a pinkish-cream stone which melts into a unifying gold. The King David Hotel, built of the same stone, is cool, colonial elegance – and the view of the most breath-taking city I've ever seen, across flowered terraces and jacaranda trees is . . . well, breath-taking. I lay on the bed and the words 'This is the life' would have passed my lips, had not my breath already been taken. I was well into my third nectarine when the phone rang.

'Mrs Rosenthal? My name is Mr Bedford. I think you've taken my suitcase from the airport.' I didn't even bother to check. I knew me well enough to know he was right. So my case was still in Tel Aviv; my baggage-check was with Pat; and Pat was Lord knows where. My sleepless night was almost compensated for by the beauty of dawn breaking over the Holy City.

Before hitting the suitcase trail I hit breakfast. This was a stroke of genius. Breakfast at the King David is like lunch, dinner and supper anywhere else. Fruit I didn't know existed, breads of all shapes, fish of all flavours, sculptured yoghurts, every known egg, and a heaven of herrings – all arranged as though Constance Spry had also been up all night. I overdosed as demurely as possible, then chased over to Mr Bedford in Tel Aviv with the suitcase and a litre of gin. I traced Pat, chased back to the airport, got the case and chased back to Jerusalem. Day one, and all I'd acquired was an expert knowledge of the Tel-Aviv-Jerusalem road, no gin and very creased clothes.

On day two, I spent two and a half hours in the Museum of the Holocaust at Yad Vashem. I was deeply moved. It is stark, unsentimental and a *must*. The visit had its lighter side. I watched three guides give totally different interpretations of the same mosaic. That's Israel – three Israelis, four opinions.

In the Shrine of the Book Museum – again superbly designed – I pored over the Dead Sea Scrolls. It's the mundanity of some of the ancient letters which moved me – 'Dear Sir, you still have not paid me for the water jugs I made . . . ' In the event of war, the whole edifice containing them retreats into the ground. It would be nice if we could all do that.

With the walled Holy City having so much to offer, I decided to wait until Jack and the kids arrived. Twenty years before, on my last visit, it was still divided between Jew and Arab and therefore inaccessible. One day an old Arab was leaning out of the window when his false teeth fell out. They dropped into the No Man's Land of the street below. Hostilities were suspended until a UN officer, a Jordanian officer and an Israeli officer found them. Sounds like one of *my* tricks.

At the Hadassah Hospital, there are twelve stained

glass windows made by Chagall, one for each of the twelve sons of Jacob. In the Six Day War four of them were smashed. Chagall said, 'Listen, you take care of the war, I'll take care of the windows.' A year and a half later, he replaced them with exact copies. Their beauty makes you cry.

An hour's drive away, and 400 metres below sea level, the Dead Sea is a brilliant turquoise with what appear to be either glaciers or meringues floating on the top. Yes, it's salt. *Now* you understand about Lot's wife. She just went swimming too soon after a 'King David's' breakfast. In fact you can't swim at all, you just flail about helplessly while the mineral-rich water and the purest air in the world tone up your body more than a lifetime's worth of Jane Fonda. Then, up the cable car to Mount Masada, where 950 Jews killed themselves rather than surrender to the Romans. In the ruins on the plateau, you stand in their synagogue, walk through their living quarters and marvel at their ingenuity in storing food and water during the three-year siege. You gaze down on the site of the Roman camps below, feel something of what they must have felt and somewhere inside you history stirs.

On the way back we popped into Jericho. It's a seven-thousand-year-old city. Eat your heart out, Stratford-on-Avon. And that's only at its youngest. There are archaeological digs all over it, uncovering deeper and ever deeper layers of civilization.

The next stop was Nazareth, a beautiful town of winding streets. In the cool marbled Church of the Annunciation a Romanian nun was selling hand-made lace squares, 'for blouse, for blouse'. I, who can't sew up the end of a chicken, bought a job lot.

Now, if you think Christmas is commercialised, take a peek at Bethlehem. 'The Ninth Station Boutique' and 'The Manger Pizzeria' say it all. Despite that, the story of Jesus, the man, began to come alive in an exciting way.

In Haifa, after gorging on much too much gorgeous fruit, I began to suffer from Montezuma's Revenge. Now I could write a Good Loo Guide to Israel. One of the loos that wouldn't be in it is in the brand new Daniel Towers Hotel in seaside Herzliyya. The hotel has four restaurants ranging in style from mock-Cleopatra to mock-Polynesian. The whole is Florida kitsch with a slice of kiwi. Here your stomach-clutching travel writer found a not-completely-completed loo and was washing her hands when the lights went out. I groped round the walls to the door, couldn't open it, assumed the workmen had gone home, and did what any grown-up locked in a lavatory would have done. Screamed! Until a passing Swede switched on the *outside* light, pushed the door open and pointed out that 'push' in English means the opposite of 'pull'. So ended my chance of spending the night in a million dollar rest-room learning to read 'Air Freshener' in Hebrew with the help of lighted matches.

Later, over pumpkin-and-almond soup and sea-bass with fresh herb sauce (to settle the stomach), I suddenly missed the kids. It was the dessert that did it. It was jelly. I phoned home: 'Get here soon, Jack, before I'm deported for silliness.'

On my one free day I said 'shalom' to Avraham and raced to the poolside with shades, coconut oil and panama to do my beached-whale impersonation. Two seconds later, through closed eyes, I had an uncomfortable feeling that someone had their face very near to mine. I opened an eye and got a whacking great close-up of a beaming, elderly Jewish lady's mouth which heavily stage-whispered, 'I'm not going to disturb you 'cos I know you're here on holiday, but I just wanted to say *I know who you are!*' For the next hour, I heard about her son's business, her husband's life-story and her operations. Listen, what you lose on sunbathing, you gain in entertainment.

The morning after the family arrived, we hired the lousiest car in Israel and headed for Tiberias on the Sea of Galilee. We chugged out of Tel Aviv, through streets, the story goes, just wide enough to manage two camels turning at the same time – which would have been *all* we needed. I'd phoned the hotel to say we wouldn't be there the previous night as arranged, but the message didn't get through. When the car finally spluttered up to the foyer, Shula, the manageress, confessed that not only had *she* been up all night, but that from 3 a.m. to 6 a.m. the police had been combing the road from Tel Aviv with searchlights. We resolved to dump the car and hire an ass.

At the Tiberias Club, a time-share hotel, we swam and ate and relaxed as though we were actually on holiday. No mean feat for the Rosenthals who tend, like home-made wine, not to travel well. By the pool we watched a fashion show. Suddenly the compère, speaking in Hebrew, made all four of us jump out of my skin by saying two words in English – 'Maureen Lipman'. Four years old again, I tried to disappear. What was he expecting me to do? Recite 'Mary had a little lamb' in Hebrew? During the remainder of the show he said 'Maureen Lipman' three more times, and three more heart attacks were had by all.

After the show I asked him why. 'Because it's the name of one of the models,' he replied. So flabbergasted was I that I waited for my namesake to come out of the changing-room and asked her if that was really her name. 'Yes,' she said. 'So is mine!' I yelled. 'Oh,' she said, and strolled off. Pretty laid back, these Israelis.

At night the red sun drops dramatically into the Sea of Galilee turning the surrounding hills a spectacular vermilion. We bathed in the lake, ate St Peter's fish fresh from it, visited an ostrich farm and the ancient Roman hot springs at Hammat Geder. On the way back the car finally croaked its last and the kids ended up pushing it while Jack did his somewhat English version of a whirling dervish until we got another one.

Among the ruins of Capernaum, another ancient Roman site, we saw St Peter's house and the synagogue where Christ preached each Saturday. It's run by bad-tempered Franciscans who don't like tourists with bare knees, but it's absolutely spine-tingling. Adam disagreed. 'Why do we keep having to see interesting things?' he yawned, bowling an imaginary leg-break at a monk.

Back in Herzliyya, at the Dan Hotel, we had cool, airy bungalow rooms opening straight on to the lawns, the pool and the Mediterranean. Fifty yards away, we watched an open-air wedding, the bride and groom under a canopy with the sea and the sky as a back-drop.

The proximity of the Bible prompted philosophical thoughts from the kids. 'What do you think God looks like?' Amy: 'Well, he's got a blue outline, a long beard and he's not as *fulsome* as us.' Adam: 'He's not bald though, is he?'

The next day, God patted his head a little too enthusiastically and Adam got a headache. We rang reception for a pain-reliever, and the manageress arrived bearing the tablets, Sabbath wine and a tray of titbits. Jack said only in Israel can you ask for aspirin and get chopped herring. He now wants to emigrate.

Our last day was spent, fittingly, in old Jerusalem. In the burning heat we stood by the holiest of sights – the Western (or Wailing) Wall. Every crack is filled with pilgrims' prayers written on scraps of paper. The Jewish, Christian, Arab and Armenian Quarters actually feel like the cradle of life. The wailing Moslem chant washes over the city as tiny Arab boys push their postcards in a hard-sell campaign rarely seen outside Madison Avenue. Sombre black-clad Jews brush shoulders with ebony Ethiopian priests at the doorway to the tiny, atmospheric Coptic Church which stands on the site of a church discovered below it – and another church below that one. Like Israel itself, an endless story.

At the risk of being labelled (libelled) a Zionist and having Vanessa Redgrave never speak to me again, you don't have to be Jewish, you don't have to be Christian, you don't even have to take my word for it. Just go. But don't go as a would-be travel writer – go as a human being.

Rain Stopped Plane

AT LAST I'M a journalist. I feel qualified to rank as a triple high insurance risk, along with actor and after a fashion, musician.

It started with an invitation to join an inaugural flight to New York, with a new Scottish Airline, hereby entitled 'Fly the Kilt' and probably run from some tiny tartan office by Billy Connolly's aunty. They were offering for the weekend of June 5th, flights to and from the Large Apple and one night's stay at a posh hotel which boasted an arboretum in its foyer. Who could resist? My first trip to New York, my first travel piece on America, my first guilt-free weekend! My first big mistake.

Daughter Amy, pride and joy, has this one annual birthday. I know because I was there at the inaugural one. June 7th. It was a warm day from what I can recall through the haze of Pethidine, and not one to be missed thirteen years later because of a wretched freebie! 'You *go*,' said my mother, long-distance, adding ominously, 'You can sacrifice yourself now – but they won't thank you for it later!'

I tossed a coin, then tossed it again because it came out wrong. 'Best of three,' I muttered. Jack was keen to accompany me as he had a mini-musical showing off off-Broadway (not far *enough* off as it happened), and moreover he wanted to show me NY. I phoned the mother of Amy's (then) best friend and she agreed to give my daughter the birthday of her life. I then booked a box for *Kiss Me Kate* – dinner at Joe Allen's for seven – and two identical dresses for Amy and her friend. The combined cost of all this guilt was enough to fly me to NY on Concorde.

So, plans were duly laid, phone calls made to old pal Simon Jones (Arthur Dent in *The Hitchhiker's Guide to the Galaxy*) in Central Park who says 'Don't use a yellow cab – they're all certified criminals – I'll lay on a car', domestic arrangements of the complexity of Oliver North's Filofax all efficiently executed – freezer filled to bursting etc.

A week before our departure, the tickets and the itinerary arrive, including promise of piped bands to greet us and a tour of Manhattan. Astrid has given me details of where to go to put on pounds and where to go to lose dollars. 'Don't take the carriage ride round Central Park – it's a rip-off!'

On Monday comes an ominous message from the lady who's fixed me two nights at the Barbizon Hotel. She's had a letter informing her that the flight has been cancelled. I phone Scotland, where the boss's secretary tells me brightly, 'Yes, it has been cancelled – we were unable to check over the plane at Kennedy because it was raining.' I express some surprise at this piece of logic on the grounds that this is 1987 and if the mechanic is worried about getting his hair frizzed he could wear a plastic hood. When I ask her what are the chances of another flight she says even more brightly, 'Well, I suggest you phone your travel agency.' I then speak to her boss who says '*You're* in Show Business. These things happen.'

It's too late to retrace my steps and I'm too over-excited, so I book two standard British Airways flights, tell myself it's the money I saved not bidding for the Duchess of Windsor's jewellery, and with enough clothes for two months in Paris, we're off.

All I can say for British Airways is that they don't need Joan Collins. The flight was wonderful. The food was nice. I'll repeat that. The food was nice! On an aircraft! The staff were even nicer and actually organized a birthday card for Amy back home. And guess what *I* got to do? Sit behind the pilot whilst he landed at Kennedy! Seeing New York State spread out like twists of lace on satin right beneath my quivering nose was magical. The Captain patiently explained some of the myriad buttons, switches and keys in his brand new module and I tried to make intelligent-sounding noises in reply. I, who am wont to fly with one hand on the inflatable life jacket beneath my feet and the other over my eyes, was completely reassured by the sight of all those wonderful butch arms in their short-sleeved white shirts.

On arrival at Kennedy in boiling sun we were met by a peaked hat and a gleaming double limousine, courtesy of Simon Jones. 'My God,' I whispered. 'It's playing "Bridie" in *Whatsit Revisited* – it's turned his mind!' The driver closed the door behind us, saying 'You'll find the drinks in the cabinet by the door, TV and phone to your left. Enjoy your journey.' We sank into the air-conditioned depths of the car. I sniffed the first of two crystal carafes. It was bourbon. The second was clearly water as it had no smell. I poured a full tumbler and drank half of it greedily. It was neat vodka. The last thing I recall of the journey was Jack trying to pour half a tumbler of liquid back into the narrow neck of the carafe in a moving vehicle.

The Barbizon Hotel on 63 and Lexington is reasonably central and appears in the National Register of Historic Places. It was in the 1920s a

Professional Women's Club Residence for 'ladies of good breeding', which meant it welcomed gentlemen in its lobby but ladies only upstairs. Rumour has it that Burgess Meredith made it to the 14th floor, and I'd *love* to know for whom. Grace Kelly and Liza Minelli stayed there and Veronica Lake worked in the restaurant. It's fading beauty has been tastefully renovated in the 'America out of Yoorope' way, and the result is smart, pretty, restful and chic. The rooms are small but comfortable. Apparently we were in one of the larger ones – in some of them you can sit on the bed with your hands on the walls on either side, which could be handy if you've just driven from Kennedy with half a tumbler of neat vodka inside you. There are, of course, some magnificent suites and apartments, but who needs them with the whole of NY to conquer. Quite my favourite part of the Barbizon charm is the fact that some of the original 'gels' from the late Twenties are still there as sitting tenants – much to the chagrin of the hotel owners. They just won't go! They drift through the foyer in imposing hats and mysterious veils and hover around the piano bar at 'happy hour' like vintage ghosts. I longed to ask them if Burgess M. really made it!

During the course of the weekend we saw four shows. First we went to Neil Simon's *Broadway Baby* which concerns the trials of a Jewish family in the Forties as seen through the eyes of a young man writing for radio. Then we saw *Radio Days*, Woody Allen's affectionate but jerky account of a Jewish family in the Forties as seen through the eyes of an adolescent boy obsessed by the radio. We then whizzed over to see a disastrous production of *Bar Mitzvah Boy*, a musical set in the Forties concerning a Jewish family as seen through the eyes of a pubescent boy who's nothing to do with the radio, and finally we saw Jacky Mason's superb one-man show based on a lifetime's hilarious observations of the Jewish way of life. Quite frankly I think the same audience moved round en masse to each theatre. 'Look,' I whispered to Jack outside one foyer. 'Two thousand people have gone in and only one thousand noses!' The whole audience was like Louise Brooks's hair – bobbed.

An elderly lady came up to me outside one theatre. 'You wanna buy a ticket?' 'No thanks, I have them!' I replied. 'Shame. I gotta spare. My husband ya know . . . ' she broke off. 'He's ill . . . ' 'Oh, I'm sorry,' I said, sympathetically I hoped. She seized the opportunity and leaned closer. 'Yeah,' she drawled, 'diarrhoea.' And added graphically, 'Yeurrghew!'

To add salt beef to injewry we dined at Reuben's Deli (massive portions but tasteless), and the opulent Russian Tea Rooms where I had a stroganoff I could talk about for weeks. Then over to Saks on 5th Avenue, where we were sprayed with at least twelve of the strongest perfumes known to Frenchman or beast on the corner of every counter. We countered this by taking the aforementioned rip-off ride through Central Park, amidst the richest scent of fresh horse droppings you've ever – well, encountered.

For sentimental reasons we visited Greenwich Village, scene of almost all of *Wonderful Town*. More of that later. (Much more!) Lyric writer Adolph Green invited us up to his Central Park West apartment, from the terrace of which we gazed down at the collage of the park. The trees look like broccoli threaded through with lines of spaghetti, with the occasional jewel or jelly for the lakes. And over it the ants run and jog and wheel their babies and waggle their Walkmans. Adolph's neighbours in the apartment are Isaac Stern and Beverley Sills – so who needs a Walkman?

Final morning, last-minute shopping – window

only, the stores terrify me! – and down to the last instruction on Astrid's list: lunch at the Oyster Bar underneath Grand Central Station. Had I world enough and time I would describe the menu. All fish. The best. Ever. Tiny lights set into the arches of the basement ceiling. Red checked tablecloths. Fish soup. Red snapper salad. Oh be still my husband's heart! Then out to the airport to the accompaniment of the entire, fascinating life story of the Czech cab driver. On the plane they showed *Children of a Lesser God*, which is perfect plane viewing as you only need to lip read. I was too exhausted to sleep and too fat and happy to care.

Re the cancelled plane. I heard the true story from the hotel manager. Apparently it was an oldish Boeing and they were having it resprayed for the inaugural flight. The story goes that the Puerto Rican doing the respray sprayed not only the plane but all the windows. He'd chipped out five of them by the time they reached him. So it's not just you and I who have trouble every time we get a man in. I wanna be a part of it – New York, New York!

3

Womenopause

If the Cap Fits

I WOULD LIKE to shake the hand of the sex counsellor on LBC's afternoon problems programme the other week. Having done that, I'd like to poke two fingers in his eyes, yell *'Big mouth'* in his ear and Sellotape his lips together. 'Pourquoi the hyperbole?' I hear you chunter. Okay, are you sitting cross-legged? Then I'll begin. My son and I were. Sitting comfortably, that is, driving to Acton. I had one ear on his rendition of *Stille Nacht*, the other on the sexual shenanigans of Sharon from Upminster. 'What kind of contraceptive were you using prior to your pregnancy?'

'What's contraceptive?' came the reply. Only it wasn't Sharon from Upminster, it was Adam from the back of the car.

'Erm . . . it's, er – .' Gulp. 'You know when I explained about, erm, making love . . . '

'No.'

'Well, I did.'

'No, you didn't.'

'Did.'

'Didn't.'

'Well, Amy knows, ask her!' Silence. Gulp. 'Contraceptives, darling – sorry' (dropping voice to normal register), 'contraceptives . . . '

Ten minutes and a good deal of inarticulate burbling

later, the subject, not to mention the driver, had been thoroughly exhausted. Pills, coils, caps, sheaths, rhythm methods, blues methods, Mrs Gillick *and* the Papal Bull had all been ruthlessly exposed.

'Oh,' said Adam. And recommended *Stille Nacht*. I breathed again and turned left into Acton with right on my side. As I parked he said, 'How does the little bag stay on the end?'

'Shut up and tie your laces,' was my considered reply.

Later that day, driving with his better-informed, older sister, I mentioned the episode by way of a joke. 'So he said: "What kind of contraceptive . . . " and Adam said, "What's contraceptive?" and *I had to explain the whole thing to him*! Arf, Arf, chortle, chortle.'

'What *is* contraceptive?' Amy enquired.

Gulp. 'Well, darling, you know when I told you about . . . ' Etc. There's a lot to be said, I've decided, for my mother's method of dealing with sex education – which was encompassed in one single word – 'Ugh!'

But wasn't I a mother who believed in dealing openly and honestly with her children's questions? After all, when Annie from New York was over, it was *my* advice she sought. It seemed her two-year-old daughter Elisabeth wanted labels for all the little bits and pieces she had seen hanging around and Annie didn't know whether to favour a generalised 'willy' situation or what. I was adamant – 'I've always used the proper medical words,' I assured her. 'I call a penis a penis, and a geneva a geneva!' Thus, in one malapropism I had convulsed Annie, confused Elisabeth, and renamed the world's banking centre 'Vagina'.

Which reminds me of the tea party I once gave as a slip of a mother with a single, delightful two-year-old, and a hint of the other around the midriff. I'd invited six or seven couples round for English tea (one Earl Grey bag in amongst the Typhoo, and home-baked scones from Lindy's). The conversation and the tea were flowing, and the tinkle of cups and laughter intermingled as a small piercing presence made itself felt.

'Wot's this, Mummy – can I play with it?' One small hand clutched a circular plastic container, and the other held the always welcome sight of a cervical diaphragm. My sudden high-pitched laughter was of the theatrical variety associated with French windows, French maids, and French lettuce. I pushed, hissing. She pulled, screeching; 'I wannit, 's'mine. Gimmyit!' All the party needed was Lady Bracknell, a quizzing glass and a few choruses of *My Old Dutch*.

Once, in a similar vein (jugular), I took a diversion through Soho for the purpose of buying a red, white and blue crocheted 'willy-warmer' for a friend's birthday. The sex shop which stocked the invaluable article sported a 'Back in a minute' sign, so I had to spend ten shifty minutes outside. After roughly twenty seconds I'd been spotted by two youths and, two bars into the *Agony* theme, I'd dived into the delicatessen next door. I emerged carrying a large can of nut oil. No, I don't make these things up for effect, *they happen*! The shop was still closed. I studied my feet, and the lettering on the can for several seconds. Or hours, depending from whose point of view you're experiencing the story.

Finally, a taxi drew up spilling out a George Coleclone in a leather blouson, who unlocked the door, went in via a rack of rubber ladies, and switched on the lights. After a seemly interval, looking neither to right nor left, I slid in after him and made my request in a small but noticeably foreign voice.

'Hello, Maureen – oooh, it's *Agony*, ennit? Right. One willy-warmer coming up. Large or extra-large? It's very nice to see you, Maureen, yes, we get a lot of your sort of people in here, Maureen, that'll be £4.50 please, and if you have any *problems*' (this in the doorway) 'just come back to me, Maureen, eh, anytime.' At that moment I wished my friend and his willy in Hades.

As youthful drama students, all our family planning or no-family planning was cared for by a Welsh doctor in Earl's Court. Within the space of two terms, he'd fitted out the cast of *The Cherry Orchard* and was well into much of *Arms and the Man*. Apart from being a little over-inquisitive as to your 'romantic inclinations' and tending to examine the palms of your hands for hairy growth, he was a first-rate doctor, and I recommended him strongly to a friend of mine who had a large wart on her neck which her own family doctor had refused to remove. She blithely went along to Dr W. and, having mentioned that I had recommended him, proceeded to tell him of her wart.

'I see, Miss Cameron,' he smiled knowingly, 'now, have you got a steady boyfriend?'

'Er, not really – I've just got this wart . . . '

'Now don't be shy, Miss Cameron, are you involved with one or more persons?'

'No, I've just got this wart. It's on my n . . . '

'*All right*, Miss Cameron, now if you could just remove your skirt and tights . . . '

Sandy was never known for her speed, but she was out of the rooms before you could say Mac-flash and within a few weeks her wart had dropped off from shock.

Finally, a word of advice. Should you find yourself in an American city, trying to finish some written work, but with nothing to erase your mistakes, do not pay a visit to your local stationery shop and ask for a pencil with a rubber on the end. They will ask you to repeat your request, stare blankly, mutter 'Damn English' and direct you to the nearest drug store. In America, of course, it's more than possible that someone has marketed a pencil with a rubber on the end. So that's what they mean by 'Here's lead in your pencil!'

Accessories after the Fact

IT WAS THE day of the Woman of The Year Luncheon and the taxi was ticking away outside. Inside, my heart was ticking more irregularly from within a fashionably mustard silk blouse, so new that the plastic security tag was still wedged in the back of the collar in such a position that neither arm was long enough to retrieve it.

The crisis was apparent before I'd ever put on the mustard tights, mustard hat, mustard bag, black skirt and black and white dogstooth jacket. Mustard is terrific on a mackerel. On me, admittedly without make-up, at nine o'clock in the morning, it made my skin look like the inside of a new-born baby's nappy, and my teeth, even the ones the dentist rather than God had given me, became a fetching shade of green, not unlike a territorial army uniform.

Obviously, the whole ensemble had to go. 'You can put anything with black and white,' I heard my mother's voice telling me as I mounted an assault on the walk-in wardrobe. 'Not if you haven't got another hat, you can't!' I snapped back – and certainly not if your only other pair of unladdered tights is aubergine and grey horizontal stripes reminiscent of old Mother Riley on washing day.

Back on went the mustard skirt and tights. I glanced

warily in the mirror. Now it was principal-boy time. 'Three years and still no sign of Dick!' I cried, climbing into elderly black shoes livened up considerably by the two mustard and black shoe-bows. Such economy, I thought gleefully. Such stupidity, I should have added, as the second bow laddered the mustard tights. Frantic hunt for mustard nail-polish. Found only orange. Not entirely convincing in the centre of a yellow foot.

I should point out that throughout this pantomime my hair was wet and dripping and so was the bathroom carpet from the faulty shower-head. I blow-dried the hair, head fashionably upside-down, turned the right way up again and keeled over from a combination of low blood pressure, no breakfast and an unusually long period spent upside-down. Because I now looked like Ken Dodd's understudy, I plugged in the Carmen rollers and started on the face.

As the eyes were tiny slits in a sea of puff-pastry, I covered the whole area in a foundation tactfully labelled 'Extra Help', and could immediately have been mistaken for an employee of any Japanese Geisha house. In Israel. The mascara ran out, not weeks but months ago, so it had to be the royal blue one bought me by an au pair whose colourful eyes I'd once admired. Within seconds the royal blue was everywhere but on the eyes. 'Swabs, Nurse, and plenty of 'em!' With the addition of the new 'Bronzer' came a feeling that perhaps everything might be less disastrous than I thought. It costs a fortune and, if used sparingly, lasts a lifetime and is worth it. If used as I use it, impatiently, it covers your face, your clothes and your mantelpiece and _never_ comes off any of them.

The taxi in the drive was revving pointedly.

I started to yank out the Carmens and most of my hair. The phone rang. It was _The Daily Telegraph_.

Would I write an article on 'Getting Ready', five hundred words? I laughed hysterically, told him to call back, arranged the hair on my head and removed the hair off the suit, and jammed on the remaining mustard and black accessories. I glanced in the mirror and saw a fashionable and highly-bronzed bumble bee. I flew out.

Bzzz. At the Luncheon I gave a ten-minute talk on the subject of 'Hope'. The other speakers were Princess Anne (who was marvellous) and the Queen of Tonga. I sat beside the latter's lady-in-waiting, a startlingly statuesque lady in colourful national dress. Rather stumped for conversation, I asked with exaggerated enunciation, 'And where exactly is your home?' She smiled benignly and replied 'Wembley.'

There is a tremendous spirit at the Woman of the Year Luncheon, engendered mainly by the power-house spirit and energy of 'Toni', the Marchioness of Lothian, who works tirelessly for the Greater London Fund for the Blind. Partially sighted herself, she wears a rakish black eyepatch and has a way of making me want to run to the ends of the earth for her. The room is packed with women of all types, creeds and glove size, and the atmosphere is delicious. I wouldn't have missed it for all the Royal Jelly in Barbara Cartland's bathroom cabinet.

Whoops Apocryphal

THEY ALWAYS START 'This friend of mine was telling me about his wife's sister-in-law, Debbie, and her car . . . ' The story which follows is so far-fetched and improbable that it has to be grounded in relatively familiar territory to preclude an immediate response of 'Oh, get off! I don't believe it – pull the other one, it's gone to gangrene. No, it's really a joke, though. Isn't it?'

Debbie's car, it would seem, kept breaking down and one Saturday morning finally found her husband in his old blue denims working, somewhat reluctantly, under the chassis. Well pleased to have laid him so low, she goes off shopping with a cheery 'Goodbyee.' On returning an hour or so later, she sees him in the same supine position. Feeling rather touched, she decides he should be, too, and creeping up, in one deft movement unzips his fly and gives him a grateful pat on what could be described as his 'wedding tackle'.

One can only assume these were the heady, early days of their marriage. Given another eight or nine years, there's many a husband of my acquaintance who might have tersely responded with 'Oh, hello, love – I've put the carrots on a low light and did you remember the hosepipe extension?'

Where was I? Oh, yes, Debbie. Well. Off she toddles

into the house, delighted by the diligence, not to mention the responsiveness of her husband, who she's now somewhat surprised to see making two cups of Typhoo in the kitchen. One for him and the other for the mechanic he'd called in who was now outside working under the car. Wearing good old reliable blue denims, presumably unzipped.

Debbie's embarrassed. She and her husband shuffle outside to explain and apologise, only to find the abused mechanic lying in a pool of blood. His own. Obviously when the assault on his lower half took place, his upper half had jerked into direct contact with acres of hefty car-part and he's been knocked unconscious.

Believe it or not, the story continues. The couple phone 999 for an ambulance. The ambulance men drag out mechanic, put him on stretcher and start to leave, stopping to ask how the accident occurred. On hearing the couple's honest account, they start to laugh, try to stop, become hysterical and finally drop stretcher and mechanic, breaking arms of both. True or false? Only Debbie can tell us and she's probably sitting in a circular glass room somewhere trying to catch her own thumb.

Then there's the dinner party. Let's call her Deirdre. (Funny how often the perpetrator of these acts is the 'little woman', isn't it? 'Silly-ol'-self-deprecating-me' stories. You hardly need Betty Friedan to explain their derivation . . . or do you?) Intercourse, as it were, conversation flowing well between high-profile guests, she goes into the kitchen to garni the whole poached salmon. Unfortunately, she's been pre-empted in this en-devour by her cat, Nelly, who is garni-ing the fish in the only way it knows how. Desperate, Deirdre wrestles with her scruples for a whole thirty seconds before kicking the cat out, rearranging the chewed bits, covering the whole with a cucumber, six lemons and a parsley bush, and making a flushed re-entry into the dining-room. The dinner party's a wow. Everyone especially loves the salmon. Back in the kitchen to make coffee, Deirdre opens the door to let in Nelly only to find the cat stone dead on the stone steps, feet and legs rigid with mortis.

Collapse of Deirdre into roughly the same position. Husband (they're never named . . . interesting?) and she decide that possible salmoNelly of high-profiles is unthinkable; they confess crime. Whereupon twelve of them go to local hospital and are unceremoniously stomach-pumped. Odd cries of 'Thanks for an unforgettable evening!' ringing in her ears, Deirdre and husband return home, lift cat from doorstep – to find note underneath, as follows: 'In haste – I apologise most dreadfully but your cat leapt out in front of my car. Nothing I could do. Saw you were entertaining and didn't want to disturb the party.' Signed by A. Neighbour.

Even more silly women people the mother/child story circuit. (And why not? We are never more certifiable than when attacking or protecting our young.) The woman on the bus whose child is wiping her lolly back and forth on the fur collar of the lady in front: 'Don't do that, Tracey! You'll get hairs on your lolly!' Or the woman on the country bus whose sixth and final child has just started school. She breathes the sigh of the long-last rid and finds herself grabbing the sleeve of the elderly man beside her, pointing wildly out of the window and shouting 'Look, darling! MOO-COWS!' She's the self-same 'friend of mine', no doubt, who was so anxious to impress her husband's new boss as being an active and supportive wife in spite of the six appendages, that she sent them all to her mother's on the night the boss was due for dinner. The house was spotless, the food divine, the conversation stimulating. It was only after the boss had left and she was congratulating herself on being a perfect hostess, that her husband asked her what the hell she'd thought she'd been doing – leaning over and cutting up the boss's meat into tiny pieces while holding a conversation with his wife on the Post-Impressionists? Ring any bells?

In fact the only male protagonist in the world of the Apocryphal crops up in a story about a famous actor-chappie (could've been Ralph Richardson – he's at the centre of most actor-chappie stories) who was invited to the legendary country mansion of two moneyed theatregoers of limp-wristed but impeccable taste. Let's call it 'Smacked Bottom Villa'. He is housed for the night in the Peacock Room – so called because of its hand-painted silk murals of peacock motif, each panel being of custom-design and exquisite delicacy. During the night and needing the bathroom, he gropes his way towards the light switch, knocking over what he takes to be a vase of water. He continues groping along the walls till he finds the switch. In the glaring light he looks down at his blackened hands and realises it was not a vase he'd tipped up but an ink-well. And there all over the silk mural are his fingertips to prove it. Without pausing for breath, he dresses, packs, and under night's cover he leaves the house and thumbs his way back to London.

He lives with this on his conscience for many months till, at last, he writes an explanatory letter to his hosts' London home with an invitation to his approaching first night. A letter arrives inviting him to tea the day after and mentioning neither peacocks nor ink. He arrives at the portals of the Eaton Square house, is ushered by the butler into the satin drawing-room and sits heavily in a large wing chair to await his hosts. After a while he rises to adjust what he takes to be an intrusive cushion and finds he has totally suffocated the couple's pet chihuahua.

Legend also has it that a family drove their estate car across to the continent. In the car were mother, father, three children and paternal grandmother. They reached the South of France and for a few days all was sun, sea and beaucoup de plage, when after a particularly full bowl of moules marinière, the elderly grandmother collapsed. They got her to the nearest hospital, but it was, alas, too late. Grandma had passed on.

To bury her on French soil was out of the question. There was nothing for it but to drive her body back to – well – to English soil. But how? The car was full of kids and it would be too unsettling and, let's face it, too pungent to sit her in her normal seat next to the baby. In the end they hardened their hearts, wrapped her up in a groundsheet and tied her on to the roof-rack. Then off they went at a somewhat sedate pace. After several hundred miles, they drove into a motorway café, to fill up both family and car. They ate well, washed and freshened up and returned to where their car was parked. Except it wasn't. It was of course disparu, vanished, kaput, stolen, filched, GONE. With a roof-rack full of late Grandma.

It has to be said that this macabre story is only funny from the villains' point of view. They see the bulky roof-rack, spend furtive minutes breaking into the vehicle, drive off like madmen, and finally stop at a safe hideout to unpack the booty. Except the booty is one very dead old lady in a groundsheet. Then, how does the family explain the theft to le gendarme? Franglais gone frantic: 'D'accord, Monsieur, est-ce que vous me dites que votre grand'mere 'as been, 'ow you say, remové de votre roof-rack? Encore une fois, s'il vous plaît?'

Sometimes a shaggy dog story can be told with such dead pan that you believe all the way that it's factual. There's a hair's breadth between shaggy and apocryphal. Which reminds me – only the other day, driving back from the country, I hit something large which felt like a dog. I stopped and got out, only to find a huge hare lying by the front wheels. It was a pitiful sight, shocked into a quivering, twitching paralysis. I was luckily able to flag down a police car and a vet was called. I felt sure the hare would die before he arrived but somehow, the creature lived. I explained the accident to the vet in trembling tones. 'Don't worry, madam,' soothed the vet, bringing out from his medicine bag an aerosol can with which he sprayed the surprised animal. A moment later, and to all our amazement, the hare jumped to its feet, shook itself, hopped blithely over the fence into a field of buttercups and, waving his right paw in the air as if to say 'Cheerio', disappeared from sight.

I was stunned, and turning to the vet, said, 'What on earth was in that spray?' 'Oh, that,' he replied nonchalantly, 'was a new kind of hare restorer.' 'But,' I wanted to know, 'why was it waving its right paw at us like that!' 'Oh, well, you see, it's the hare restorer with the permanent wave!'

Yes, I know it's awful. But in its defence – it was told on *The Des O'Connor Show*. Les, my fireman friend, told it to me as though it had happened to him. I was practically weeping at the plight of that poor hare. He gets me every time, too! Only last week I was ga-ga over the saga of one of his mates at the station who'd been taken seriously ill with food poisoning after a meal in an Indian restaurant. Apparently, the only dish the guy had eaten which his friends hadn't was an onion bhaji. So when the Health Inspector visited the restaurant he checked the ingredients the chef was using. To his horror, instead of using onions, they'd been using daffodil bulbs, which were cheaper and tasted similar.

My jaw hit the lino. 'My God,' I whispered. 'What happened to the man who'd eaten them?'

'Well,' said Les gravely, 'he's still in hospital.'

'But is he going to be okay?' I persisted.

'Ye-es,' grinned Les. 'He's a bit yellow, but he's coming out in the Spring.'

Total collapse of silly little woman in kitchen. Ever been 'ad?

Finally, the one I hope is true. A reporter asks Mikhail Gorbachev, 'What do you think would have happened, sir, if Mr Krushchev had been assassinated instead of President Kennedy?' Comrade G thinks for a moment before replying, 'I do not think that Mr Onassis would have married Mrs Krushchev.' If it's true then he has a real sense of humour. And, if *that's* true, what in hell did he find to talk about for nine hours to Margaret Hilda Thatcher? Surely not silly, defenceless women stories?

Childspoofs

AFTER *HOW WAS It For You?* I received a complaint from one reviewer about including cute sayings from the mouths of my babes and chucklings. I never thought of my kids as 'cute'. Acute maybe. Eccentric, certainly. If ever I doubted that, confirmation came one hot summer's day when I found them sitting on the hall stairs wearing man-sized wellington boots, woolly hats, scarves and gloves, fishing with twigs and twine in a bucket of water for a plastic lobster and a plastic crab. This would have been normal enough, had they not been singing in unison, in very slow dirge-like voices, 'There's no business like show business'.

Or the time when they announced they were leaving home after some dread confrontation regarding the trimming of fringes or the losing of more than one anorak a term. 'Adam and I are going to leave home,' announced Amy, furiously packing furry animals into a tote bag. 'We're going to dig a hole and live in it. But,' she said, interrupting the derisory expression I was about to assume, 'it will be a *detailed* hole.' I knew what she meant. I've been living in a detailed hole for years – I'm still trying to dig my way out of it.

My son is an obsessive creature and his current obsession is astronomy. His knowledge of the workings of the universe turn me into glazed chintz within two minutes of his engaging my interest. A free telescope was dispatched at enormous expense from kindly friends in Massachusetts, and binoculars purchased to tide him over the wait. The first night as a binoculars owner was spent in a deck chair in the garden gazing at the moon. He was there for hours making the kind of noises Christopher Columbus must have made when confronted by the Statue of Liberty. 'My God!' he cried. 'I've got an incredible terrain! Pfwah! I can see everything!' He was beside himself with excitement. 'The Sea of Tranquillity – yes, look – I've got it!' It was only after three hours and a faint drizzle that we discovered his binoculars were trained on next door's fluorescent garden light.

My kids' knowledge of the acts of life have fortunately not been any of my responsibility. Any time I tried to broach the subject I was told to knock it off in no uncertain terms and would I please not embarrass them further. This puzzled me at first. I never had a sex education as such – I mean, I knew from the girls at school roughly what went on, and could laugh and crack jokes along with the most ribald of them. But I was a good nineteen (very good) before I actually *believed* it! I swore then and there that my children would be enlightened from an early age. Frank, open discussions around the family table. Full access to our bedroom and bathroom and all unspeakable questions answered with a story, a hymn and aplomb.

Wrong again. They don't want this. 'Mo-o-od – can we change the subject, please? Look, we don't want to *know* – I mean, we know – sssh – it's *The Colbys*.'

The Colbys. Dynasty. If there's a finger worth pointing it's in the direction of those oil-filled oleogarchies. 'Who's that?' I say as yet another wide-boned smoothy oozes blandness across a 'Le Mirage' table.

'Oh, that's Adam,' murmurs my enlightened eleven-year-old. 'He's her brother-in-law. He raped Jeff's old wife and now he's pinning the blame on Stephen, but he's gay. That's his boyfriend, Luke, anyway it's not the same actress playing Fallon . . . Oh, yucky kissing, don't look!'

'Why is she having breakfast with him if he raped her? How do you know about rape? I mean, do you understand the seriousness of it?'

'Shhh, Alexis is undoing Dex's trousers again – urgh, yuck, geroff – I'm not looking . . . '

I used to adore Susan Harris's *Soap* because it went as far as your imagination's boundaries could travel and was screamingly funny along the way. Will you ever forget Jody telling Jessica he was gay, and her despondent question as to why so many people had suddenly decided to be homosexuals? Jody says, 'No, Mom – there have always been gay people throughout history. Socrates was gay. Homer was gay. Plato was gay.' 'Plato was gay?' Jessica interrupts. 'I don't *believe* it.' 'S'true,' insists Jody. 'Everyone knows that.'

'*Plato* was gay? Plato was *gay*? No – no, I can't handle this.'

'Mom, I'm telling you, Plato was – '

Jessica's eyes are popping. 'Plato gay? You're telling me Mickey Mouse's *dog* was gay?'

Crazy, yes. Funny, certainly. Ironic – the show had real irony. Something most Americans can't even pronounce. So what do they do? They take it off the air on grounds of 'moral indecency', leaving the field open to Dex's bulging trousers, Alexis's heaving upper lip, and lines like 'You wrapped her in dreams. Your dreams tried to make her in your image' and 'I'm trying to leave a failed marriage with as much dignity as I can muster.'

What worries me is that our kids are learning the

fiction of life not the facts from the television programmes they choose to watch.

'Why do you watch this rubbish?' I asked them, knowing that to ban it would make it more tempting.

'Because it's so terrible,' said Amy. 'Besides, we always close our eyes and sing when they start doing yucky kissing things.'

But they don't.

Recently I came back from New York and told the family about a newspaper report concerning a demonstration against Reagan's Aids policy. There were, of course, many homosexuals among the protesters and apparently the police had been issued with yellow rubber gloves to wear for the occasion. We were laughing about this when Amy spoke out in a puzzled sort of way. 'But I don't understand. Are homosexuals afraid of yellow?'

It's the logic of children's response to our mode of speech which intrigues me. And it's not just children who respond in a child-like way. There was a recent report in *The Telegraph* about a girl assistant in a jewellery shop, selling a cross to a customer. 'Which sort did you want to look at, sir?' she enquired. 'We've got the plain silver, the plain gold, and the patterned gold. Oh, and we've got some others with a little man on.' A little man! Two thousand years of solid symbolism and it's come to that.

Or take the conversation recorded on a bus in 1959 and exhumed for the BBC radio programme, *When Housewives Had the Choice*, in 1987. Two women on a bus, one showing the other family snaps.

'That doesn't look a bit like your Brian.'

1st Woman: 'It's not our Brian.'

'Isn't it? Well I never, it looks just like him.'

1st Woman: But you just said it looked nothing like him.'

'No, well, I meant it doesn't look like him if it is him, but if it isn't it does.'

Maybe one of the things I felt I had in common with the late great Joyce Grenfell was her obsessive people-watching. It's also Alan Bennett's and Victoria Wood's great occupation, and we can overhear their over-hearing in the dialogue they write. Joyce once overheard one waitress whispering to another as they came through the revolving doors from the kitchen: 'Well, he's *eaten* it!'

Many years and the Irish Sea between us, I was filming *Educating Rita* in Dublin and an extra line of dialogue was called for in a waitressing scene. Director Lewis Gilbert suggested I walk up to Julie Walters and whisper darkly, 'Well, he's eaten it!' Could Joyce Grenfell and Lewis Gilbert have eaten in the same restaurant, or is that line and all that it implies the most common of restaurant parlance? I suspect the latter. Restaurants breed good dialogue, as in 'Waitress, I want a coffee, without cream.' *Waitress*: 'We haven't got any cream, so you'll have to have it without milk.'

Still on a culinary note, Adam and his two friends, David and Daniel – sounds like something out of *Genesis*, I know, but very trendy round these parts – the Bible Belt, we call it – it came to pass that they were discussing school dinners. Adam mentioned something that David hadn't eaten at lunchtime, and, contrary to the empty plate rule, had got away with. Daniel sprang to David's defence. 'He *can't* eat it, stupid!' he bellowed. 'He's allergic to adjectives!' So is my publisher, funnily enough.

Or, straight out of Luke, I give you Matthew, aged 6, who is my dresser's godson. 'Mummy, don't think I'm being economical with the truth, but you really are the most cleanest loveliest mother a baby boy could ever have.' Now, if one of mine had said that I'd have had it cross-stitched on to a sampler and hung for life in a place guaranteed to embarrass the bum off him when he brought home his first girlfriend or boyfriend. Or laptop desk module, with meaningful interface and floppy discs. Whatever the 1990s equivalent is – I'm ready. Loins akimbo, shoulders girded, chin receding, teeth out, breasts plated (not to mention deflated), and mind so *open* you can hear the wind coming through the wry.

N.B. I've just found a note from my daughter who I now think is writing for posterity. It says:

'Hello friendly Mod and Dod!

We had a yummy Chinois (or slitty-eyed meal as Prince Philip would say), didn't we?

What shall we call the new word-processor? How about Marguerite? Cute, eh?

Thanks for a jolly existence. Love, Trog.

I blame the father. Whoever he is.

Getting to the Beetroot of the Problem

I WAS INHALING a cup of warm beetroot juice through my right nostril last night, when I suddenly thought of my readers. Would they believe it if I told them? They've accepted my eccentricities in the past, I mused. They've had me doing three rounds with the bank service till, force-feeding a sex-starved tortoise – why should this new hobby be anything but normal? But beetroot? Up the nose? And warm? Is this gag a long-running one?

It was all down to the osteopath. I'd returned from having my crick clicked, bearing 'a couple of daily exercises' to reduce the puffiness under my eyes. Now, we all know that as you approach 40 the bag under your eye starts to feel like the one over your shoulder, but when I'm at the studio at 7.30 a.m. and I look like a cross between Willie Whitelaw and Rocky Racoon, I have been known to utter the odd expletive. I've tried sliced cucumbers (they dry up into little, hard courgettes), tea bags (they dye your skin ochre, which is hell to match), egg white (reputed to be what the women of *Dynasty* wear under their make-up, which probably explains why their acting is such a yolk), and every eye gel, most of which cost more per pot than a session with a good plastic surgeon.

Talking of which, I met an American plastic surgeon at a party the other night. He held court on the stairs, sporting a hair transplant which looked like one of those experiments where you grow mustard and cress on blotting paper, and always referring to himself in the third person. As in, 'So they wanted the best in the world, so they called Fritz, and Fritz said, "Sure, send her over" and twenty minutes later, Fritz had pinned back her ears and repositioned her nipples.'

His wife, who was blonde and luminous, hung on his every word as he explained that when they'd married Fritz thought her 'a boodiful woman, who needed nothing doing but her upper eyelids'. So he did them. He then did the lower ones, gave her bigger cheekbones and a tighter chin. Then he remodelled her nose. So much for above the neck.

'Don't you ever worry about all those operations?' I ventured.

'Are you kidding?' she grinned, showing a couple of hundred perfect teeth. 'It's better than a vacation. You just close your eyes and before you know it, wake up looking like someone else.' And I don't think she meant Willie Whitelaw.

Obviously, the lady had anaesthesia addiction, and pretty soon she must have shouted, 'Come on down!' because then he reupholstered the rest of her. He enlarged her breasts. Then he made them smaller again. Or they deflated. I like to think he did it twice because the first set wouldn't fit her last year's Calvin Klein. Then he sucked the fat from her stomach and buttocks. I asked him why he didn't refrigerate her so that the fat would rise to the surface and he could just skim it off like I do with chicken soup. He looked at me with suspicion, but didn't entirely dismiss the idea out of hand.

Finally, the pièce de non-résistance. So that she would wake up in the morning looking as perfect as she did at night, he tattooed eyeliner on to her lids. 'How did she look?' I hear you croak. 'Ordinary' is the answer. Like an attractive saleslady. She admired my socks and when I raised my skirt to show her they were tights, she moaned, 'Oh, but you have great legs; I have these tree trunks!'

Fritz shook his head miserably. 'Yup,' he volunteered, 'and there's not a damned thing even Fritz can do about *them*!'

Later, at dinner, he stopped with the hard sell and seemed genuinely convinced that he was doing a real public service by giving people the features they long for. A sort of Louis B. Mayer of Silicone Valley. Sometimes, he told me, at a party, while chatting to someone's neck wrinkles, he'd drive downtown, open up shop and do a quick carve-up as a favour. Like you and I might give a lift home, he'd give a home lift.

The most intriguing aspect of all this was how easily – in spite of the demeanour, the dead stoat on his head, the encyclopaedia sell, the wife and the mildly deranged air – he could have persuaded any woman in that room, however attractive or intelligent, to go in for an alteration. We are, as a breed, dreadfully insecure when confronted by anything that was once a medical student. I always cry at the doctor's. Even when I just take the children for their ears or Belgian measles I'm near to tears.

When my gynaecologist told me he'd have to induce my first baby because he was going on holiday the day she was due, I said, 'Oh, thank you, yes, that'll be fine.' Which, roughly translated meant, 'Why, you rotten hound, didn't you tell me that during the last nine months? Will it hurt? Will it affect the baby?

Where are you going for your holidays? And I hope there's a sodding earthquake.'

One avuncular naturopath with a scarlet flowing beard brushed in opposite directions at the bottom, asked me copious questions about my preference for light and shade, warmth and cold, mountains and valleys, then, without further ado, filled me full of pins. Or, rather, I allowed myself to be filled with pins. He placed his little needles in my head, in my hands and in my feet. A week later I had pneumonia. I'm not saying it was his fault. Intellectually, I know I didn't get it from wind whistling through my pinholes, but in my heart I blame him.

Another memorable medic was the allergy specialist who accused my body of being allergic to wheat. Every complaint is food related, he proclaimed, producing a myriad of home-made charts with spirals, arrows and circles. He, too, asked lots of questions. Which food did I like to eat? When? And how? I was intrigued throughout by the number of big, white pills he kept popping in his mouth. Finally, I asked him what they were.

'Bisodol,' he replied. 'I suffer from appalling indigestion.'

'But surely your allergy diet would stop that, wouldn't it?'

'Oh, no,' he replied, burping. 'No, it doesn't do a damn thing for it. No, Bisodol's the only thing.'

As my confidence in him began to dwindle, I paid my £40 and rushed out for a wheatgerm sandwich.

The vital thing to remember about alternative medicine (which I'm extremely 'pro') is to keep an open mind and a straightish face. I mean, it wouldn't do to say 'pull the other one, it's got dumb-bells hanging off it' or 'I'll believe that when Nelson gets his eye back!' when told to rub aboriginal mud on your top four vertebrae for arthritis, or masturbate for migraine. (I have actually *heard* both of these suggestions from quite serious sources. Oh, wouldn't you like to know?)

Another treatment I tried on myself was cupping. It was done by Minoru, a Japanese friend of mine who is an Aikido Dan and Shiatsu masseur. It centres round a mysterious black box with tubes attached to a series of sort of wine glasses, which are placed at strategic aqua pressure points along your back, buttocks and legs. A current is then switched on which somehow sucks the flesh into the wine glass, or in my case whine-glass, turning the blobs of flesh a lurid magenta colour.

Is the question 'Why?' springing to your lips? Well, I'll tell you. It is a fast way of encouraging the toxins to leave your body. More than that I cannot say because I do not know and I'm obviously fare game for anyone who fancies the sight of quivering Beaujolais-coloured flesh in a goblet. Does it work? Well, yes, it made me feel more energetic and look considerably more patterned. It also made my husband lose several years when he walked into the bedroom to find me lying naked on the floor with blobbing glassware all over my torso and a robed Japanese gentleman squatting beside me, twiddling his big black box.

'Oh, hello, love,' he said after a momentary pause. 'It's the *Give Us a Clue* office on the phone – shall I tell them you're tied up?' In my cups was probably more to the point.

Actually he's fairly blasé about Minoru and me. Once I cut my thumb rather badly on a tin of corned beef (Orthodox Jews please don't write in – I know!) whilst he was here. I was all for the killer Casualty Department and some stitches but immediately Minoru took hold of the bleeding digit, pressed the cut together extremely hard and began shaking it above my head. He did this for at least forty minutes, which was an interesting experience in itself, since I lost all sense that the hand or arm was any part of me, and felt only this hefty lump of dough being kneaded over my head. After a while Minoru said, 'I go to car now, fetch black seaweed toothpaste.' He actually said 'brack seaweed toothpaste,' which was even more confusing, but we'll have no racial stereotypes in these pages and I'm very fond of him. 'Jack – you hold thumb and shake it while I go,' added Minoru over his shoulder. Jack rather warily took the shocked thumb and proceeded to shake it rather forlornly about. As he went through the door Minoru popped his head back and said, 'Bend the knees, Jack – bend knees.' Jack bobbed smartly into a half bend and carried on shaking from this rather uncomfortable position.

'Why do I have to bend my knees?' he asked me.

'It's probably to do with the energies coming from the lower part of the spine – it probably gives you more manoeuvring power,' I said knowledgeably.

Minoru returned with the toothpaste. 'Very good Jack,' he smiled, unscrewing the cap.

'Tell me,' said Jack, 'why do I have to do this shaking with bent knees?'

Minoru looked blank. ''Cos you too tall,' he answered with Eastern logic. He then smeared brack toothpaste on my cut and I disappeared through the fixtures and fittings with the pain. Something to do with the salt? And the healing, of course. The thumb did repair but it has retained a curiously flat look like a depressed whoopee cushion and is a bit slow to spring back to life when pressed, which rather goes with the rest of me these days.

Then there was the chiropodist who berated Jack for not eating enough oranges – for his feet; the hypnotist who told him that if he never again picked up another cigarette he wouldn't smoke, thank you, £50 please; and the local osteopath who said, 'Can you come back next week please?' – for a year.

I recently spent a weekend at a Natural Healing Centre in Dorset. I was full of cynicism when I arrived, particularly when of four guests, three were journalists and one was a theatre-masseuse. However, I thoroughly enjoyed my two-hour aromatherapy. They dowse to discover which are the best ones for each individual. Two of mine were marjoram and rosemary. I came out smelling like a leg of lamb. In fact, they dowse for a lot of their diagnoses, using a small crystal on a chain and contact between the dowser and patient. My eyebrows were well-arched when I saw this thing start circling then suddenly reverse directions, but it turned out to be very accurate about foods which I can't tolerate, and in prescribing remedies. I knew chocolate, cheese, red wine and some dairy and wheat products were not good for me but you should have seen the pendulum when confronted with me and peanuts. It went bananas! Oddly enough, it went bananas on bananas too! Must make a note: don't spend inordinate amount of time with Jimmy Carter or the Premiers of small republics.

The remedies prescribed for my general health were the Bach Flower Remedies. And I must say I have a lot of time for these plant- and herb-based cures. Whatever you do, though, don't read the book on how Professor Bach discovered them or you'll never take another. It seemed as though my big problem was 'Over-enthusiàsm and enforced jollity, and taking on other people's problems!' This will come as no surprise to those who've ever encountered me on a bus or in print, and indeed I spent most of the healing weekend listening to the problems of almost everyone there. I am after all the woman who told an entire risqué

Dress by Murray Arbeid, Armpits by Mum

Trevor Leighton

Above: Hatmaker David Shilling took literally the 'trousers optional' invitation to the launch party for *How Was It For You?* Julia McKenzie, Anna Carteret and Derek Nimmo look amused. The other actress is cock-eyed with shock

Anthony Gran

Left: A review from the *National Gay* said: 'Emily Morgan plays the Beauty, and Maureen Lipman plays the *Brians*'! *Right: Best Side Story*. In the clutches of the maestro, Leonard Bernstein

Christina Burto

Is this woman a) in a West-End musical, or b) auditioning for the Stork Club? This is *Wonderful Town*

Above: Julia McKenzie and I, real friends playing
Absent Friends in Alan Ayckbourn's BBC television play

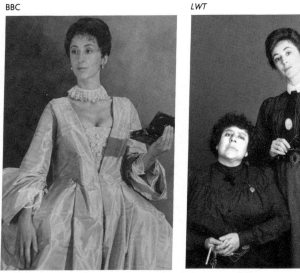

Left: Love's Labour's Lost – the Princess of France.
Une Princesse juive, deja? Right: Miriam Margolyes and
I in *The Little Princess.* The long and the short and that's all

Above: Not the Arab-Israeli conflict – just a *vehicle* for Tony Alleff and I. The BBC film *Shiftwork* by Lesley Bruce

Underplaying to the hilt, Lesley Joseph, Patricia Hodge and I in TVS's *Exclusive Yarns*

TVS

Age 14, Musical Festival, Hull, Rubberlegs Lipman, perfecting her craft

Loot – Watford Palace Theatre 1969. Who did she think she was?

'Sitwell, don't I?'
Posing as Dame
Edith
Anthony Grant

'Kiaay!' Getting
rid of all those
Pentax feelings!
Dave Lee Travis

Above left: Mother giving daughter the elbow . *Right:* My pride and my boy

Happy ever laughter . . .

joke under intra-valium anaesthetic. I have no memory of doing so but I vaguely remember hearing roaring medics and much dropping of sterilised instruments.

The best form of relaxation I know is reflexology. Amazing to think that points on your feet can directly affect the rest of your body. So, if they press a certain spot under the sole, your stomach starts rumbling. Its curative and diagnostic powers are almost a certainty, but what you don't anticipate is the sheer sensual delight of having your feet rubbed. Parts of your inner toes which have never felt the pressure of anything other than a winkle-picker or a corn plaster, start positively beaming with pediatric pleasure, and you walk out with a Spring in your step and a Fall in your arches.

Anyway, for the moment it's beetroot juice. The leaflet says you retain it in the nose, then expel it, repeating several times, and this will facilitate the elimination of large quantities of mucus. It certainly did. It also eliminated the sangfroid of my husband who entered the bathroom just as a quarter of a pint of red liquid was coursing down my nose, mouth, chin and nightie. He thought I'd cut my throat and was all for calling Casualty until I explained the root cause for my appearance. Whereupon, he was all for calling a psychiatrist.

At the end of the day, as David Coleman might say, the best tonic you can have is a good laugh. Maybe there's a small business for me – a 'chuckle clinic'. I can see it now: the front door revolves on itself so you walk inside and find yourself outside again. You finally get in, and it's decorated to look exactly like the outside did. The receptionist says, 'Good morning, can I interest you in a mother-in-law joke?' The doctor has an array of custard pies and invites you to throw one in his face after you've disagreed with his diagnoses. The in-house shop stocks tickling sticks, whoopee cushions. Mucky Pups and banana skins – all in constant demonstration. Non-stop videos show the best of Lenny Bruce, George Burns and Gracie Allen, Lucille Ball, Les Dawson, Billy Connolly, Woody Allen and the Marx Brothers, episodes of *Soap*, the original film of *La Cage aux Folles*, and *Monsieur Hulot's Holiday*. Oh – and early Australian afternoon TV runs concurrently, and such classics as Ian Nairn walking backwards towards camera and John Cleese walking anywhere are on request buttons. In fact, you can dine at Fawlty Towers and even have your head slapped by a Basil clone.

If all that is too bellicose for you, Madam, may I suggest a private interview with a Margaret Thatcher look-alike, who will explain her policy for keeping the NHS alive, quite sincerely and with a straight face.

There will also be places where you, the patient, have to keep a straight face: simulated models of church when someone has just farted during the vicar's sermon, and the headmistress's study when her bra strap has just snapped, sending one breast hurtling south at an alarming rate in the middle of her lecture on personal hygiene.

And if all else fails, there's always jokes: non-stop, we-never-close, stop-me-if-you've-'eard-it jokes. 'A man runs into a pub clutching his hand between his legs. "Oh my God, oh my God, oh hell, oh – oh – aaaargh – etc," he writhes and twists in agony. "What on earth is it, Fred?" asks the barmaid. "What have you done?" He groans and twists, doubled over in pain. "I've been hit by a bleedin' cricket ball," he manages to gasp out. "Oh dear me," says the barmaid. "Have a whisky – there, now how does it feel?" "Oh – grrr – oh God – it's still terrible – aargh." The barmaid looks at him, then says, "Oh, come on, lad – I've known you long enough. Come into the back room and I'll give it a rub." Off they go into the back room, where she proceeds to undo his trousers and give him a rub better. "There now," she says, surveying him. "How do you feel now?"

'He smiles wateringly. "Well, I feel a bit better," he gasps out, then, holding up his thumb, he added, 'but I still think the nail is going to go black.'''

To apply for membership of this élite organization, please send an old, abused and graffiti'd copy of any article by Hunter Davies, or ticket stubs from any Ray Cooney farce in which the hero never loses his trousers. No, seriously!

In the meantime, if there's anyone out there who's had puffy eyes which suddenly went away without recourse to vegetables, needles, or Fritz and his Swiss Army knife, please send me details in a buff-coloured envelope, and I promise to make us both a very rich man.

A Shortage of Screws

WHEN I WAS asked to write a foreword to a *Punch* book on sex and marriage, I decided to mis-hear the brief and wrote a short but emotive piece on Saxon Marriage, which was easy to research if one had access to my son's last history project.

Traditionally, sex was not a big subject in my family home. If *really* pressed my mother would admit to 'only having done it twice' and her look implied this was three times too many. This grossly permissive attitude ensured her daughter would be something of a late starter. (Not for nothing was I placed somewhere between Janet Street-Porter and Margaret Thatcher in a 'sex appeal' list. I blame our dentists.) While my schoolmates squirmed over Cliff's top lip, James Bond's rigid weapon and a few Humberside acne cases, I worked on a veneer of carnal sophistication as underdeveloped as my chest. The worst moment of my 16-year-old life was when my best friend and fellow wallflower found passion at the Polytechnic. There's only so long you can endure being part of a threesome, two of whom kept swapping tongues.

I must have grown up during the Sixties, because my memory positively ripples with tales of bedding strange-fellows. This one did because *Cosmopolitan* magazine told one to. Or at least told one everyone else was. It was the sexual equivalent of the whole class wearing their school berets inside-out in order to be different. There was Helen Gurley Brown telling us the world was at it like cutlery. There was Germaine Greer using rallying phrases like multiple orgasms and erogenous zones, and there were Masters and Johnson doing a Desmond Wilcox on our intimate moments in 3D, full colour and marks out of 10.

And there were we. In satin bell-bottoms, cowbells and enough Indian cotton to empty Madras, sitting cross-legged on the parquet, rolling unpleasant substances and gazing meaningfully into each other's tinted granny glasses to the sounds of Leonard Cohen, who, in retrospect, should have kept to the family tailoring business.

And you know who benefited most from the sexual revolution? _Really_ unattractive men, that's who. Fellas who'd never got so much as a snog or a fondle of a Maidenform at the Hammersmith Palais half a decade before were rolling in clover. Fellas with huge T-shirted beer bellies ballooning over obscenely buckled cowboy belts. Fellas with bald pates, meandering jowls and long wisps of facial hair, who donned owlish specs and an all-seeing expression, grabbed a cheap copy of _I-Ching_ and a phial of frangipani, and suddenly became 'Desirable'. The bigger the nose, the more gravy in the droopy moustache, the more the frizzy-haired, bandeaued, loose-breasted maidens hung on to their every 'Peace, man'. Every A-string they plucked was a heartstring.

Where are they now, those profits of mood? All living peacefully in Surrey, having sold the record business to finance the water beds and moved fluidly into jacuzzis at the drop of a trend.

This is the sadness, of course. By the time permissiveness had filtered through from the Big Apple to the

Small Seedless, say Keighley or Cockermouth, the Germaines, the *Tatlers* and the *Cosmos* were all into celibacy – just as the car keys were about to hit the Casa Pupo shagpile rug.

I got sidetracked, as usual, by the Sixties. I meant to tell you the story of Jack's stay at the Algonquin in New York where, as he puts it, the walls were made paper-thin so that everyone could hear what Dorothy Parker kept saying. He arrived at the same time as a large, pheumatic Nordic beauty who checked into the next room. In the night he was aroused from his cross-word by a piercing shriek. 'This is New York,' he reasoned, 'and the woman in the next room is being mugged and raped!'

Without further thought, he cleared his throat and rapped out Britishly, 'Are you all right, madam? Can I help you at all?' There was a silence, broken only by a girlish giggle, a man's murmur and the sound of flesh on flesh. Then they resumed what they were doing and Jack withdrew beneath the duvet. He spent the following three days skulking round the hotel to avoid meeting her, and took all his meals alone in his room.

God knows, sex is no joking matter, so here's the latest which neatly combines sex and hotels. A man checks into a brand new multi-storey hotel in New York. The bellboy says, 'Anything you want, sir, just ring.' Then – nudge, wink – 'And I mean anything. Service is our motto.' The man sits on his sumptuous hotel bed, thinks, and phones down . . . 'I'd like two brunettes, two blondes, two redheads. I'd like an assortment of whips, a leather collar, a bag of chains and a cactus.' 'A cactus?' says the bellboy doubtfully. 'Now that may be difficult at this time of night . . . ' 'Well, in that case,' says our hero, 'I'll have a coffee and a prune Danish.'

Talking of service, only last week I had the kitchen

specialist service department in my basement, examining their faulty extractor fan. (The only way I got them round after three months of 'All parts required for your machine are in West Germany' was to send a letter in fluent German saying, 'Where are the sodding parts for Maureen Lipman's lousy extractor fan?') While the mechanic was down there, I was in the kitchen being interviewed by a publishing gentleman about women. (No, really. Feel free to yawn – I did.) It was exactly at the point of his asking me about women's sexuality that 'the dialogue exchange I will never forget' occurred . . .

Me: 'I simply don't understand why so many of the interesting, bright, caring and beautiful women I know are hooked on the most dismal, selfish, boorish, philandering, egocentric, unattractive men . . . '

Mechanic's voice from basement: 'Mrs Rosenthal, I think you'll find a shortage of screws here. That's your problem.'

So there you have it. Or not, as the case may be. Just remember, every four hours a woman is being sexually harassed on the streets of this great city – and she's getting damn fed up with it.

4

Musical Chores

Diary of a Showbody: Part 1

DOING YOUR FIRST musical is like having your first baby. There's a conspiracy of silence. Oh, people will tell you how fulfilling it is to hold this glistening prize in your arms, to feel the waves of love and admiration, to know that you've accomplished the most natural and most unnatural of openings. But no one will tell you how it hurts. Or when to breathe, or how not to push when there's no one in the theatre but your husband and twenty-five Japanese medical students.

Nor will they tell you what an excellent contraceptive it is. Just about the only thing that could have lured me into bed in those days was a large tube of Algipan and a heated pad. In fact I reckon you could solve the problem of world population explosion in one season, if you put the Third World into a musical. And don't imagine Andrew Lloyd Webber hasn't thought of it.

Dan Crawford sent me the script of *Wonderful Town* saying, 'This is the Cleopatra of women's parts in musicals.' I wrote back saying, 'You bet your asp', and booked a crash course of singing lessons with Ian (The Larynx) Adam. David Torugi of *Guys and Dolls* fame was asked to choreograph. We spoke on the phone. 'I'll do it if you do it' was our mutual promise. Martin Connor was to direct, having done a production already at the Guildhall of Music. We met and immediately established a rapport which was to continue throughout the wonderful, gruelling, whirlwind days to come. The story of two 'girls' (since the part had been created for Rosalind Russell in her heyday – i.e. in her 40's, and since Lauren Bacall played it only nine years ago in Boston, I felt suitably qualified for girlishness) who leave Ohio to find fame and fortune in New York's Greenwich Village, was a familiar one. One sister was blonde, dumb in a knowing kinda way, and gorgeous. The other was me. Smart, wise-cracking, plain and funny. It was a part for which I'd been auditioning for forty years.

Prior to rehearsals I met the lyricist Adolph Green's wife, Phillis Newman, and her friend Jean Kennedy Smith, the youngest of the Kennedy dynasty, for dinner at the Savoy. They were to invest in the show, and along with producers Dan Crawford and Bob Fabian, we all discussed the project with barely suppressed excitement. We were to open at Watford, the scene of my first-ever professional performance (good omen), after only a taut four weeks of rehearsals. As with every new show, I felt both pleased and apprehensive, mostly the latter. I voiced my growing feelings of inadequacy to our director. 'I'd like to sing the songs with a pianist to see if they're really in my range' – my range being about as wide as my knowledge of rugby union players between the two world wars. This was arranged in my back room with Jack Owen Edwards, who later didn't become our musical director, having bigger fish to conduct for.

The great thing about singing is that it gives you an enormous buzz. Just opening your lungs wide and making a loud noise is enough to make you feel quite high with joy, even if the ensuing sound is like the cry of a baby otter in search of its mother. After singing through the score in front of another human being I felt relieved enough to sing in front of the cast and ultimately in front of thousands. Funny thing, confidence, you know. It's so fragile that one discouraging word can silence a voice for ever, just as an encouraging one can give you Ethel Merman-itis. Potential critics, take note.

Just a few weeks before we were to begin, tragedy hit the project. Bob Fabian, the delightful, urbane, silver-haired New Yorker who was co-producing, died of a heart attack. I hadn't known him long, but had liked and trusted him instinctively, and felt an ominous sadness at his untimely death. Indeed, financially the show lost some of its investors and Dan had to fight tooth and nail to find the necessary money to fund the out-of-town try-out. There was still no promise of a London theatre, but throughout the days of rehearsals we pushed this firmly to the backs of our minds.

The fronts of our minds were taken up with learning the dancing. David Toguri is the kind of man who asks as much of you as he would ask of himself. He particularly excels with actors who are untrained for dance because he somehow works around their personal eccentricities of movement. He watches what you can do and uses and improves upon it rather than asking the impossible. I claimed in *The Stage* that he could make a Volvo Estate look graceful. He certainly had me doing stuff my 40-year-old body had only had nightmares about.

In the Brazilian Conga number, where Ruth (my character) attempts to interview some Brazilian sailors whose only word of English is 'Conga', he calmly suggested that I leap sideways into the arms of three of them, who then pushed me upwards into a standing position on their hands and thus slowly over to the top to land in the waiting arms of the other three. This overhead pendulum approach was a triumph – except that it threw my tensed body into a state of bone-rattled trauma from which I've yet to emerge. It was fine, once I'd got used to it, and if and when all the sailors were 'on'. If, however, one of them was off with a strained back or a bad throat (one boy in particular suffered badly with a strained throat which we later found was a result of days spent busking in Covent Garden), the replacement for all of them (known as 'the swinger' for reasons, I suppose, that he'd go and do it for anyone) was a man at least seven inches taller than any of the others. This, coupled with his understandable panic at dancing in six different places at once if necessary, made the line-up a rather irregular shape. At the end of the number they held me up high in the air at arm's length. This meant that wherever he was replacing someone, that particular part of my anatomy was seven inches higher than anywhere else. This was all right if it was my feet, odd but acceptable if it was my head, and downright daft if it was my bottom. My body, I found, is extremely flexible, but it drew the line at being 'humped' – in the engineering sense of the word.

There were several other sky-dives in this number as well as some extremely wild and wonderful earth-bound stuff. The number lasted about seven minutes and was immediately followed by the Conga *chase*, which involved running round the back of the set to the opposite side, up a flight of iron steps, along a grid and down another set of steps, whilst the set of our apartment slid on. Then followed a short but noisy scene leading into a reprise of the Conga, another lift, and the end of Act I. For the first few weeks I was clinging to the scenery, gasping for breath, sweat dripping down my scarlet face, and chest thumping so hard it made me feel like saying 'Sod it, you can carry on without me,' and feigning death.

Then somehow, miraculously, you get fitter and tighter and the breath comes from somewhere and you do it. This has to be an argument in favour of hard exercise, in spite of all you've heard me say before. Sally, my dresser, used to peel my dress off me and drop it in a wringing heap on the floor, whilst I sponged myself off all over, there being no such convenience as a shower in the dressing-room. *Shower*? There was scarcely room for a flannel, but knowing the old Watford Palace well, one can't really complain. It's not the first time a theatre's exterior and auditorium have been gloriously refurbished at great expense, with the money suddenly running out before it can reach the actors' dressing-rooms. My room adjoined the boys' room. (Are you kidding? After all that running and dancing?) So I could hear the lowering of voices that indicated a particularly filthy joke or the lowering of bums into whoopee cushions or whatever they'd decided to do for intellectual stimulation, bless 'em, whilst I was dripping into a washing-up bowl. Strangely enough, I only had one major migraine in the whole year of doing *Wonderful Town*. It was a matinée day, after we'd moved into the West End, and it was bad enough to make me miss two shows. Apart from that I was trouble-free – which has to say something about the relationship of exercise to migraine. Certainly during the seven weeks between Watford and the West End, working on a television series, *The Little Princess*, I was back to my normal one a month, and since the end of the show, it's been the same story.

Has this discovery galvanised me into a life of aerobics, jogging, long-distance hula hooping and Kendo? Has it buggery! Same good intentions – one day's jogging, next day rain stops jog, next day imminent delivery of school blazer stops jog, next day slow walk down to Lark Pet Stores reveals twisted bit in foot, and jogging ceases for ever. Still, if it really seems, as I'm told, that exercise is good for the liver, which is the sluggish organ that causes migraine in the first place, then you'd think I'd be up to my ears in leotards, like a veritable Green Goddess on steroids, instead of hunched over this page with a throbbing pate and a green skin.

I'd sat in on some of the auditions for chorus and featured roles, and I found it unbearable. There is something heart-breaking about the sight of young kids on their best behaviour, desperately wanting their talent to show in its best light, in a five-minute spot. Everyone was very kind, the lights were on in the theatre and there was no suggestion of the barking voice from the stalls shouting 'Next!' but even so, there was still the strong feeling of slave begging for freedom or groupie currying favour. The worst part was when David Toguri would say, 'Do you dance?' Always the same response – a giggle, a shrug, then, 'Well, yes, I mean, I can move a bit.' The next few minutes are then torture as the flustered individual attempts to pick up simple steps and rhythms with his brain in command and his feet in total mutiny.

I was reminded of Jack's story of the auditions for *Bar Mitzvah Boy*, the musical version. After a back-breaking afternoon watching acres of ethnic women singing 'Sunrise, Sunset' in headscarfs and pained expressions, a little lady came on in a purple cocktail dress. She had a red face and very shiny black hair piled into tortuous coils almost as high as she was. She was very definitely not Jewish, but she'd *heard* that this was a Jewish show, and amended her lyrics accordingly: 'Love is where you find it (I should be so lucky), Don't be blind it's all round you (oy veh) everywhere (Have I got a daughter for you!), Love is where you find it – (Have I got a daughter for you!), Love is where you find it (already) – ' etc. All this delivered through a fiendishly animated face and accompanied by wild shrugging and bartering gestures.

Gradually the assembled team, director and producer crept out of the darkened theatre leaving only Jack directly in her line of vision. With his hand clamped round his mouth he nodded and smiled and finally thanked her in a clenched voice for coming in and for her song, and all the research she'd put into it. Then he laughed till he was sick.

My friend Lesley Joseph was on the receiving end of such an encounter. She turned up at the tail-end of a day of auditions for a West End musical, walked on stage to a wall of apathy, and heard a voice call out, 'Well, Miss Joseph? What have you got for us?' to which she replied, 'I've got rhythm and You can't take that away from me.' Wearily the voice drawled, 'Nobody's trying to, Miss Joseph, nobody's trying to.'

Pity the poor actor, for we know precisely what we do. The story goes that three men went up to Heaven and were greeted at the gates by St Peter. 'How much do you make a year?' he said, naturally enough, to the first one. To which the man replied, '£300,000.' 'Go and stand over there with the surgeons and lawyers.' Then, to the second man. 'And how much do you make a year?' 'About £50,000,' replied the man, and was promptly told 'OK. Go and stand over there with the accountants.' St Peter then turned to the third man. 'How much do you earn a year?' he asked. 'About £3,000,' admitted the man. St Peter stopped in his tracks, looked at him keenly and said, 'Would I have seen you in anything?'

Or in the same vein, there's the story of the director

who goes to Heaven and is met by – you guessed it –
St Peter at the gates. 'Before I go in,' says the director,
'just tell me something. Trevor Nunn's not in here, is
he?' 'No, of course he isn't,' soothes the saint. 'Now
just pop in there.' 'You're quite sure?' 'I'm quite sure.'
In he goes and immediately sees before him on the
walls every poster ever printed of Nunn's productions
– *Macbeth*, *Nicholas Nickleby*, *Chess*, *Les Misérables* – his
mouth falls open in disbelief, he turns to protest, then
sees through the window a huge triple limousine draw
up. A chauffeur leaps out and opens the door for a
small neat man with a dark goatee beard, black floppy
hair and beady little eyes. The director swings round
in fury and yells at St Peter, 'That's unfair, you
promised me faithfully that Trevor Nunn wasn't here.'
St Peter smiled. 'No. No,' he says firmly. 'That's not
Trevor Nunn. It's God – He just *thinks* he's Trevor
Nunn.'

Meanwhile back Watford way the show was finally
cast – the full quota. Cast, orchestra, musical director,
stage management and all. At the time I wrote the
following:

'I am a bit pushed for time this week, as I'm doing a
musical. We open next Saturday and I'm not a bit
worried. The other night I had this dream. We'd
moved house and the new one was a converted
optician's. There was a large shop front window and
situated in the middle of it was a toilet. I kept pointing
out that there were no curtains, but no one seemed
concerned except me. Also, I had told my son Adam
the new address before he went to school and he
hadn't returned. It was now one o'clock in the
morning. Oh, yes, and I had syphilis. The doctor told
me what to do, but I'd forgotten on the way home. It
had something to do with the toilet, I think.

'I woke up in a muck-sweat and told Jack about it. "It's all right, love," he said sagely. "Everyone has that dream when they're doing a musical. It's what we in show business call 'The Doing A Musical Dream'." I felt much better after that.

'Last night's dream was an improvement. I was merely an undercover spy in the home of Ferdinand and Imelda Marcos – only everyone knew. It was while wandering through Imelda's bra cupboard that I discovered a cache of children tied to their beds in conditions of horrible neglect. Well, you hardly need a coat of many colours to interpret this, do you? Give me a few ears of corn in alien bleedin' fields and I'll give you a decent night's sleep.

'Anyway, this musical – I'm not going to go on about it because by the time you read this it'll probably be a pile of old spangled tights, a maribou waist-clincher and fifteen empty wage packets in a dusty skin in Bushey. Suffice to say that your lumbering and graceless correspondent spends eight hours a day *dancing* and, at the time of going to press, my feet look as though they've been eaten. By a Dobermann pinscher. With a Cruft's medal for savagery.

'We start each day with a fifteen-minute warm-up, by the end of which I'm so knackered I want to lie down for a year. Then we have a vocal warm-up, which is a hell of a shock to the system as I'm not used to speaking before 10 a.m. – and then only to say, "Did the kids get off all right?" or "Where are my eyes?" Then we rehearse until 7.30 or 8 at night.

'The show is *Wonderful Town*. We open in Watford. I'm very fond of Watford. Twenty years ago, the Palace Theatre gave me my first job. I played the Genie of the Ring in *Aladdin* with a blue Afro, a Liverpool accent and a pogo stick. The height of understatement. Of course, in those days, Watford didn't have a traffic-free town centre and a ring road, and so I didn't spend a fortnight driving round and round the town's perimeter in search of a car park without a "full" sign until my petrol tank started whimpering for Bob Geldof's phone number. Nor did I have all four tyres slashed in the car park I finally found. Of course, twenty years ago I couldn't afford the convenience of a car.

'Mind you, I knew this musical was coming up last October. I started running again to get fit for it. Straight out of the house at 8.15 a.m. Round the block past John the greengrocer, who dropped a box of "ten for the price of two" courgettes at the sight of me moving at something other than a meander.

'Then, as *Time* lurched by, and Christmas and three weeks' filming added volume and density to the craters on my hips, I decided to book a few days at a health farm. Peace and pampering were all that I required, and Inglewood in leafy Kintbury was happy to fit me in for a few days. I chose Inglewood because it's quite proletarian as health farms go. By which I mean not too many Sloanes quaffing pink champers in the jacuzzi or Arab potentates pumping iron by the pool. It's warm and accessible and rather middle class . . . not unlike myself, I suppose.

'So there I am in the sauna, forcing a bead of sweat to my surfaces, when I hear a chandelier-shattering theatrical laugh, and the unmistakable voice of Joan Turner says, "I'm a real water baby, me – always have been – ooh, me towels are slipping – ooh, look at the state of me!"

'For those of you too young to remember the effervescent, zany opera-buffoon, put down what you're reading *now* and take out a subscription to *Bunty*. Miss Turner's act could best be described as cheeky, as in "tongue in", the high spot being a rising

With some feeling, I drew this cartoon for opening night cards.

arpeggio to at least Top C, followed by a scream to the audience of ''All together, now!''

'Strangely enough, at the very first health farm I went to – seventeen years ago – who should be there but Joan Turner. And I hadn't seen her since. We had a lot of giggling to catch up on.

'The peace part of the peace and pampering retreated rapidly. Not that I cared. Health farms can bore the bum off you if you're not rapt by calorie counts. Actually, I ate rather well, by dint of regular circumvention of the buffet table, and thus managed to stay pleasantly pear-shaped. Not so a lady from Michigan who had lost nine stone! Not in a fortnight, mind you, but in a year at Weight Watchers. The health farm was a sort of golden handshake. Ever the opportunist, I had her correcting my Mid-West accent for the musical in the evening, while a plump, kindly lady from Bristol taught me how to meditate during tea break. I stuck her address label in my slipper, for future reference, and promptly mislaid it en route to my next venue.

'Now this was the *real* treat. Two days at The Miller Howe, by Lake Windermere, with Denis and Astrid. Oh, and Jack. A visual and gastronomic paradise which I can scarcely describe without dribbling on my foolscap. ''Breast of chicken with apricot and hazelnut stuffing and coffee-cream sauce,'' said the menu. ''Eat your heart out,'' it should have said. I think I'd rather be there than anywhere on earth, except Robert de Niro's knee. In between banquets we waddled round Wordsworth's cottage and afterwards, walking round Tarn Hows, lo! the Muse struck us. Gentle reader, this was it . . .

> *Oh great slumb'ring Tree-Trunk*
> *Torn from the bellie of the Earthe*

What is the Soule of Man?
What is a Man's Soule worth?

O vast, reproachful Tarn
Like unto a silent Tear,
Oft-Dabb'd by Nature's hanky
Oh dear, oh dear, oh dear.

'Any road up, I expect you're deeply moved, so I'll
sign off and discreetly back out of the room. I'll let you
know how the musical goes. I'll drop you a line from
the Hospital for Aged Thespians. I'll be in the Ginger
Rogers Recuperation Wing. In leg-warmers and a
surgical truss.'

Wonderful Town at Watford was wonderful. Everyone –
audience and critics – loved it, and we seemed set to
transfer to London. As the four weeks came to an end,
however, there was still no producer prepared to put
his money into a revival with an untried (in a musical)
star in the lead. The papers complained daily about the
number of revivals in the West End. A funny kind of
snobbery about American classics grips theatre critics
from time to time. In terms of the musical theatre,
shows like *Annie Get Your Gun, Cabaret, West Side Story*
and *Wonderful Town* represent the cream of the most
productive and prestigious period of the art form. Of
course such shows should be revived. To my kids they
are as fresh as a new pea and, what's more, unlike
today's megabuck musicals, they have a book. A play.
With words. Often very witty and well-constructed
words. Why do I never hear, 'I see the National are
doing *another* revival of *The Orestoeia*' or 'Looks like
Triumph Theatres are reviving *King Lear*'? Oh no –
quite the contrary. They can't *wait* to pit Hopkins' Lear
against their memory of Wolfit's Lear and Sher's

Richard III against Olivier's version, and thus show off their erudition. When does a vehicle cease to be an 'old banger' and become 'vintage'? How old must it be to achieve classic status?

Kiss Me Kate is playing to packed London houses and has done so in theatres throughout the land. Possibly this is because it is under the auspices of the Royal Shakespeare Company, which gives it a certain air of legitimacy. Everyone knows that when the RSC does a comedy, other than a Shakespearian one, the critics suspend disbelief, so bowled over are they by the fact that actors they've seen in the classics can actually say funny lines – out of tights! It's like watching the end-of-term show – *everything* is hilarious, and the laughter has that same quality of exaggeration.

At this period in our West End history, what the critics and the people wanted was *Chess*, *Les Misérables*, *Cats* and *Starlight Express*, all in their ways operetta. Shows without books – with, of course, the glorious exception of *Me and My Girl* which is Cinderella in Lambeth-land, and you can't argue with that! Meanwhile, we played to packed and rapturous houses at Watford and prayed for the right sugar daddy to come along before the four weeks were over and set us up in a place of our own.

One night, as the curtain came down on a wall of delight from the audience, Ray Lonnen, my co-star, said, 'I hope Lenny liked it.' Is Lenny Henry in, then?' I asked, pleased that the cast had kept it from me as I *hate* knowing who's out front. Even the knowledge that my next-door neighbours are in makes me self-conscious. Ray smiled and said, 'Er, no – Lenny Bernstein, actually.'

Once they'd picked me up and resuscitated me, I was fine. We all lined up around the stage, as in the Royal Variety show, and awaited the maestro. He came with his daughter and an entourage. He wore brown leather trousers and a peacock blue sweater. He gave me a king-sized hug, said two or three unrepeatably flattering things, and introduced me to his daughter, to pay for whose birth he had written the score of *Wonderful Town*. In three weeks. I carried away an image of a man more leonine, less tall, more dynamic, less American, more zoftig, more showbiz, and more or less the maestro.

On the same bill came Adolph Green, half of the legendary Comden and Green, book and lyric writers, whom I'm now honoured to call my friend. One day at lunch he filled me in on the days when Betty Comden, Judy Holliday and he were a singing act in Greenwich Village. I sat there like a kid at the pantomime while he 'did' their first visit to Hollywood, when Judy had the contract and said, 'Not unless my friends come too.' It was great hearing it from the source's mouth. In his exquisite and truly 'lived-in' apartment in New York there are memorabilia to make Barry Norman's mouth water – silver pillboxes, engraved 'Frank and Mia', Eleanor Roosevelt, Noël, etc. What's more, the man doesn't seem to have an egocentric bone in his body.

The original author of *My Sister Eileen*, the play on which *Wonderful Town* was based, Jerome Chedorov, I would meet at a later date. He's a dear, gentle man, but his reaction to my costume for a routine called 'Swing' was classic. It was a black and white tango frock, covered in musical notes, which was wired to light up when I pressed a switch. 'Marine,' he said kindly, 'you look *obnoxious* in that outfit.' 'That's not really very constructive. We open tomorrow,' said the designer. 'That's OK,' said Mrs Chedorov. 'She's a pro. She can take it.' (She couldn't but she did.)

Producer Dan Crawford is as straight as the day is long, but he does have some eccentric habits. I think he learned all he knows at the Zero Mostel school for would-be producers. One night after hoofing our combined socks off, I was scraping away a few layers of old skin in my dressing-gown, when some friends came by. They had loved the show, they said, and were amazed that we couldn't get enough money to take it into the West End. 'How did you know that?' I asked, then fell backwards out of my chair on being shown a strip of paper in the programme saying, 'If you have enjoyed this show and would like to invest money in its future, then please ring the following number.' It then listed Dan's number. I was mortified. I'd thought the applause was out of genuine appreciation. I hadn't realized it was tinged with pity.

Two days later a friend rang to ask me if I'd seen the *Financial Times*. Being as how I still keep my weekly wages in the brown envelope in which they come, at the bottom of my bag, in the belief that I then know I've been *paid* and that anything else – cheques, banker's orders, giro etc, does not count as real money (can they buy you a savoy cabbage and a pound of fig Newtons? Exactly. Not real money) – I told him, 'No, it's not part of my set reading.' He then read me an advert headed 'Lipman and Bernstein – do you believe in this combination?' Initially I had to ask myself if Leonard and I had agreed to open a firm of solicitors – however, the advert went on to ask for investment in a future West End production. That night on stage was the closest I've ever come to empathy with Cynthia Payne. 'What the hell,' I thought, 'why don't I just take the straw boater off my head and pass it round the audience?'

In the last ten days of the show, rumours grew like so many 'Next' boutiques. By then I was on the 'day-job', working at London Weekend TV on *The Little Princess*, in the role of the fiendish headmistress Miss

Minchin. The last Saturday of *Wonderful Town* was my fortieth birthday. I spent it doing two shows, with half an hour and a lot of cake in between. I can recommend it strongly as a way of ignoring the sudden onset of middle age and should you chance upon six young chorus boys, a revolving iron staircase and a thirteen-piece orchestra, it could be the same for you.

Re the orchestra, a small detail that had escaped the notice of this novice chanteuse. I had foolishly imagined that, like actors, once a musician was employed it was for the run of the show, excluding serious catastrophes such as sudden amputation or loss of instrument. However, with musicians it's more a case of 'Yes, I'll be there for the first three nights and after that I'll be there if nothing better turns up. In which case I'll send along a dep', as in deputy, who'll busk it for the first half and learn it in the interval. Admittedly, it's a dreary job sitting in a deep black hole unable to see what's going on around you for two and a half hours a night, which is why they're mostly reading *Trout & Angler* in the arc of their anglepoises, and in some lamentable situations, chucking orange peel at Wayne Sleep. In our first week in the West End we had seven deputies and I tell you now that a complex and sustained trumpet solo in a Bernstein score, as played by someone who's just rushed in from having a quiet herring supper in Sydenham, is something I hope you never hear. There's a strong argument for having the band on stage where they can feel like part of the show, or at least join in the jokes. At Watford we all felt part of a big snappy family; ever after it was downhill.

The Little Princess kept me occupied in whalebone and pince-nez whilst most of the cast hung on, without benefit of a retainer, waiting for news. It was a tedious job, probably because my heart was in 'Ohio' but also because it was painfully over-rehearsed on account of the number of children involved. The kids were lovely, particularly Amelia Shankley who played Sara, the little princess, and, once they'd got used to my deeply irreverent attitude, we got along splendidly. My sister was played by the irrepressibly avuncular Miriam Margolyes. (Yes, I know what avuncular means and I stand by it!) If I'm irreverent then Miriam is positively anarchic. The children got used to her scatalogical conversation and quickly arranged a swear-box for rehearsal purposes. They made a fortune!

Jack first encountered Miriam when he was a producer at Granada TV. One day he answered his office phone to hear a voice say, 'Hello, Mr Rosenthal, my name is Miriam Margolyes. I'm an extremely brilliant actress and I would be wonderful in your plays.' Shaken but not stirred, Jack replied that he was sure she was and would . . . 'and, er, thank you for, er, letting me know'. 'Well, you really ought to see me, you know,' she went on, 'particularly if you don't know my work.'

Jack agreed enthusiastically. 'Yes, I'm sure I should. I mean, I will. Please come and see me if ever you're in Manchester.'

'Do you mean that?' she asked and when told that he did said, 'Goodbye, I will.' As Jack put the phone down congratulating himself on how he'd handled the call there was a knock on the door and in walked Miriam. She'd phoned from an office down the corridor. That's the way to do it!

She really is the most extraordinary shape: short and round like a benign biscuit barrel. She would be the first to point out that her breasts make Dolly Parton look like a War on Want poster. Her story of trying to get just one breast on to the slab for a mammography actually stopped the Ruby Wax TV show one night. With me in tight corsets, a bun and a high Victorian collar and her in her undulating bustles, we looked like an antique cruet. One hot day at the studios, on our way to the canteen, we encountered Jack with Les Blair and Paul Knight, director and producer of his film *London's Burning*. I introduced them to Miriam, who said, 'God, it's hot inside these corsets. My tits are completely stuck together. Do your balls get like that in the hot weather?' This was in lieu of 'Hello, how do you do?' I've never seen two more shaken men.

Naturally enough many of our scenes were left to the end of the studio day, as it's more sensible to get the children's scenes in the can because of their short working day. Consequently we'd both be in a seriously wilted state by the time we got on, and much prone to silliness. There was a scene in which Miriam told me about Sara's extraordinary behaviour on being parted from her father. 'That new girl, sister – such a quaint serious child,' she said. 'She asked to be quite alone and went to her room.' I made some villainous remark in reply and the scene progressed to us both talking about her clothes and her wealth and how useful she would be for the school's image. We rehearsed this scene for a week by the fireside in the study with fire-poking by way of emphasis. Unfortunately the studio day was over long and the scene was cancelled. We then rehearsed the scene all week until the following studio day, when once again there was no time to shoot it. Unfortunately the study set had to be cleared after this episode, so thereafter we rehearsed the scene in the hall and the stairs area, with the odd dust-finding gesture and grandfather clock business, and sudden hushed silences when a maid walked past in the vicinity. Once again, come studio day there was no time to shoot the scene, which by now Miriam and I could hardly begin without recourse to mirth.

We did shoot the scene, finally. In the kitchen pantry. It was the only set left. The scene, of course, was rewritten. It now read, 'That new girl, sister – oh, we need more lentils – such a quaint serious child – the rice is getting thin – she asked to be quite alone – I see we're about out of tea.' Both actresses kept their backs to camera as much as possible, and four quivering bosoms strained inside their whaleboning with the effort of staying dead pan. Well, six bosoms if you count Miriam's quota as four.

I must say the finished scene was lovely, a treat to the eye and a credit to director Carol Wiseman and producer Colin Schindler. Many people have asked me how I could possibly have been so unmitigatingly horrid. I refer them to my children, who think I was being pretty nice compared to the way I am at home!

Meanwhile the race to Shaftesbury Avenue was still on. We had a West-End producer, Bill Kenwright. I finally heard that we were going to open at the glorious Queen's Theatre. (I heard this through the usual showbiz channels – Julian Holloway's barber told Julian, who told Denis King, who told me.) It was a touristless summer and our box-office advance was so small the Manager could carry it home in his Filofax.

As openings go it was just fine. The right mixture of adrenalin, joie de vivre and terminal terror. Actually a dentist I once frequented told me, after I fainted during an injection, that I was allergic to adrenalin. You could have heard my laughter from here to Sydney Harbour. Allergic to what I spend my entire life summoning up! We partied at Stringfellows where

several members of the press hung round until I
opened my mouth wide enough to swallow an ibis,
crossed my eyes and showed my bra-straps – then
snapped away merrily. The result hit the supplements
on Sunday. The reviews were a smashing mixture of
rave and resist. 'There are musicals around that are
more glamorous, more pretentious or more bizarre,'
declared the *Sunday Times*; 'this one wins by telling its
story well, knowing its business, and not least by
having captivating music.' 'Maureen Lipman stars, and
I mean stars' said the *Sunday Times* 'like a likeable
predatory bird . . . half urchin and half vamp!' (Play
that!) and in the *Express* 'Maureen Lipman is no great
shakes as a singer but her special brand of comedy is
reminscent of the immortal Fanny Brice'. (I should
definitely be so lucky.) The *Listener* – 'This isn't
escapism – it's a life affirming treat'. My favourite

WONDERFUL TOWN!
EMILY MORGAN *as Eileen*   MAUREEN LIPMAN *as Ruth*

PUNCH

came from the *International Gay Times* which said 'Emily Morgan plays the Beauty, while Maureen Lipman plays the *Brians*'.

Gradually, through the clout of Lucille Wagner, of the Bill Kenwright organisation, and through word of mouth (mostly mine) and some more great reviews, we built up to the stage where we had to buy our own 'House Full' sign for Saturday nights instead of sharing one with the NCP car park. We needed, but couldn't afford, many more actors to fill out the bigger stage – in the Broadway version they had scores of chorus – but somehow by dint of lighting, changes of persona and hats, the actors we had managed to give the impression there were three of each of them.

I flogged my number, 'A hundred ways to lose a man' across the *Wogan Show*, Breakfast TV, and anywhere else they'd have it. Radio and newspaper interviewers filed in and out of the dressing-room like so many emery-boards. *Shiftwork*, Lesley Bruce's tautly-written comedy thriller about a woman minicab driver, was broadcast to excellent notices. *The Little Princess*, too, and the paperback of *How Was It For You*? It was all publicity for our homespun extravaganza. Still, we weren't an unqualified hit in the Lloyd-Webber vein, and the production company were not sure enough of our staying power to risk doing the cast album, although their loyalty towards and love of the show was unquestionable. The word of mouth was still terrific, and compared to much of the rest of Shaftesbury Avenue, we were doing fine. After five months we were nominated for two Olivier Awards (about which more anon), audiences were up, and I said to Bill Kenwright one night after the show, 'How about doing the cast album, then?' He looked at me as though I'd just had the most original and weird idea on earth and said, 'You want to do a record? OK, we'll do one. Next week all right?' So we did. In two afternoons and more often than not, one take. David Steadman, our musical director, steered us through it and filled in whenever an actor was missing because of laryngitis or otherwise engaged doing 'voice-over' for a commercial.

By now there was a British Rail strike, appalling weather and rampant 'flu working against us. In one week we had ice, a thaw, floods, and a drought. (It's extraordinary in this country, isn't it, how the weather is a constant source of amazement to us. Cries of 'Isn't it terrible?' when the Siberian wind blows in February – or winter, as I like to think of it. 'Nationwide shortage of thermal underwear,' scream tabloids. 'Crocuses and old people hit by worst frost since *last* year.' Same with summer: 'Phew, wot a scorcher! See how shapely Tracey 39, 21, 36 gives a wet string vest a-peel!' 'What's that you want, a fan!? You must be joking, missus! I got less fans than Des O'Connor. There's a world shortage, dontcha know?')

On three successive nights I played the same scene with three totally different members of the cast. Everyone was moving around to fill in for the missing few. Also, because (in a long run) furniture has feelings too, the set representing our apartment had begun to misbehave. It slid ingeniously on its castors, but occasionally it stopped, put its little feet down and said 'That's it – no oil, no performance.' This meant that half the playing area was still in the wings and there were no doors to go through to say 'The bathroom's a little small and the kitchen . . . ' Of course, once the audience know what's wrong there's nothing they like more than seeing you get out of it. On one occasion after it had stopped in mid-move, Emily Morgan (who played my dumb-blonde sister) and Ben Stevens decided to carry on acting the scene regardless of the fact that they were playing in a quarter of a doorless apartment. Suddenly the whole set juddered into action and slid on to its prescribed marks. With miraculous presence of mind Ben said, 'Gee, I see you girls are still moving in.' It got a roar of laughter and the best applause of the night.

The following day the tracks were oiled but someone omitted to clean up the oil from the stage. When Emily and I walked into our apartment we could well have been mistaken for Torville and Dean on an off-night, as we slid about the set clinging to the door posts for the sake of our equilibrium. Emily was fortunate; she got to sit on the bed looking pretty and confused. Muggins, on the other hand, had to unpack two cases, swan backwards and forwards from the bathroom, and dance and sing a number. Many people may have pondered that night whether my apparent Max Wall impression was absolutely in character, or, indeed, necessary.

Chest microphones hate me. At Watford I wore two because the first one broke down so frequently. This meant two large battery packs on my backside, which complemented the bias-cut Forties dress line not at all. So I wore a tight pantie girdle to flatten them down over support tights (for support), and stockings and suspenders for authenticity. On top of all this went French knickers for the purists in the lower stalls. I must have lost a stone in four weeks – the Maureen Lipman sweat-your-way to slimness method. Still the mikes played up – I think my magnetic field must have an irregularity. Why not? All my other fields have. Of course, at Watford I blamed the unsophisticated system, but when, during a 'Tribute to Leonard Bernstein' evening at the Barbican, the same thing happened, I had to admit the responsibility was all mine. Four minutes before I was due on stage to sing

'A hundred easy ways', two strange young men came rushing backstage and without so much as a by-your-leave, yanked my dress above my head, unpacked my battery pack, plugged a new one in, and pushed me on stage as the announcer's voice said 'And now from the Watford Palace Theatre . . . ' I was a nervous wreck. But audible.

The great mike problem has apparently been solved in *Les Misérables*, where they wear tiny throat mikes on their heads, just under their wigs. The resonance is said to be marvellous, but it was ruled out for me on the grounds that I might have looked unusual in a Forties strapless evening gown and a powdered periwig.

Prior to Christmas, business went steeply downhill, with theatregoers presumably, to a man, either in Selfridge's basement or with both hands wedged firmly up a turkey's bottom. The excuses for small houses ranged through too hot, too cold, too wet, too icy, too near the Budget, a leaked death in *EastEnders* or a Royal circumcision, no tourists (care of Colonel Gadafi Ltd), children off school, back to school, the January sales, the February and March sales, you name it – audiences are affected by it. Our advance sales were still some of the best on the Avenue, but theatre managers want to hear the thud of cash in the till, not the promise of distant Access cards.

I remember hurrying through the back of Covent Garden in between a Wednedsay matinée and evening show, in cold icy weather. My mind was miles away, somewhere in the second act, and I was mumbling the lines that used to get a laugh and suddenly didn't. There's a story about the legendary Lunts going through a similar trough. Alfred Lunt just couldn't understand why he'd ceased to get a laugh on the line 'Could I have a cup of tea?' He'd tried it fast, he'd tried

it slow, he'd changed the inflection, he'd emphasised
different words, he'd said it fortissimo and barely
audibly, and still it failed to make the audience laugh.
'What am I doing wrong?' he demanded of his wife
and co-star, Lynn Fontanne. She looked him firmly in
the eyes and said, 'Darling, have you thought of
asking for a cup of tea, instead of asking for a laugh?'

Suddenly the sound of running footsteps interrup-
ted my reverie. The narrow street was badly lit, and as
the footsteps got nearer I turned to see a young man in
a long raincoat running towards me. I froze, then
turned back and started to walk more urgently. Still he
ran towards me, his arm outstretched until I felt him
touch my shoulder. I'll never know why, but I spun on
my heels, assumed a vague karate stance recalled
from one or two distant lessons and a deal of exposure
to the _Karate Kid_ video, and let out the longest, loudest,
rawest cry you've ever heard this side of Berwick
Street fruit market. 'Kiayeeee!' I roared from deep in
the gut. Even _I_ was shocked. As for the young man, he
was paralysed. He went quite green in the gloomy
light and stammered, 'I'm sssorry – I didn't mmm-m-
ean to fffrighten you. I'm a ffan of yours and I wwork
in that hairdressing salon over there. I thought if you
ever wanted a haircut I'dd-I'd do it for frfr-free . . . '
He petered out and I thought for a minute he was
going to be sick.

My turn to apologise – I tried to laugh it off, but I felt
such an idiot. On the other hand I was pleased I'd
made a sound at all. Women generally don't, can't.
We're taught from the cradle that anger is amusing in
boys and unattractive in girls. Better to whine and
whinge than to have a tantrum. More girlish. We fear
the reaction we'll get if our rage breaks forth. A friend
of mine's life was saved in a Glasgow park by the
power in her lungs. She was attacked from behind, in

broad daylight, and thrown to the ground. Her first instinct was to scream (many women open their mouths to do so but nothing comes out). In her case, having been trained as a singer, she made quite the loudest noise either she or her attacker had ever heard, and in an instant he reeled back and fled.

As for me, when I reached the theatre I was quite hoarse and had to breathe steam and go heavy on the Lockets. Somewhere in Covent Garden that young lad is probably leading a very restrained existence, avoiding all Thespians, particularly tall, dark ones with glasses and minds full of martial arts. Shame really – I could use a good haircut.

My Wad and My Staff

QUITE SUDDENLY, AND with varying degrees of prior warning, my entire domestic staff deserted me. My Mother's Help went to Vienna, my secretary to Hastings and my cleaning lady into publishing. It must have been something I said. Now I know this is the kind of problem that would only beset a *Guardian* reader like myself, but you have to understand that, without the help and support of the women I love, my life could never run as choppily as it does.

Actually, I knew Simone was going to Vienna. I took it characteristically well. 'Don't go!' I howled, throwing myself full-length on to the kitchen lino. 'They've got a Nazi President! You have to click your heels at bathtime! You'll overdose on Sacher-Torte and come back spherical with a husband called Wolfgang!' My protests fell on deaf but nicely pierced ears. And who could blame her – faced with the ghastly prospect of her own flat in a country mansion and her own little Fiat to run around it in? Anyway, I'd be all right. After all, wasn't a nice Hull girl desperate to be my Mother's Help after reading my book and falling, in her own words, 'in love' with the Rosenthal family?

I called to check she still loved me and arranged that she would meet the kids and me at the theatre between shows. She seemed nice and bright and offered to take the kids to MacDonald's for yuck-burgers whilst I had a rest. Six minutes after they'd left, every drop of blood in my body hurtled to my face as I realised that I'd just delivered my children, my pride and my boy, into the hands of an unknown and undoubtedly ruthless terrorist.

Common sense immediately took over as I reasoned that if there was kidnapping to be done they'd pick on someone with a bigger stake in the Abbey National than me, and one who didn't drive a B registration Ford Escort with a dented bumper and no petrol cap. By seven minutes, I was praying: 'Anything, God! I'll do anything! I'll never do a musical on Shabbos again! My understudy will go on on Fridays! I'll only work for Orthodox managements!' By fifteen minutes, I was chewing Kleenex and something had to be done. *I* couldn't go after them. Not because I had on three layers of greasepaint, false eyelashes and a Thirties' wig – so did everyone else in Soho, even the women – but because of my verruca.

I'll repeat that. Because of my verruca. Which had, understandably, taken against the acid crystals being used to destroy it and had swollen up into a throbbing asteroid where my heel used to be. This had been particularly fetching during the matinée, and seemed set to turn the evening show into a saga of two sisters, one a beautiful blonde who sings like a bird – and the other an agitated brunette who hops like one.

Finally, Ray Lonnen, my trusty co-star, agreed to go round the corner and stage a one-man siege-break. Five minutes or five hours later, depending on whose dressing-room you were hyperventilating in, all four of them returned, two of them covered in ketchup and wearing badges saying something like 'My friend Ronald gave me this stomach-ache' and wondering why their erstwhile self-absorbed mother was clutching them to her microphoned bosom in such a humiliating manner.

A week before Simone was due to leave, the girl who was so in love with us wrote to say that she still _loved_ us but couldn't get a divorce from her mother. I set fire to her letter and phoned _my_ mother, the North London Nanny Agency (tantamount to the same thing), and _The Lady_. Me and twelve thousand other nanny-needers . . . 'Wanted: Caring NNEB for Feargal, 3, and baby sister, Sigourney 1, own magnificent apartment with balconies, use of Range Rover, Bang and Olufsen CD, other domestic help kept and household robot. Hours of work to suit you, weekends in Venice. Nine-figure salary to start.'

One girl from Glasgow travelled down to meet me. I told my, by now, distraught mother of this and she reacted strangely – 'Glasgow? But she'll speak Scotch!' 'Er . . . yes, mother, she probably will.' 'Well, Jack won't want _that_!' she protested. In broad Yorkshire. 'Actually, mother, he's almost over his Scots prejudice now – he's had aversion therapy and he can walk past a Tartan shop now without head-butting the windows.'

Finally, the Chosen One arrived. Let us call her Patsy. Buxom, to say the least, pink of face and merry of mien. 'Ah,' quoth I, 'herein lieth the home-baked pie, the smell of new-mown laundry and the dashing-away of ye olde smoothing iron.' Plus – she had her own _CAR_! No more 'Is it all right, Jack, if I borrow the car to visit a friend?' without mentioning that the friend lives in Shepton Mallet. Plus – _PLUS_ no boyfriend! No Qantas pilots on staircase in wee small hours for wee's. And she liked reading, sewing and cooking! I could almost feel my verruca healing over.

However, this is me, remember. Not Patience Strong. Two weeks later, when Jack had driven the

7.30 a.m. school-run with her daily, when she'd finally grasped the dishwasher, washing-machine and burglar-alarm procedure, when the kids had proclaimed her 'Brill!' and we'd passed Choice No. 2 on to a family round the corner, when we'd merely smiled when she'd had the initiative to take the car to the car-wash without having the initiative to take down the car aerial first, and when she'd gone off cheerily for a weekend at home, saying 'See you Monday!' – then came the phone call. You know the one. The hysterically-sobbing one with words like 'They can't, *hic*, manage without me, *sob*, Dad has lost a stone, *sob*, and what's more, me cousin's been shot.'

'Shot?' I retorted. 'When?'

'Two months ago, *howl*, *sob*, but he's got worse . . .'

Complete collapse into gibbering heap and end of phone call and employment. So it's all down to Limping Lipman now. Cooking, cleaning, washing, tote that barge, lift that bale, have a little drink and you land in . . . and, guess what, I'm *enjoying* it. No, don't throw empty canisters of Jif at me. It's only the novelty. Roll up, roll up, see West End artiste shampoo tuft-pile carpet with one hand and turn duck's giblets into stock with other! See family taste duck soup and scream 'Carpet shampoo!' See me ring North London Nanny Agency, grovelling for help for ageing and faded Thespian, not to mention ageing and faded carpet.

Postscript. One night, the whole cast went to a black-tie party after the show, given by the Management. Outside my dressing-room I could hear every chorus boy and girl whooping with delight at the glittering wardrobe of each stage-hand and electrician. Shouts of 'See you there, darling heart!' and 'Say, you guys look *fabulous*!' and other such theatricalities. And where was I? The star of the show? Was I encased in kilo-

metres of Jean Muir having my nails lengthened by Mr
Garth of The Kindest Cut of All? Was I buggery! No, I
was sitting alone, wearing a grey (once pink) towelling
robe, one foot in a bucket of salt-water, feverishly
awaiting a girl who lives above one of the actors, who
just happens to be a flying chiropodist.

She scraped and probed – and I screamed. Then she
packed a large wad of foot-fleece round my crater and I
hobbled homewards to change the cat-litter tray. Once
more, in the glamorous world of showbiz, something
was afoot.

The Humber Lyrical Chord

'DON'T FORGET WEDNESDAY,' my mother said breath-lessly, and not for the first time that month, reminding me of the joke about the sane man in the lunatic asylum. I'll return to that later. 'Wednesday,' she added unnecessarily. 'You know. I told you. They're coming. To the theatre. *The Women.*' I hadn't forgotten. In fact, I'd bought twelve plastic teacups and a Madeira cake, and the Margaret Thatcher teapot was standing sincerely, in my dressing-room, waiting. For these were no ordinary post-matinée visitors. These were indeed *The Women*. Eight women, to be exact. Freda and Lily and Sadie and Lilly and Flora and Nora and Connie and Muriel, to be more exact. All from Hull, all of a certain age and all as intrepid and bold as Dame Freya Stark, and considerably better dressed.

Their expedition to see *Wonderful Town* had been planned with the military precision of an armed landing on foreign terrain, which, of course, it was . . . Rise 5 a.m., survey skies for signs of weather, make nice cup of tea. Dress in very smart suit and blouse, add collapsible umbrella and mac. Check watch, peer out for signs of approaching 'lift'. Remove unneces-sary articles from handbag. Put articles back in handbag. For fear. Check window. Make nice cup of tea. Turn off every switch in house. In darkness knock over nice cup of tea. Attack tea stains with wet cloth as horn sounds outside. Rush out, get into car, fasten seat belt. Get out of car, unfasten seat belt while still attached to car. Rush back to check gas is off, etc. As dawn breaks, *The Women* meet at the bus station and swap identical departure stories. Much waving to a few bewildered husbands, abandoned at the bus station at 6 a.m. in downtown Hull on a wet Wednesday.

Four and a half merry hours later, they disembarked at Victoria and headed straight for the security of Graham's Fish Restaurant in Poland Street, where apparently none of them was 'going to eat a thing'. Well, maybe half a portion of plaice lightly grilled with a salad . . . listen, I'm not hungry, I had a slice of toast before I left . . . ' Several hundred chips and ten jumbo haddocks later (for by now they had been joined by the organiser herself, a lady I can only describe as my mother, and her trusty cohort, Helen, both already in London for staying-with-their daughters purposes), they helped prise each other, groaning, giggling and plucking helplessly at waistbands, from the tables and headed off to the Queen's Theatre. Via Soho.

Picture the scene as the Mob descends, armed with combs, compacts and clutch-bags, sending the Soho Mafiosi scuttling in terror. *The Women.* Past signs reading 'Erotic Bed Play! Naked Raw Sex! Step inside – 50p'. 'I ask you, Helen, what can you get nowadays for 50p: you can't even get a jar of gherkins!' Past crotchless knickers and peephole bras, past Love Machines and Kebab Machines – the relentless click of twenty patent leather heels on patently sordid pavement.

Meanwhile, the show must go on – including the full curtain call as previously demanded by one Z.

Lipman, related by birth to your singing author. Now this is a trade secret, but usually on Wednesday afternoons we did a short 'call' due to the fact that the foot-stomping Conga reprise might outlast the clapping expected from a dangerously elderly house. This Wednesday, however, was to be different from all other Wednesdays. We'd had our orders, and they included the full Conga. *The Women* expected it. Go fight City Hull! Two thirds of the way through the show, Emily Morgan and I sang a reprise of 'Why-Oh-Why-Oh-Why-Oh, Why did I ever leave Ohio?' and I suddenly found myself watching *The Women* watching me. As they'd watched since I was grass high to a knee hopper, up on the sideboard doing the Alma Cogan impersonations, shepherding their daughters into *Sunday Night at the London Palladium* line-ups, my mother showing me off, me showing her up, school plays, Purim plays – Me: 'The Queen faints!' Them: 'Well, she said her line nice and loud.' Misty-eyed now, I knew through tribal instinct that they, too, were misty-eyed somewhere in the front stalls.

Afterwards, in my dressing-room, we all shrieked and hugged and Sally passed round the cake as *The Women* passed round the compliments. Coffee and ketchup stains were rubbed furiously off the shoulders of spotless blouses and lurching buses shouldered the blame. Like kids, they giggled helplessly and, like kids, they went to the loo in batches of three for fear of getting lost in the backstage corridors. 'I'll end up in the middle of the Conga! That's all you're short of!'

And, like a kid, I looked at them proudly. None of them looked a day older or a mite different from how they'd looked from my vantage point on the sideboard. Unless more beautiful, more animated, more vivaciously chic. *The Women*. Pre-liberation, pre-feminism, their husbands, their kids and their communities came first. No talk of personal fulfilment, independence or 'finding yourself'. Yet not one of them looked lost. 'Bloody magnificent!' I thought, on the verge of becoming maudlin, when the getaway cars arrived.

The long march was nearly over. A sudden flurry of crumbs to the floor, more kissing and the urgent signing of programmes and photos for the bewildered husbands. More lipstick and compact clicks and more joyous, shiny noses made matt and sober again – and, quite suddenly, they were gone. Back to the station, the bus, the four and a half hour journey, the lurching coffee cups and the lifts home.

My dressing-room was never so empty and never so full. Thanks, ladies, and here's to *The Women*. It may have been an exciting day trip for you, but for me it was better than having your name in lights on Shaftesbury Avenue. It was having your feet firmly on the ground you came from.

Oh, about that joke: Lady Mayoress is being taken round a lunatic asylum. She meets a friendly, intelligent patient who tells her that his presence there is a complete mistake. He is totally convincing and she agrees to bring his case up at a council meeting on Tuesday. Very moved, she walks on. Suddenly, a huge brick hits her with tremendous force on the back of her head. She spins round to see the 'sane' inmate smiling at her. 'Don't forget next Tuesday!' he calls.

No Prizes for Dressing

SHOPPING FOR THE perfect dress for the perfect occasion leaves me fraught and overwrought. I don't know about you but I go cataleptic in departmental stores and positively nymphomaniac (buying-wise) in boutiques. In John Lewis I hang around the carpets, the children's department and the fabric department and emerge heaving plastic-coated shoe racks. Whenever I buy clothes for Amy, they usually go back. *You* buy clothes for a thirteen-year-old!

'Yucky.'

'But, darling, it's with it, it's – '

'With what? It's not me. You like things like that but I don't. Look, I'm sorry – but it's no use my telling you I like it when I don't. I mean, NOBODY wears those any more.'

I once bought a suit for Jack in Harrods. I was on my way back from a singing lesson and feeling high, as I always do after taking in all that air and making such a loud noise with it. I cut through the men's department and saw a Prince of Wales check, single-breasted, double-vented designer dream. With no idea of the suit size of the man with whom I'd lived for twelve years, I held it up against a variety of benign salesmen, who obliged me by adopting a variety of Jack-like postures – i.e. typing, frying fish and lighting a fag –

and bought it, along with shirt and tie. It fitted like a glove and on reflection it's a pity I didn't buy him a pair.

I know a lady who shops for all her husband's clothes right down to his shoes. In fact, he sits in the car whilst she rushes out to fetch a left one, and if that fits then she rushes back in for the right one and takes that one back to the car too. Given that this routine goes on enough times to find him a pair that he not only likes but that fits him, this is hardly her idea of a day out. Yet she does it. You may be tempted to think perhaps there is something wrong with this relationship, but you would not necessarily be right, as it's one of the longest-standing ones I know. Just as well the shoes fit.

Actually, I understand how the man feels. For the 1986 Olivier Awards Ben Frow (the man who created my favourite dresses in *Wonderful Town*) and I went to Jacob Gordon and bought several yards of black and yellow chiffon without really knowing what we were going to do with it. As the occasion drew nearer he would pop into my dressing-room at the Queen's Theatre in between shows and throw the material at me till it landed in roughly the shape of a woman's body. (No wonder the idle rich in days of yore spent so much time with their dressmakers. It's like dressing up dolls. Remember cutting the paper doll from the back of *Bunty* and choosing her wardrobe?) However, the black and yellow number never got made due to a tragic death in his family. It certainly wasn't the time to say 'But what about my dress?', although the thought crossed my bad side and had to be ferociously quashed by my good side, which sometimes isn't as powerful as I'd like.

Both *Wonderful Town*, the show, and my performance as Ruth were nominated for awards, and we were to perform the Conga scene, where six Brazilian sailors and Ruth do violent acrobatics, whilst Ruth attempts to interview them. I could, of course, wear my show dress for the number, but what to wear to lose in afterwards was a worry. With only a week to go, I remembered wearing a fantastic midnight blue and silver tulle dress by Murray Arbeid, for some photos in the *London Standard*.

Clutching my forelock, I rang his salon and blurted out my plight, and to my delight he agreed to lend me the dress, provided I insured it for £1,500. I tried to swallow but something seemed to be stuck in my throat. I think in retrospect it was an advance apology. I called at his salon to pick up the dress, which came with an incandescent midnight blue cape, fastened at the neck with diamanté. The dress was somehow constructed like a moulded skin and clung wonderfully to my new streamlined body down to the knees, and then fantailed out, Hollywood-style. I felt I looked like a Jewish mermaid – but a star one!

Mr Arbeid, with his white coat and rather severe manner more like a dentist than a designer, turned out on further acquaintance to be charming and urbane, and wished me luck for Sunday. Then, like Cinderella's Godmother and Al Pacino's Godfather rolled into one, he reminded me to have the dress back at the salon by 9 o'clock Monday morning as it had to go to America to be copied. In other words, what I had in my trembling hands was a priceless original. I laid it reverently on the back seat of my infested B reg. Ford Escort and drove funereally to the Queen's Theatre, where I hung it lovingly amongst the rest of my costumes – leaving the wardrobe door wide open and a sign on my door saying 'Step in and marvel at the most expensive consolation prize you'll ever see on a leading lady.'

Sunday came and by then we'd done eight shows and two rehearsals of the Olivier show in our spare moments. I was due at the Royalty Theatre for further rehearsals on Sunday morning at eleven. By ten-thirty I'd just eased my creaking body on to Sue Cook's massage table – there was simply no way I could get through each week without that luxury (no, necessity). So I thought, 'Sod it – they can have me when they get me.' This attitude lasted until eleven-thirty, when I panicked and fled the table in a taxi to the Royalty where the rehearsals were so far behind that the Conga wasn't performed till two o'clock.

The BBC had thoughtfully provided coffee, which would have made me throw up, and ham sandwiches (75p), which would have made my rabbi throw up. There were hundreds of Thespians crowded into the backstage of the Royalty, a theatre used only for TV quiz games and other such televisual art forms. The last time I'd been there was for Simon Williams's *This Is Your Life*, which I'd adored, if only for the chance to see the handsome rascal again. If my memory serves me right, Eamonn was wearing a commissionaire's outfit in which to petrify his subject, and by golly he certainly succeeded in Simon's case. The man went the colour of a wellie. He seemed to enjoy it though, finally, which is all that counts. I've always had a pact with my agent and husband that if Eamonn's squad ever rang either of us, we'd squeal. This has twice saved me from crying uncomprehendingly throughout and remembering no one but the people against whom I bore a tremendous grudge. Needless to say, this is the biggest disappointment of my mother's life. A fact she never fails to remind me of. Every Wednesday, actually, after the programme's finished I get a call. 'Well, so-and-so was on, and she's not even famous!'

Simon's mother, Margaret, the still glamorous and

charming half of the eminent playwrights, Hugh and Margaret Williams, gave me my best after-dinner story, for which I will thank her eternally. She'd been brought over from sunny Portugal for the event, and looking bronzed and handsome, she seized me by the hand, and said 'Maureen, darling, you look *soo* pretty.'

'Well, thank you, Margaret,' I beamed, not used to being linked with such an adjective, 'and so do you!'

'Yes, darling,' she retaliated swiftly, 'but *I* was *always* pretty!'

Where was I? Back in the Royalty Theatre, cramped into a tiny dressing-room, with my absolute heroine, the American singer Barbara Cook, and the dry and witty singer, Angela Richards. Now Barbara, who has a voice which one critic described as making him think he'd died and gone to heaven, would be the first to admit that she is no Nancy Reagan sizewise, and between all our dresses and my dresser, and her hair-dresser and Angela Richards's boyfriend, there was not the room to swing a virus round, nor were there any windows nor a tannoy system to tell you when you were requested some three floors down. The corridors were jam-packed with gorgeous pouting drag queens from *La Cage Aux Folles*, and after the *Wonderful Town* boys and I had rehearsed our number, there was nothing to do but sit on my butt in my room, pile on far too much make-up, and panic until 8 o'clock – when the fun really started. One of the high points of my day was hearing two young BBC assistants comparing clipboards in the corridor. One said to the other 'Have we got the Vanessa Redgrave replacement, yet?' 'Yes,' breathed the other one, 'she's in dressing room 4, and her name's Athene Seyler.'

During the rehearsal I was given my cue very precisely by the director. 'When the white gauze goes up you make your entrance, Maureen, OK?' 'When the white gauze goes up? Right,' I confirmed and complied. The orchestra struck up, I walked on, did a bit of dialogue then swept into the business of being thrown from one sailor to the next and tossed over the heads of all six.

'Fine Maureen, just fine,' called the director. 'Then after the number you'll have about seven minutes to get back to your dressing-room, change and be in your seat for when your nomination is announced.' 'Fine. Just fine,' I gasped, short of breath and long on disbelief. 'And don't forget – when the white gauze goes up – ' 'I come in,' I cut in, and slowly climbed the flights back to my dressing-room and to my heroine Barbara, calmly reading a book and eating an apple.

Hundreds of hours and a bottle of Rescue Remedy later, I stood in the wings with my sailors, awaiting the cue to go. My heart was doing a Buddy Rich impersonation, only faster. I turned to Denis Quilley who was MC'ing with Angela Rippon. 'Denis,' I said vehemently in reply to his whispered '*You* OK?', 'The last time I felt this bad I was having a Caesarian.' We hugged, and almost before I could extricate myself Angela Rippon had begun the introduction, the white gauze had gone up, the band had struck up and I was au milieu de l'étage (as we say in the world of nervous diseases). The only problem was that all these things happened simultaneously. In other words, I was doing *my* words in the middle of Angela Rippon's words. In even plainer words, I'd been given a duff cue.

Well, what's a girl, in front of nine hundred of the top brass of London theatre, to do? Turn around Eric Morecambe-style and walk off again, thus bringing the house down and Angela's morale with it? Answer – yes, that's exactly what I should have done. What did I *actually* do? I soldiered on, 'The show must go on' being engraved on my lower colon. On I went, to the relief of the band who rewarded me by playing the Conga at roughly three times its normal speed. Apparently to the naked eye I looked like Halley's comet and sounded not unlike the National Westminster Bank Piggy.

When the number finished I seriously thought I was going to have a stroke. On stage. In front of major luminaries and Angela Rippon. I collapsed against a pile of old scenery, or old actors, God alone knew the difference at that point in time, and somehow my sailors got me out of star-bored and into a large port.

Someone was flapping at my wrist. A young PA. 'Can you hurry, Miss Lipton, I've got to take you to your seat?' *Hurry*? There was more chance of me making a choux pastry than there was of me hurrying. My throat and chest were making a strange husky whistling sound and my sweat was such that the Conga dress had to be peeled off me like the shell off a quail's egg.

Somehow I got into the Murray Arbeid. Someone or other, maybe Sally or maybe Sir John Mills, who knows, zipped me up. I ran my hot sweaty hands through my 1935-ish hair-do to try and bring it into the Seventies if not the Eighties and stumbled down the corridors in warm pursuit of my minder. We finally reached the back of the darkened auditorium, just as the number from *La Cage* was announced. I hitched up £1500 worth of dress, and leaping over TV cables and prone sound-men, I just made it to my seat in time to hear 'And the nominations for the Best Actress in a Musical are . . . ' at which point the screen split into four and there were Lesley Mackie, Elaine Page, Angela Richards and a wet rag in glasses and a gorgeous dress. I just had time to smile excitedly and (I hoped) generously as I lost to Lesley Mackie. As I squeezed Jack's hand I felt the damp piece of Filofax on which I'd scribbled headings for my acceptance speech.

No, you're wrong. You *have* to prepare a speech. It isn't arrogant or unlucky, it's professional. Even if you're up against Maggie Smith, Judi Dench and the Archangel Gabriel – if there's a cat in a laboratory's chance of your taking home the dong then you must, in my opinion, have the odd word prepared. I don't mean you should do a Sally Field and proclaim, 'This award means you love me – you really love me', whereupon you want to phone in and say, 'Actually, before I saw this, I quite liked you, now I bleedin' *hate* you!' Nor do I favour the Tony winners' approach of thanking *everyone* they've ever known by name, including their mother's sister's aunt's upholstery man with the funny eye. I just mean it's part of the job to say 'Thank you' either simply and sincerely or with a bit of wit and preferably no political gestures, and above all no mention of the Almighty, who is after all not strictly in show business.

Whatever you choose to say will offend someone and please others. At the Nominees' lunch a month before, there was a sort of Press Conference. 'Are awards the most important part of your profession?' I was asked, and stupidly, rose to the bait. 'Well, of course not. They're far less important than *anything* in our profession. What's important is doing the job well. Pleasing audience and critics and most of all satisfying your own standards. Everyone knows,' I added, 'that you seldom win an award for your best performances – you win it the following year as a consolation prize for not winning it when you deserved to. You win it for surviving blows, marriage bust-ups, illness and flops. Of course, being nominated is thrilling and of course winning is sheer delight, but the best and only reason for braving such an occasion is to bring people into the theatre, to increase business, to show the show of "shows".'

The following day the headline said, 'Nominated Actress Knocks Awards'. See – you can't win them all. Particularly when you lose.

When the ceremony was over we stood up to let the winners past to be interviewed, and made our weary way to the front, past the phalanx of no-longer snapping photographers, into the cold streets, clutching the hem of my skirt all the way to the car, with Jack carrying the make-up and the costumes and the Carmen rollers like the regular roadie he never minds becoming.

On arriving at the Grosvenor House for dinner we felt a little brighter and smiled without a hint of disappointment for the Press corps, who somehow managed to be in both places at once. What happens to all those photos I'll never know, there must be hundreds and hundreds of them lying in a huge vault under the streets of Fleet, labelled 'also-rans' or something.

I tidied up a bit in the ladies – the dress suddenly looked sensational in a full-length mirror, and with a relaxed face, I felt I could pass muster with the best of 'em. I swept down the curving stairs on the arm of my trusty cohort, reached the bottom, and moving merrily towards my allotted table, felt the first foot of the evening wrench the hem of the £1500 dress from the train. I nearly died. Looking behind me I saw a hoop of detached tulle. Looking ahead of me I saw any fun the evening might have had to offer go clean up the balustrade.

I grabbed the rest of the train and forged gingerly on. The next sound I heard was the sound of chair on tulle. Arbeid tulle. Again I died. This time I could tell that my foot was now encircled by torn hem. I started to cry, then stopped myself viciously for fear everyone would think it was disappointment rather than sudden penury.

My feelings during the rest of the evening were a sort of resigned despair. All I could think of was the dress and Mr Arbeid's face. The *Wonderful Town* table had more of a decayed city look about it, anyway. I tried awfully hard to perk up, but was oh, so glad to come home, remove the offended article and sink into a deep and guilty sleep. The last thing I did before laying my head on the pillow was to write Mr Arbeid the world's most grovelling letter.

The next morning Jack returned the dress, Bill Kenwright sent me glorious flowers and the *Wonderful Town* company gave me a pretend Oscar. Back to square one, the square with the proscenium arch, the sliding set and the kids in the chorus. All's almost right with the world of Showbiz. And Murray Arbeid? Like the perfect gent, he never mentioned 'the rent', and if only I'd bought that dress it would've been money darn well spent.

Another occasion loomed ahead during the *Wonderful Town* run – that of the Water Rats' Ball. I'd never before attended such a theatrical fandango, and for my first appearance I'd been asked to sit at the top table and propose the thanks to the King Rat on behalf of the ladies. For some unknown reason this seemed to me to indicate that the King Rat's speech would be something of an eulogy to the ladies. I spent the Sunday lying on the bedroom floor composing an ironic twist on the standard reply to such flattery.

'It may not be obvious to you why I have been chosen for this honour, but the Grand Order of Water Rats is 98 years old this year and after eight shows a week in my first musical, I qualify as someone who feels the same age.' I added, 'One should never trust a woman who tells you her real age. A woman who tells you that would tell you anything' and went on to say that I wasn't entirely sure whether the quote was from Oscar Wilde or Coral Browne. 'I know that it is hard for you gentlemen to believe that the incandescent creatures you see before you this evening are merely mortal, and I'm not going to disillusion you. The fact that I have to be cranked out of bed in the mornings like an old Austin 1100 should in no way be applied to my youthful sisters here this evening.

'We may sometimes flag, gentlemen, after a hard day crouched over a cold microwave; when the man from British Telecom has confiscated our new £200 phone and told us, "It's a defunct model, get another, from Lewisham. On foot." When the bank machine has eaten our card for the second time this week and given us in exchange a slip of paper saying, "Coutts the Bank that says Ya"; when we overhear one of our children say "I've found a condom on the patio" and the other respond, "What's a patio?" But I assure you it's nothing that can't be cured by a gold-rimmed invitation, a chance to fumigate the floor-length, and a dinner which has the distinction of being washed up entirely by other people.

'Gentlemen, we are delighted to accept your compliments and are as ever bewitched by your charm, that elusive quality best described as "the ability to get the answer 'yes' without ever posing the question". I'm not sure who said that either, but I expect it was Warren Beatty.'

The speech continued in this vein, then went on to praise the Water Rats for all their great good works, and concluded by carefully thanking the gentlemen for so thanking the ladies. I quote the speech merely to illustrate the dilemma in which it was to place me.

The Grosvenor House ballroom must have been host to a thousand people that evening. They were hanging from the balconies. The world of Variety was out in full regalia. Ruth Madoc, Barbara Windsor, Esther Rantzen, bejewelled and begowned to my right; Danny La Rue, Frank Carson and several Ronnies to my left. We sat down just off-centre of the fifty-foot long top table, and I began to feel distinctly queasy. Then came the cabaret, starring Bernie Winters, Bernie Bresslaw and probably Bernie Grant for all I know. I was by then too nervous to notice. I do remember Frank Carson's version of the 9 o'clock news. 'The Argentinians have declared war on the Irish. They've removed all the keys from the tins of sardines.' Then I vaguely remember a hilarious interlude when all the men sang a song about Rats and leaped up and down waving their handkerchiefs. Jack by now was having the time of his life. I don't remember eating but I guess we did. I do remember the sound of my heart thudding against boned taffeta.

Suddenly it was speech time. The King Rat, Alan Freeman, was on his feet delivering his speech. The one I was to respond to. I kept waiting for him to mention 'the ladies'. He kept talking about his year in office. My left eye began to twitch like mad as I heard him winding to a close. Still no mention of anything remotely feminine, not even 'fluff'. I grasped Jack's hand violently. 'What am I going to say? My speech is totally irrelevant. What can I *do*?' For once he panicked with me. 'I don't know, luv – I don't know what the HELL you can do!' Then together, 'Oh my Go-o-od' as Alan sat down to tumultuous applause and the lady toast-master banged her gavel. 'My lords, ladies and gentlemen – pray silence for Miss Maureen Lipman who will – ahem – reply to the toast to the ladies.'

I was on my feet. Clutching my redundant notes in my frightened fist. There was a two hour pause for a couple of seconds, then a voice said, 'Chief Barker, my lords, ladies and gentlemen. I would like you to imagine you have just heard the following speech: ''My lords, ladies and gentlemen, it is my honour and privilege to give you a toast to the lovely ladies gracing our tables this evening. Yes – where would we be without them? Oh my, what wonderful women, etc. etc.'' Yes, he has showered us with praise which has made us pink with pleasure, he has gone *right over the top* and back again in adoration of our splendours! Right, have you got that? Are you sitting comfortably? Then I will respond.' Hugh laughs and sigh of relief. 'King Rat, my lords, ladies and gentlemen: I have the honour to reply on behalf of the ladies to the rose-tinted toast given so fulsomely by the King Rat . . . ' and followed with the speech.

Drenched, I sat down amidst comforting applause. The toast-mistress stepped forward and announced Mr Ted Rogers to reply to the toast on behalf of the guests. His first line was: 'Follow that. I wish I were married to Jack Rosenthal.' I laughed along with the other 1,999 people till it suddenly hit me what a chauvinistic remark it was. Obviously Jack had to have written my speech! I'm just a woman, I couldn't possibly have done it. Beside, it was funny. It took me back to the launch of *How Was It For You*? when the standard question was, 'How much of the book did Jack write?' To which my standard reply became, 'Between you and me – he wrote all of it.' Then, when they'd written that down: 'I, on the other hand, wrote *Bar Mitzvah Boy*, *Spend Spend Spend*, and *The Knowledge*.' Claire Rayner came foaming at the mouth to my table to object to Mr Rogers's remark, and it even made the Ann Robinson column in the *Mirror*. In the end though, it was a joke – not a great one, but one that will remain in my repertoire.

The most civilised of awards are the Royal Variety Club awards. Why? Because between you, me and several thousand other readers, one *knows* in advance. This is kindness itself to the recipient, who can have a decent lunch, prepare an articulate speech and wear a dress which is short enough not to send her flying butt over podium on the way to receiving it.

At the last one, when I won The Best Stage Actress of 1986 Award for *Wonderful Town*, I was overjoyed to be seated at the same table as Maggie Smith. After the prize-giving someone came to the table and asked me for an autograph. I was so embarrassed that they asked me first that I signed my name 'Maggie Smith'. No such thing as an accident? I know, I know!

In conclusion, my lords, ladies and patient readers, the Fellowship farrago. A saga uniting Awards, British Rail and Tupperware. I was honoured recently with a Fellowship from the Humberside College of Technical Education. Yes, me. The woman who gets a man in to change a toilet roll holder. I caught the 7.55 a.m. train to Hull, attended an 11.30 a.m. ceremony in the City Hall, caught the 1.00 p.m. train back to London for an 8.00 p.m. performance of *Wonderful Town*. Easy, right? If you think so, you haven't read the last hundred pages.

I caught the train and settled down for a quiet gawp at the world of *Interiors* and the chance to write a quick thank-you speech. After a few minutes the jovial sound of 'Tickets, please' announced the arrival of the inspector. 'Hello, Maureen,' he boomed. 'How y'a doin'?' I told him I was doing fine and showed him my away-day. 'We're neighbours, you know, Maureen,' he continued. 'We, also, live in Alexandra Park Road.' 'Gosh,' I said, not wanting to tell him that *I* didn't.

'Fancy that.' 'My wife she is a good fan of yours,' he beamed. 'I will show you a picture of her and you will guess where she comes from.'

I put down my copy of *Interiors* and picked up the small passport photo he held out. It showed a pleasant, olive-skinned woman set against a background of red crushed velvet, looking vaguely uneasy, as well she might since the flash-bulb was about to turn her irises red.

'Well? Where's she come from?'

'Er – would she be Greek?'

'No no no no no,' he laughed in a falling cadence.

'Well – er – French, then?'

'No no no nooo. Try again.'

'O, sh . . . I mean, she's not Belgian, is she, at all? No no no no no,' we chorused together, then I threw in the wet wipe. 'I give in.'

'Yes. She's an Iraqui Kurd.' He looked absolutely delighted.

'Well, I never,' I breathed. 'Do you know, I don't think I'd have known that if you hadn't told me.'

Well pleased, he beamed, tipped his cap, called out 'Tickets, please' and disappeared.

I picked up my pad and wrote, 'My Lord Mayor, ladies and gentlemen' and looked up to find a tall, middle-aged gentleman standing opposite me. He introduced himself as the Dean of Recreational Studies from Edinburgh University, travelling to Hull for the same ceremony. I asked him to sit down and we chatted for the rest of the journey. He was charming, urbane and interesting, and before I knew it we were at Paragon Station. I was to be met by Pat, courtesy of the college, and whipped to the City Hall in a hot Fiesta. Sure enough, on the platform stood a short, cheery lady waving wildly.

'Hello, you must be Pat. This is Mr – '

'So you've managed to pick up a fella already then!' boomed Pat, grinning.

I died slowly and painlessly drilled myself through a hole in the platform.

Within minutes we were on the platform of City Hall, where hundreds of graduates received their graduation certificates and I strained my eyes and back in search of my parents in the audience. Finally I received my award. 'Shall I say a few words?' I whispered to the Dean of the College. 'No time,' he mouthed back. I sat down again. He then gave a long and extremely detailed report on the progress of Science and Technology in the college, after which the ceremony ended. We piled into a room for pre-lunch drinks. I found my parents and said goodbye, and leaving them to lunch I headed outside to await my taxi. It failed to arrive. I had ten minutes to catch the only train to get me back in time to be on stage at 8.00 p.m. Pat came out to join me, then went back to phone the cab firm. The minutes ticked by. No cab. The square was filled with thronging, exultant students. My mother appeared, white-faced, on the City Hall steps. 'Don't tell me the taxi hasn't come! OH, MY GOD – OH, NO. I CAN'T BELIEVE IT – WHAT WILL YOU DO? YOU'LL MISS THE SHOW! SHE'LL MISS THE SHOW! SHE'S ON STAGE TONIGHT IN LONDON! OH, MY GOD! (This last to total strangers on either side.) WHAT ARE YOU GOING TO DO? OH, MY GOD!'

Ignoring this constructive advice I raced on teetering high-heeled shoes in pursuit of what looked like a yellow cab. It was. I leaped in and leaped out again at the station just in time to race on to the smallest train you've ever seen outside Hornby-land. Apparently they (BR – Barmy Rail roads) have decreed a three-carriage train to Doncaster with bus-like seats and no bog, on which I was privileged to stand all the way wearing a large yellow hat, matching stockings and black and white suit, and carrying a floral display. The train was full of men, women, children and assorted livestock. I got some quite unusual looks from the good people of Humberside.

Seconds before the train left I heard a shriek and saw Pat, red-faced and running, brandishing a Tupperware container and some bulging tin foil. I was too hemmed in to get to the window, but someone – a shepherd, I think – pushed it down, revealing a hot Pat, who yelled, 'Your mother packed you a couple of fish patties and some iced buns. She said to ring her when you get in.'

'Thank you, Pat.' And thank you, MUM. And especially, thank you, British Rail. For you are jolly good Fellows. And so, it seems, am I.

Diary of a Showbody: Part 2

IN FEBRUARY THE family and I had lunch at the Holiday Inn, Chelsea. Roast beef and yorkshires around the poolside. Outré? OK! For some reason, after my swim my knickers had disappeared from the changing-room. In the same week *Wonderful Town* was given its notice. Somehow the two events seem inextricably connected. The audiences had never been better, and after I received the Variety Club of Great Britain Best Stage Actress of 1986 Award, they soared. The show was a delight to perform. Still, the notice was up and although the Kenwright office tried to dissuade the theatre owner from doing so, he booked in Griff Rhys-Jones in Brecht's *Arturo Ui*. It lasted a few weeks, then the theatre went dark for most of the summer.

During the last three weeks I moonlighted once more on a TV play called *Exclusive Yarns*. Lesley Joseph and I researched each morning at the Oval and sped back for the show each night. It was madness. One night, standing in the wings, she said to me, 'I've got a blood blister on my finger. Do you think it's Aids?'

'No, Lesley, it's a blood blister. Why would you possibly think you had Aids?'

'The man in the bagel shop round the corner. He cut his finger as he was slicing my bagel. Can you catch Aids from a bagel?'

'No, Lesley. Jewish people have a different disease. It's called Maids. If you don't have one, you die.'

We were both exhausted but determined not to let the day job affect the night-time one. During the last week I was asked by the *Daily Mail* Features Department if I would write eight hundred words on 'My Perfect Weekend'. I laughed out loud. 'I don't have them. It's just not something I have. I have, on the other hand, just had an atrocious one – prize-winningly so. I'll write that for you if you like.' A fee was agreed and I spent two bleary mornings and the three precious hours in between the last Wednesday matinée and evening show correcting it. It seemed that because my piece would be topical, since it ended at the BAFTA awards, it had to be in that very week, replacing the advertised celebrity's piece. Somehow I got it to the *Mail* in time to print it for Saturday's edition. On Saturday I opened the paper to read 'My Perfect Weekend' featuring Diana Rigg on fly fishing. Beautifully written, but not the one I'd broken my neck to write.

Flowers and weedy apologies followed and promises, hand on heart, to print it the following Saturday. This time it was 'My Perfect Weekend' by Lord Montagu of Beaulieu – on castle-polishing or some such thing. I was quite cross. I seem to remember telling the pleasant young man in Features what to do with his column. Looking back at it now, it seems to sum up my feelings in those last weeks:

'Of course,' I wrote, 'a lot depends on your definition of "perfect". The Greeks called it "arete" – something perfectly true to what it is. Few things could be truer to what *I* am than last weekend. Read on.

'Friday 3.30 p.m.: I'm driven from Southampton to

London after a day at TVS filming *Exclusive Yarns*, a comic gem in which I play a Soap Queen. The rest of the cast are staying for the party, but I'm going back to do *Wonderful Town* in the West End, as I've done each night for almost a year. At 8.45 that morning, in Make-Up, I was so overtired that I began to howl like Steppenwolf, and although I blinked, barn owl fashion, to stop the flow, there were soon thin white rivers meandering through the Clinique Extra-Help. The make-up lady tried hard, but my face still looked like the set of *Starlight Express*.

'By 10 a.m., I was back on camera, cracking jokes and over-acting like a trouper. Everyone said "Mahvellous, Dahling", and I slipped out of my jewelled shoulder-pads and into a hot getaway car.

'6 p.m. London: I'm in my dressing-gown, heart banging like the bedsprings in *Dynasty*, convinced I'm going to faint, forget my lines and start crying again in the Conga. 8 p.m., I'm "on" and beaming like a wet headlamp. 11.30 p.m., I'm home, bathing my bulging feet and unwinding till 2 a.m. with *His Way* by Kitty Kelley. After two chapters on Sinatra, I realise what a lovely person I am, and sink into sleep. Jack's in Los Angeles, and the last thing I remember before oblivion is that tomorrow is my Mother's Help's day off – and matinée day. No point in crying. No one to see me but my Maker, and he's blasé about blubbing.

'Saturday 2.30 p.m.: En route to the theatre, I take my ten-year-old son to buy a new Rubik's Magic. He's solved the old one to death. He can transform it in two seconds, and no wonder. It's all he does. You can hear him coming for miles, clicking like the croc in Peter Pan.

'5 p.m.: The marathon begins. I dance, sing, wisecrack and sweat. One of the actors is off – necessitating a shifting-up of two others. In the Conga, I'm about to leap into the arms of three of them when I notice one has the prop book in his hands. I know of old that he'd much rather drop me than the book. So I don't leap. This throws the rest of the routine. A spectacular sky-dive becomes a fumbled lurch (there's a giggly end-of-term feel to the show – we close in a week). I try manfully to give the nice audience as much as they deserve. I think I try too hard.

'7.25 p.m: In the dressing-room, I peel off sodden clothes. ''This is your half-hour call!'' comes over the tannoy. I would cry but it would embarrass my clicking ten-year-old. I lie down, get straight up again, dress and hit the second show. Two and a half blank hours later, I crawl up to the Stage Door, desperate for a bag of chips. ''Stop in Old Compton Street,'' I plead to my cab-driver. I leap into the ''Fish & Doner'' and demand ''Chips – and can I have *one now* while I'm waiting?'' I salt and devour it. Suddenly I see myself, mother of two, name in lights, forty years behind me, standing in Soho *sucking* chips. I realise, of course, that I'm dehydrated. It's the salt I need. Half-way through I lose interest in the chips and start licking the bag. Ah, the glamour! The cab smells like Hull Fair. The driver's well pleased.

'Sunday, 1.30 p.m.: I assuage my familial guilt by cooking a traditional lunch, which the children disappear for. All my good intentions fly out through the microwave. I scream at them, saltily, like a fishwife. They shake wise heads, tap resigned foreheads and ignore me. I clear up and stay in a hot bath till it's cold. For Sunday night is BAFTA night.

'5 p.m.: I wash my hair, apply a ton of mousse – mostly to the floor – and scrunch-dry till I look fashionably yak-like and my fingers are stuck together. I squeeze into the new basque and even newer gown, then squeeze out again as the basque shows at the back by about a foot. Does this make me a basque separatist?

'5.30 p.m.: Jack jet-lags in from LA and Jane Fonda, so ravenous for a cuppa that he doesn't notice his wife in yak's apparel. "There's braised steak in the oven. God, I missed you, darling. Goodbye," and I exit into the night towards the Great Room at the Grosvenor.

'6 p.m.: Flashbulbs pop as I enter alone. "*Rosenthal marriage in turmoil!*" . . . "*Is Jack Fonda of Jane . . . ?*" I envisage, and hastily make entrance with Nigel Havers. In the cloakroom, a lady asks me if she looks all right, then bursts into tears. She's had a crash on the way in and is in shock. I comfort her and avoid saying I've been in shock since Friday and crying is good for it. I apply blusher to my face, standing between Susan George and Stephanie Beacham. I feel like a "Spot the deliberate mistake" cartoon.

'6 p.m. till 11 p.m.: The awards are interminable, the meal indigestible and *The Singing Detective* is the victim of a massive injustice. I soothe Dennis Potter with my theory that the prizes reflect a post-Aids vote for "Romance", but I know he'd have felt better for a good cry.

'Midnight: Home for the cup that cheers and an up-to-date briefing on Jack's week that was. Another warm body beside mine. Just Jack's – I don't know what happened to Nigel's. All's almost right with the world.

'Just before I fell asleep, the following poem breezed through my brain:

> *Sunday evening. Went to BAFTA,*
> *Pair of Ronnie's. Lotsa LAFTA.*
> *Potter loses. Nothing's DAFTA!*
> *Evening endless. Quel DISAFTA!*
> *Why'd I go? Felt I'd HAFTA –*
> *Expensive dress. Bleedin' TAFF'TA!'*

*　　　*　　　*

On the last Friday night before closing, the emotion hit me straight between the eyes during 'Why-Oh, Why-Oh, Why-Oh did I ever leave Ohio?' I couldn't finish singing for the lump in my throat and the stinging in my eyes. Sitting on the front row was Irene, our 'company fan', who'd seen the show 129 times, with and without broken arms, and the floor was awash with end-of-term emotion. At Saturday's matinée I was determined just to enjoy myself, without indulgences. It was a lovely show, as fresh as the first time we'd played it and the audience reaction was wild.

The evening performance was, if anything, rather better. Everyone was on their best, most delicate behaviour. It's odd how, after a longish run, so many bad habits creep in. Extra lines, heavier emphasis, more frills, coarser acting – we're all guilty of it. It staves off boredom, we think. Then along comes a special occasion, in our case the sadness of a last night, and all that's extraneous drops away revealing the straight lines of the book, lyrics and songs, portrayed as the authors intended. Then you see why everyone was so well cast in the first place. At the final call two little Rosenthals, dressed up and carrying a bouquet, trod gingerly on to the boards and caused their beaming mother to force out a tear or two before rallying the whole audience to join us in an abandoned Conga round the stage and the theatre.

Afterwards, amidst hugs and swapped promises, Jack, Sally and I crammed eight months' worth of make-up, letters, clothes and general domestic garbage into the back of his car. Jack headed home and Sally, the kids and I took my car around to producer Bill Kenwright's flat where he and his vast Liverpool family were in mid knees-up. It was a wonderfully gregarious way of forgetting my sadness, and I blearily recall telling the famous old 'You don't have a vase?'

joke (see *How Was It For You?*) into a mike before staggering out into the night in search of a taxi. There wasn't one. The taxi drivers of London must have all been in Fuengirola on a cab drivers' awayday.

One ex-West End star, one ex-West End star's dresser and two very over-tired ex-West End star's children stood, loaded down with flowers, in the Marylebone Road at 2 o'clock in the morning, flagging down anything with a light on it. Any cabs which did stop refused to go as far as Muswell Hill. Finally, I bent the truth. 'Highgate, please,' I said, shoving my yawning babes inside. Once in Highgate I said, 'Just straight ahead – no, a bit further please – er, just on to that roundabout,' until we were within distance of the Hill itself.

'This isn't bloody Highgate,' shouted the irate driver. 'No, I know, but if I'd said Muswell Hill you wouldn't have taken us, would you?' 'No, I bloody wouldn't, and you can get out now!' 'Thank you very much – we are within the six mile limit and you'll take us there or I'll report you to the Carriage Office. I know my rights.' 'And I know my bleedin' rights – you can clear out of my cab or I'll – ' 'Right, I won't pay.' 'You'll pay or I'll – ' 'Don't you threaten me – I'm just about ready for you – ' By now the cab had stopped and the driver and I were about to crack each other's jaws. The kids were pulling me, 'Come on, Mod – don't fight with him – we'll walk.' They pulled me away from the driver's jugular and we limped home yelling abuse back at his proffered two-fingered V sign.

It was a perfect metaphor for the last eight months. I can't exactly explain why. Something to do with being in the right place at the wrong time, knowing you were right to have gone there in the first place. Or the other way round.

Suddenly, horribly, there was nowhere to go in the evenings. I'd planned to see every play in town, dance the night away, sleep the days away and grow fat and placid. Instead I just sat there with not a thought in my head until I finally picked up my left arm – which in turn passed my right arm a pen, and the result was this. It's what your left arm's for, really.

5

Home, Home and Deranged

Not on Your Wellie

I'VE GOT TO get away from it all. It's no good, I've had this city life up to here (gestures to twenty-eighth vertebra – the quivering one) and frankly I'm sick of the sight of my own skin pallor.

Sally O'Sullivan, editor of *Options* magazine, started it. It's all her fault. I'd popped into her office for a screech on my way from dropping the kids and Karen (new Mother's Help from Bridlington and ace, also cuts hair and enjoys playing with the children – *my* children – present employer recommends – no you can't she's ours) at Kings X for visiting Humberside purposes. It was my first free day since *not* being in a West-End musical. Feeling light-headed with sudden lack of responsibility, light-fingered with sudden lack of earnings and light-footed with lack of ever having to dance on my verruca again, I purchased a bottle of champagne, some paper hats and a blower, and, illegally parked and wearing a knee-length orange cardy and leopard skin tights, I erupted on the Editor in Chief calling 'Party! Party!'

Tea and the rest of the staff were summoned. It was Friday and it sure beat working! I showed them my endangered legs and blew my little hooter for them all. This led to the swapping of gossip, anecdotes and finally clothes, as Sally plied me with a plethora of pleated skirts (an *Options* special offer) as a going home present, though I demurred all the way back to the car.

It was during the obligatory 'What are you doing for the hols?' exchange that Sally mentioned 'The Country'. She, I was informed, was swapping her gorgeous, groomed, something-in-the-city look for a pair of green wellies and a parka with a dog attached to it. What about me? Oh, well – I was just happy to be at home really. Indeed, the world being my oyster during this period of rest and recharging my Duracells, I was just dying to shop, cook, reintroduce myself to the kids and pamper Jack. The girls in the office all looked understanding, although I thought I caught a twitch of the dubious in Sally's eye.

Afterwards, on the way home, I thought, 'The Country, eh?' I'd heard of it, of course. I'd even seen bits of it from the train window. Novelists always started chapters by describing it for a paragraph or two. Those were the paragraphs I skipped. In Bertolucci's films it looked ever so lush, and once, in the Dordogne, we wandered into it by mistake and had a really good steak au poivre.

Oh – and health farms tend to be in it. You can tell this because they ask you on the brochure to take a taxi from the little leafy country station, and the eggs are bigger. But of course once you're *in* a health farm you could be slap-bang in the middle of Leicester Square or Limoges for all you know. They all look like stately homes with long curving drives, but then, so do most of the houses in The Bishops Avenue, Hampstead. And once you've located the light diet room, the swimming pool, the torture chamber and the TV, then the next whiff of air you'll be having is the one you'll draw at the front door with your head between your legs, after you've seen the bill.

As a child, the words 'a ride out' were synonymous

with the words 'family row'. Mother suffered from car sickness and had to travel sitting on a folded copy of *The Daily Express* (an *incentive* to throwing up, if you ask me), and the shooting brake had to have a chain dangling from the back. To *earth* it. Not being of a scientific bent I didn't understand it then and I don't understand it now. Dad never quite knew his way outside a radius of three miles from Hull, which was apparently my mother's fault. (I thought map-reading was anti-Semitic till I was twenty-four.) Meanwhile my brother and I began fighting over who travelled in the boot and got to wave at other shooting brakes. I usually won by dint of being eighteen months younger, which led him to whistle tunefully 'on purpose' till I bit him. On such occasions we would usually end up eight miles away in the market town of Beverley, where we would buy home-made ice cream from Burgess's – I can still taste it – and retired to the Westwood to eat them, by the car. It's a fact that I swore my stage name, if ever I was famous, would be Beverley Westwood.

Trying to recapture those heady days is a daunting task, but years later Jack, myself and Sara, my agent, went up to Hull for a weekend. On which occurred the now legendary 'Jewish Picnic'. Read on if you haven't just had stitches or a baby.

It was a pleasant enough day and we all declared our eagerness for a 'ride-out' to show Sara the surrounding countryside. We wanted an early start and a picnic lunch, but since it was Passover, i.e. no bread, the make-up of the picnic took a deal of discussion. Finally we buttered piles of matzos (unleavened bread) which, if you've ever buttered crackers you'll appreciate, break up into flying shrapnel when approached by a knife and go damp and soggy at the mere mention of dairy produce. We added almost hard-boiled eggs

('Aw, yours has cracked, Maurice') and salad stuff and special passover crisps (same as ordinary crisps but with Hebrew printing and a raised price), and the five of us, some rather on the largish side, wedged ourselves into the Vauxhall Chevette – 'No, honestly, I'm fine – I'll just sit forward a bit, on the edge here. Close the window? Oh, of course, sorry, I didn't realise it was blowing your hair – I just thought a bit of air might – no, no, I'm *perfectly* all right – you stay in the front and direct Maurice.'

Directing Maurice, as I'd forewarned Sara, meant Mother turning round and chatting to us, whilst Maurice drove totally erratically and without any discernible knowledge of where he was going, until such time as he'd passed the turn off, then: 'Maurice, you've missed it! I told you to go right after Ferriby Foreshore.' 'If I'd turned right after Ferriby Foreshore, we'd be in the bloody river, yer barmy bugg . . ' 'All right, Maurice, well, left then, I meant left – turn around, then. NO NOT YET!' This as he U-turned on a dual carriageway in the face of a Pickfords van and two mounted policemen. Some time later, we shuddered in anticipation in the car as he explained his predicament – and then watched navy blue arms go amicably round his shoulders, a lot of back-slapping take place. And we knew he was just about to measure them both up for a suit. All was well. Just.

Back on the road we passed Burton Constable (small world, isn't it) and I foolishly remarked that I'd never seen the 'Hall'. Action Man at the wheel swung the car off the road and down the long drive and parked on the forecourt. But it was not to be. 'Maurice, what are you doing? Sara won't want to look round an 'All – it's a lovely day, we'll miss all the weather – you don't, do you, Sara? Tell him,' urged my mother. Sara, who by now would have sold her kaftan for a chance to get out of the Chevette – agreed that no, she certainly didn't need to see the Hall this visit, perhaps on another occasion . . .

Teeth and car in mid-grit, Maurice eight-point-turned back on to the road and drove doggedly off in some direction or other in search of Hornsea. Almost under his breath I heard him chunter, 'All my life I've wanted to see Burton Constable Hall . . . ' It might have been the Great Wall of China he was wistfully regretting, not a small manor less than fourteen miles from where he'd lived for sixty-odd years.

Finally, and under darkening skies, we approached the Hornsea road. Various places were mentioned for the picnic but none was quite right. Too steep, too flat, too crowded, too deserted. A grassy traffic island with an integral bollard was suggested – then a lay-by with vehicles thundering past, not unlike a pantechnical Le Mans. At last we approached a leafy opening with white gates, a large expanse of greenery beyond, and a sign saying Private Golf Course Club. Aggravated, deprived and hungry, Dad veered recklessly through the gates and hurtled towards the Clubhouse – parked, got out, grabbed the picnic bag and strode off in search of a suitable watering hole, be it the 3rd or the 18th.

Mother rolled down the window and screamed at his retreating spine, 'Maurice, come back! It's a golf course! Come back! Maurice, can you hear me? Maurice! You can't take *matzos* on a golf course!'

With a face like a handicap and a dripping carrier bag Maurice came back, slammed the car door shut and reversed all the way down the gravel drive and on to the main road like a scene from *The French Connection*, or indeed any major American film of the last decade.

We did eat the picnic, finally. In Hornsea. No, not by the sea. Nor on the beach nor in a leafy park nor even on a cliff head. We ate it in the car park, still sitting in the car, only with the windows down. Silently. Then we rolled the windows up and set off again for more countryside, and finished off the fruit and crisps by the roadside. At which point Dad decided he needed a toilet. We urged him to use the hedge but he got back into the car and vanished in search of sanitation. After at least twenty minutes we watched him drive back towards us. Then we watched him drive straight past us and disappear in the other direction. Fifteen minutes later he reappeared, again driving towards us. This time we waved. Again he drove straight past us, and out of sight. This happened five more times until in the end we all formed a human chain and leaped up and down in unison, shouting his name and waving heads, arms, eyes, feet and crumbling sheets of matzos.

Clapped-out and crumb-strewn we somehow made it back home by nightfall. In eight hours we'd driven a 28-mile journey – only the clock showed an increase of nearly a hundred miles.

So don't talk to me about making hay while the piggin' sun shines and green hills far away. Not far enough, if you ask me. I've been there, mate. I've seen it. And I'm sticking to a deck chair in the Balls Pond Road and a take-away Indonesian. All right, as a concession I'll listen to the omnibus edition of *The Archers* once a week and grow my own basil.

Jack, too, could tell you a tale or three about 'The Country'. After eight years of involvement with *Coronation Street* as a writer, he became the show's producer and one of the first moves he made was to dream up a treat for the cast. After all, he thought, didn't they turn up, rain or shine, at the Granada back-lot for rehearsals and taping days, with tedious and unfailing monotony? Their professionalism was legendary. They made their journeys from Altrincham and Settle and Wythenshawe and Lytham St Anne's week in week out, and in hair-nets, macintoshes and their one good suit, propped up the bar of the Rover's Return, the corner shop, the Church Hall? *The Street.* Wouldn't it be *wonderful*, he thought, to get them *out to the country*. To the fresh air, to the birds and the bees. To breathe again. A treat, to say thank-you to a show which had changed the face of television. An OB (Outside Broadcast) would become the Rosenthal equivalent of an OBE. Oh, man of such naïveté.

When the plan was gloriously announced to the cast, old P.T. Barnum couldn't help but notice a rather muted reaction, ranging from the instant rolling upwards of Thespian eyes, through to heavy sighs and frantic searches for train timetables and ominous mutters of previous arrangements.

Of course it had never occurred to Jack how well the tedious monotony of 'the Street' routine suited 'the Street''s protagonists. It fitted neatly in with lives they had previously organised to fit neatly in with 'Street' life. The last thing any of them wanted was a change in that tried and trusted tradition. There were cats and dependent relatives to be rearranged and personal appearances in enterprising handbag shops to cancel. The original idea of staying overnight in a lakeside hotel was scrapped in favour of a spot within commuting distance of Piccadilly station, and the script compromised by having the residents of 'the Street' club together to visit a nearby stately home. Permission and extra budget were sought out and, with a fair amount of grumbling from them-on-high, granted.

The day of the OB dawned as days do, and the cast and crew convened in a field bordering on to the stately home location. As the first shots were being set up, a crisis revealed itself in the shape of actress Sandra Gough (Irma Ogden), who was moving rapidly from one foot to the other, lifting her knees. When asked what was wrong she revealed that she had a worm phobia. 'I can't act where there's worms,' she cried, tempting the only possible reply that she'd better get out of show business fast, then. Instead, Jack calmed her and cajoled her and diverted her gaze and probably did an ancient Hebraic worm-rebutting dance to boot, and the scene was finally in the can.

A whole new can of worms was ahead. For in the following scene the glorious Jean Alexander (Hilda Ogden) began to duck and weave in a manner reminiscent of Sugar Ray Robinson. 'Cut! What's the problem, Jean!' 'Butterflies,' moaned the actress. 'I can't stand butterflies – oh my God, there's another one . . . ' This on the move as she dashed back to hide behind a van.

Jack was mortified. His generous gesture had backfired horribly. People were grumbling and moaning all around him, checking their watches and their timetables. Nobody wanted to be there – including him by now. 'Telephone for you, Jack, in the production office,' called a PA and off he stalked, angry and hurt, to answer it, muttering all the while to himself, 'Fine, just fine. Be like that. See if I care. You do your best. Who wants thanks? Sod 'em all. Anyone would think butterflies and worms could bite you. My God, I'm a city boy if ever there was one. But you'd think they could appreciate a bit of bloody nature. It's lovely! It's a lovely day out! Nothing's gonna wound anyone or maim anyone. This is the country not Alamein! There are no hazards in the country!' so saying, he reached out for the phone and put his hand on a wasp which stung him so badly that First Aid had to be called from Manchester.

In future they filmed in the studios be it hot, cold or indifferent. After all, if it was change they wanted they'd hardly have been in *Coronation Street* for ten years.

Then there was Tum Hills. In Colne. Jack and his brother were evacuated there during the latter half of the war. It was their second evacuation, their first being the stuff on which TV plays are made. This time, it was to a town full of women, all working on munitions or in the mills, gaggles of women, giggles of women, bravely keeping the home fires and their spirits burning. Lysistrata in Clogland. No men around but shallow, callow youths in short pants, long before Joan Collins invented the toy boy.

Holidays were a distant memory, but the propaganda machine made great play of 'Holidays at Home'. Whist drives in the church halls, community dances, picnics. Breaks from the routine. During the Wakes, the mills were closed down for the week, each town taking a different week to do so. During Colne Wakes Week the women of Boundary Street and around decided their holiday excursion would be to walk down into the valley and up the steep rise to the crest of Tum Hill, where they would picnic and play a few games of Newmarket.

And so it came to pass that the twenty odd shapes and sizes, turbaned and pin-curled, thermos flasks and sandwiches clutched in bulky shopping bags, began their trek. Whooping and giggling helplessly at the difference of it all, they tottered down Exchange Street, past Patten Street and Doughty Street where Frank's Chip Shop served fish and four with scraps for free. With linked arms and lilting voices they went, May and Phoebe, Clara and Nellie, Mrs Beaumont (pronounced Bewmont) and Alsace Lorraine (named for her dad's participation in the First World War).

Trailing behind at some distance came the lads, gaping at the spectacle, willing some monstrous indignity to befall the simple outing, disappointed as finally, wheezing, short of breath and clutching thudding bosoms, the women triumphantly achieved their objective. Cloths were spread and spreads were consumed. And at last, as smiles spread too, the great moment came. Noisily they divided up into groups of five, wriggled down into position, and dealt out the cards. Whereupon the Great Prohibitionist in the Sky played his trump. And as it is said, He sent down a giant gust of wind which smote the gambling women like an avenging angel and carried off into the valley that without which they could no longer gamble. Their cards. Their whoops, rising to a crescendo, floated down to the waiting lads. Whoops Apackaloss! Then slowly they straightened their skirts, gathered up their remnants, and helpless with laughter, leaning on one another for support, dabbing eyes and blouses, they linked arms and walked home. *'Dear Alf. Just another postcard. Had a marvellous day out up Tum Hills. Me and the girls. Played a bit of cards but wind blew 'em off. Laugh? I thought we'd die. Mum and Dad send love. Take care now. Wish you were here. Your loving Edith.'*

While I've been working on this rural mural, my Mother's Help has become helpless. It's not poor Karen's fault, but on a weekend trip home she developed appendicitis, was rushed into Bridlington General, and came out eight days later without an appendix. Rather like this book, actually.

For three weeks I've shopped, washed, ironed, defrosted the freezer (which took a whole day, lacerated every finger I have, and stained the lino with newsprint). I've done two meals a day, supervised homework and piano and demanded gratitude for both. I've cleared wardrobes, drawers and sewn on name tapes. I've been to the Garden Centre and spent £75 on plants, which I've left outside to wilt and then planted. I now have no nails on the lacerated fingers. All this has made a better person of me and if anyone knows a producer of long-running musicals who needs an urgent replacement for chorus work and understudying on the Isle of Dogs, I'm *totally available*. HAS EQUITY CARD WILL TRAVEL. Otherwise I'll clean behind the guest-room beds.

Anyway, here I am, housebound and helpless. I've been to Sainsbury's – it's come on a treat since I last went – they actually helped me to pack my plastic bags and then carry them to the car, as opposed to the usual miserable faces which only brighten when holding up an unmarked purchase high in the air and screaming 'HOW MUCH FOR EXTRA-SUPER TAMPAX, MIDGE?' So that was fun. Then I went to the cobbler's and the cleaner's and the car wash, where I remembered to retract the radio aerial but not to close the sunroof. On the way home I stopped to dry out and pull out the aerial. It refused. I sang loudly to teach it a lesson, and went nose in the air to Woolworth's to buy summer shorts for the kids. Some time later I came out £36 lighter having passed the seed propagator section.

When approaching the check-out I realised that I'd lost the tickets for the cobbler's and the cleaner's, went back to the car, and found a ticket on my windscreen. Since it said Metropolitan Police on it I realised I couldn't use it for soling and heeling or re-texturing a jacket.

Americans to dinner. I've cobbled together some watercress and potato soup in spite of the colour of the watercress. It was green before I put it in the special vegetable drawer of my dream kitchen. Twenty-four hours later it's yellow, and so is the soup. But hell, I've got a salmon cooked by Monsieur Jacques, with Virgoan precision – bring to boil, simmer 10 minutes, leave to cool then skin and decorate with cucumbers and bits of greenery from what I laughingly call my herb garden. Tonight I add strawberries since I can't use them for dessert as they've started growing beards in the fruit preserving section of my dream fridge. New potatoes. Even *I* can't screw *them* up. I put them in the steamer and forget about them. They steam for about two hours till I smell them and remember. Salad, Greek bread, wine, mayonnaise are easy. Except I only remember each one after I've returned from the shops with one of the others. (You will have noted the change of tense here, used to indicate mounting tension.)

I make a yoghurt, cream and grapes dessert from a recipe written by Jo, our secretary, on the back of an envelope. I line a dish with seedless grapes, halved, whip up double cream and Greek yoghurt and try to add sieved brown sugar. The packet says Soft Brown Sugar. You could build the foundations of a channel bridge on this sugar. I bang it on the tiles. A tile cracks. I bang it on the floor; the floor dents. I hit it with a rolling pin. It rolls down the cellar steps. I take it out of the packet in a rectangular lump and try to rub it through a round sieve. It makes a neat ring of sugar all around the outside of the bowl. Jack says there's a very simple way of softening sugar. He heard it on a problems phone-in on LBC somewhere in between incest and paedophilia. He can remember the advice on incest and paedophilia but not on sugar.

I have a brainwave. I put the sugar in the food processor. The noise is like the Battle of the Somme but gradually the rectangular lump becomes a boulder, then a rock, then a pebble, and finally sand. I muse whether God created the world with a Toshiba food processor.

By 5 o'clock I'm exhausted and grey. I'll have a lie down in a minute, I think, dropping a full jar of coffee all over the Amtico. I start to chop cucumber and onion to soak in vinegar. (It's the first thing my mother does on arriving at my house. The second thing is to make a jelly. A house is naked, according to my mother, without cucumber in vinegar and a jelly in the fridge. Obviously I don't want people from Philadelphia with whom I've previously only corresponded to think I run a naked house.) My head starts to throb – I try to will it away. It feels better. I take two paracetamol for fear.

The kids are home. *Starving.* I've forgotten I have any. Kids, I mean. They see the Greek bread and cut wild slices out of it, endangering fingers and, more importantly, look of bread to visitors. I defrost and cook some smoked haddock, chuntering all the while, poach a couple of broken eggs and install them and the kids in the living-room in front of the telly with personal health hazard threats if one drop of yolk soils the velvet-pile.

I then take the world's shortest and coldest bath, paint my face with bronze tint to conceal the death mask, race back down, snatch the remains of tea from the kids – return to the kitchen – open the fridge and find they've already helped themselves to a large piece of the strawberry flan made by Earl, the potter from round the corner (to be passed off as home-made to the guests). Try to push the V-shaped gap together again to make a round. Fail. Decide honesty best policy and plan to tell the story for a hollow laugh.

Two guests, both my agents, arrive bearing belated gifts for my birthday. Phone rings and my Philadelphians are at the tube station, or in their words, 'On the corner of Lincoln and High'. My God, I think – they're in Sherwood Forest! Get into car and race to East Finchley to collect them. Since we don't know what each other looks like, I'm delighted to see a couple waving at me. For a laugh I get out of the car and, waving, race towards them and then straight past, still waving. Instead of amusing this merely puzzles them, as they assume I'm totally cross-eyed or otherwise disabled in some way, and with the politeness of our colonial cousins they don't refer to it. I sheepishly turn tail and guide them back to the car.

Once home, the dinner is a triumph. The watercress and potato soup go down a treat and seconds are ordered by weight-conscious people. When the salmon arrives, gorgeously decorated by Jack with cucumber and lemon and by me with parsley, chives and strawberries, there's a positive 'Ooooh' like in the Oxo adverts, as beautifully performed by actress, Lynda Bellingham, who lives just over the road but never has time to pop over for coffee because her husband runs an Italian restaurant down the road and she's the gofor.

Anyway, everyone eats and conversation runs smoothly until I notice Jack has no plate. 'Where's your plate, love?' I venture, adding laughingly that I often let the staff eat with us to show egalitarianism (which is like vegetarianism except you don't eat eagles). His reply is slightly shocking, more so because it's delivered in a tightly controlled monotone.

'I'm – er – not actually eating – owing to the fact that I – er – appear not to be able to swallow.'

There is a light silence.

'How do you mean you can't swallow? *Darling*?' I say, leaning heavily on the thought transference that if this is his idea of a joke it isn't mine.

'I don't know, really – something has just swollen

up and constricted my throat and I just can't seem to swallow – it's going right round to my ear now – the pain.' Then, somewhat unnecessarily, 'Don't let it spoil your meal, anyone. Just you carry on as if I'm not here', which of course in many ways he isn't.

The room is suddenly filled with suggestions. Dry bread – water – glycerine and honey – casualty departments. All I can think of is how Joseph Heller started with his Guillaume-Barre's syndrome. The one that paralysed him for two years and led him to marry his nurse! My mind is racing. This is what I deserve for letting him do the school run every morning. For letting him stand cooking fish while his mind is on a screenplay, for losing one of every colour sock he has in the wash, for – the list is endless. Meanwhile he is silently choking before my very eyes and the eyes of unknown Philadelphians. As a Punishment.

We mutually decide that his throat has been scratched by a designer crisp. This makes him feel much better. After a while, he seems to relax and although he continues merely to sip water, he can talk, and the conversation around the table resumes. The dessert is a great success and the story of the disappearing flan only adds to their enjoyment of it. Suddenly, round about half way through it, we become aware, as a group, that the non-swallowing host is now lying on the floor of the kitchen with his head *inside* the pantry cupboard, banging and crashing about and muttering to himself in a strangled fashion.

The guests and I all smile understandingly at one another, and resume our conversation. The banging and crashing goes on for about eight minutes until any attempt at conversation has petered out and I silently work out ways of passing him off as an after-dinner floor show. Finally he pops his head out, says, 'I've found it', and clutching a plastic filter, proceeds to make coffee for six. 'It's so hard to get decent staff these days,' I stage whisper to Marjorie, one of my American guests. 'He's a White Russian, actually, and he does marvellous things with beluga caviar and an oyster.'

I wrote the evening off, really. At one point someone asked me what the delicious dessert was called. Beyond politeness now, I replied 'Freda', which baffled the Americans but sent Bryn, my agent, reeling to the floor clutching his stomach. Yet it seemed that I was much more aware of the oddness of Jack's behaviour than were the others. Indeed, when I dropped off my American visitors at the tube later that evening, they said, to a man, what a charming, adorable, warm person he was. I hastened to agree, waved goodbye, then hurried home for a row.

My friend, Astrid, gourmet cook and foodie of long standing, woke in the night recently after a sweat-inducing nightmare. So intense was her distress that her husband awoke and tried to comfort her. 'What was it about?' he enquired, hoping to soothe her panic. 'I can't tell you,' she mumbled. 'You won't think it's *bad* enough.' He promised her that he would. 'Well,' she faltered, 'I was giving this dinner party. And lots of our friends were there. Mom and Dad and Arvin and Joyce were over from the States. And Maureen and Jack were there, and a whole bunch of people, and . . . ' she shuddered. 'Suddenly I realised – I had no *dessert*!' Denis tried to keep a straightish face, so that she'd continue. 'So,' Astrid went on, 'you said you'd go down into Hampstead for some ice cream, and when you came back you had this carrier bag full of dripping ice cream cones – and – oh God, it was so awful – I had to tell them there was nothing to follow . . . '

What I love is the fact that in Astrid's mind this is the

epitome of the worst situation she could imagine herself in. With me, it's going on stage at the Palladium with no idea of my lines, my song or even which musical we're doing.

How did I stray from the country into the kitchen and thus into the subconscious? Anyway, in case you fancy a lousy evening sometime, and because there's really no other way of ending this sloppy domestic saga, I give below the recipes for disaster, not to mention posterity.

Watercress and Potato Soup

Butter for frying
1 small onion, peeled and finely chopped
2 bunches of watercress, washed and finely chopped
½lb potatoes, peeled and diced
¾ pint milk
¾ pint chicken stock
Salt and freshly ground black pepper
Few reserved watercress leaves to garnish

Melt butter in pan. Add vegetables, cover and cook gently for 5 minutes. Stir in the milk and chicken stock, bring to the boil and add seasoning. Lower the heat, half cover and simmer gently for 30 minutes. Stir occasionally.

Purée the soup in electric blender. Pour back into rinsed pan to reheat, adjust seasoning, and before serving float a few watercress leaves in each bowl.

Jack's recipe for cooking fresh salmon

Ask your fishmonger to clean, descale and remove the head of your fish. Place in fish kettle and add water to cover completely. Remove salmon. Add peppercorns, lemon, onion and a bay leaf to water and bring to boil.

Lower salmon into water and bring back to boil. The simmering time is a metaphysical question which has baffled experts throughout the salmon simmering lands. I trust I am not swimming up stream if I tell you that Jack allows it 10 minutes, then goes to switch it off, then loses courage and leaves it for another minute. Others boil for as little as one minute. Still others give in and bake it, and one woman I heard on the radio cooks it in foil in the dishwasher. Straight up! On a low setting. No doubt she washes up in the toilet – however, be that as it may, Jack brings it rapidly to boiling point again then turns it off and leaves it to cool in the water. When cold he skins and decorates it, puts it in the fridge and brings it out half an hour before serving it. Then watches everyone else eat it, refusing to do so himself on medical grounds.

'Freda'

Serves approx 6 persons

Medium sized bunch of white grapes (seedless if
    possible)
1½ pints of double cream
½ pint of natural yoghurt
Soft brown sugar!

Line a fairly large round/oval serving dish (deep sided) with halved grapes. If the grapes are not seedless you must take the pips out.

Whip the double cream and fold the yoghurt into the cream. Pour this mixture over the grapes.

Sieve soft brown sugar on to the surface of the yoghurt and cream mixture until completely covered and about ½" thick. Amount of sugar needed will vary according to size of dish.

Leave in fridge for at least four hours (preferably over night).

The soft brown sugar will change colour and texture to a dark brown, wet look. Check about an hour before serving to see that there are no patches of yoghurt showing through the sugar. If so sieve more sugar on top.

At last Karen returned and I was free to socialise with the jet-set, if only they knew my number.

Actually, I went to a concert, Miklos Rosza's film themes played by the London Philharmonic, conductors Elmer Bernstein and Jerry Goldsmith. I arrived with a friend, Lyn, in good time to meet another friend, Sandra, in the bar. Parking at the South Bank was fraught and I almost abandoned the thing as the minutes ticked by. Finally, as I was being turned away from my third car park, a dapper young Indian and his colleague offered to move their car forward to the wall so that I could park behind them. I thanked them profusely and Cinderella-like promised to be out early after the concert, to enable them to get out of the space.

Lyn and I then dashed into the bar and waited fifteen minutes for Sandra, until I remembered we'd arranged to meet by the box-office. This meant we had to miss the first fifteen minutes of the concert, as owing to the presence of HRH Princess Anne, we weren't allowed to creep in late to the huge auditorium. As the last trumpet of *El Cid* played we slipped, unobstrusively in, and within the space of what seemed like seconds, we slipped out again for the Interval, where I attempted the barrage at the bar.

Worming my way to the front of the massed

punters, I tried to engage the attention of the two beleaguered bar staff by dint of an old trick taught to me by a friendly publican I once met in Ibiza. Which I now pass on to you, dear reader, with foolhardy generosity. The trick is to move sideways not forwards, which since the rest of the crowds are all surging towards him, attracts the barman's eye. So if you are ever in the same bar as a woman doing strange staccato sideways motions and dodging about from right foot to left, it's probably me – so don't queer my pitch. 'Cos I knew it before you did, so there!

Anyway there, across the other side of the bar, I see my Indian benefactor and his colleague beside him. I wave and mouth 'What will you have?' with accompanying finger and thumb wagging gesture. He signals back his thanks and the words 'Gin and tonic', and I do the same to his friend beside him, who looks amazed and overwhelmed but agrees to a lime soda.

Later, whilst having a quiet drink with my friends, the second gentleman approached me in the company of another man altogether. He clutched my hand, pumped it warmly up and down and told me what a thrill it had been when I bought him a drink.

'Well, that's the least I could do after your other friend moved his car for me,' I replied.

'What other friend?' he asked.

'The man standing with you at the bar . . . ' I began to falter.

'Oh, the other man you bought a drink for? I've never seen him before. I just happened to be standing next to him. I was quite surprised, actually, when you suddenly asked me what I wanted to drink . . . '

Sandra and Lyn were spitting their Perrier into the potted palms. I began to cry behind my glasses, with laughter, seeing the incident from his point of view.

'Going out with you,' said Lyn as I dropped her home, 'is weird. Things always seem to *happen*.'

What *can* she mean?

Even my trip to the Palace had its moments. I mentioned it earlier, but here's the full run-down, with pre-match special and action replays. First thing was the Commander of the Queen's Household ringing Jack whilst I was out and he was in the middle of Act 1 Scene III.

'This is the Commander of the Queen's Household' is not a sentence Jack is used to hearing on an ordinary damp Thursday in north London, and it prompted the reply 'Yes and I'm Dick Turpin. Gerroff the phone, Denis.' A little convincing dialogue later, and Jack was the recipient of the news that his wife had been invited up Buck House for a little light luncheon.

When I phoned in later from rehearsals in the Elephant & Castle, he received the same line in disbelief from me. 'Geroff, will you?' I hooted. 'It's Denis pulling your *good* leg.' Finally I was convinced and immediately lapsed into reverse paranoia of the 'Why me? What have I done to deserve this?' variety. I then began to await every postal delivery with the enthusiasm of a postman-hating dog. Alas, contrary to expectations, no gold-rimmed invitation arrived, and after a few weeks I *knew* it was Denis. Just to check, however, Jack phoned the Palace. It's easy – you just look up Buckingham Palace in the phone book and a rather suburban-sounding voice replies, 'Hello, Buckingham Palace. Can I 'elp you?' It transpired that my invitation had indeed got lost in the post, and the next day it arrived, as gold rimmed as a spectacle and twice as easy to read through.

How to prepare for such an event? It appeared there

would only be seven other people there besides me. 'There's no way I can help but screw this up,' I wailed, having imagined it to be more like the Royal Garden Party I'd once attended, which was memorable for the large numbers of delightful ladies from the WVS, vicars, and Lyons Cup Cakes. I phoned Barbara Dickson, who'd once attended such a lunch, and asked her the format. She told me in her soft Scots brogue what she'd worn, how 'She' had behaved and the overall thrill of it all. She advised me to buy *Debrett's Guide to Etiquette* if I was worried about that side of things, although she said the whole thing was so well stage-managed that I shouldn't really bother myself.

The night before the day after, I played *Wonderful Town* somewhat distractedly, like someone with matters of state on her mind, and a great deal of ironic bowing and scraping went on in the wings.

Ben Frow had brought round 'the dress' at the weekend. It was the old Fifties design I love to live in, made up in gent's suiting material in tiny rust and cream check with rust trim, with a circular skirt sweeping the ankles. At 7.05 I shot up in bed, peered through the blind at the cold day, and realised that none of my coats came near to the length of the dress. I could either freeze or look like a bag lady. At 8 o'clock I was rifling through Jack's wardrobe, searching for and finding a jacket in almost exactly the same check, with half its lining ripped out and a rather tweedy smell.

My Mother's Help took out her nimble needlework kit and did us both proud, then, whilst I popped into Goldilocks to have the last remnants of perm removed, she 'Palace-dropped' down at the cleaner's to persuade them to replace the nice macho pong with the heady smell of dry cleaning fluid. And there I was, booted and bespoke, man's jacket, brown leather purse – sort of Vesta Tilley crossed with Kay Kendall.

At least a week before I'd alerted the minicab company that I should need to be at Buckingham Palace at ten to twelve, preferably in a nice clean *posh* car – howzabout a Merc, I implied? The company assured me that they had a swanky line in Ford Granadas and the odd Jag. 'Fine,' I said. 'And a nice shiny driver to go with it, please.' At eleven o'clock I looked out of the window and saw IT arrive. It was a Jag all right. But shiny it wasn't, and the lanky, long-haired, blow-dried gent in a bright blue sweatshirt and jeans was not exactly what I'd had in mind either. There was no time to trade him in and I'm no snob. So I got somewhat sniffily into the rear seat and kept my mouth pursed on the subject of shirts, ties and peaked caps.

'Where to?' enquired my sartorial escort.

I gawped. This had to be the best-kept secret in North London. 'Buckingham Palace. Didn't they tell you?'

'No, I only got this job twenty minutes ago. I was on my way here. Going to 'ave a look at it, are you? You from overseas then?'

'No. I live here. And I'm going for lunch. As I informed your controller several times.'

'Blimey,' he roared with appreciation. 'If I'd known that I'd have given the vehicle a rub-over.'

I could feel my jaws rippling – I'd have to pull myself together or Her Majesty might think I was Clint Eastwood. The journey passed quite affably, actually, and the jaw didn't seize up until we drove through those oh, so familiar gates and the Palace Guards gave us those oh, so unfamiliar salute arms. Then through into the inner courtyard. More guards, more salutes. Suddenly we were at the red-carpeted steps and I watched painfully as my fellow guests dismounted from their gleaming black limos and Rolls, doors carefully closed behind them by their flawless chauffeurs. Only me, *only me*, I muttered, could be propelled out of such a banger by such an escort, straight into the waiting arms of The Keeper of the Queen's Household and at least a dozen designer flunkies.

My worries were, of course, groundless. 'Loved you in *Agony*,' whispered a scarlet-suited footman in coiffed periwig, looking not unlike Maria Charles who played my mother in the same programme. 'Would you like to wash?' The question startled me as I'd spent at least ninety minutes in the bath that morning and had to be the cleanest person in London and the Home Counties. 'Oh. Yes. Please.' My head was spinning on its own axis like the kid's in *The Exorcist*, from trying to take in all the surroundings at one glance. It's a bit like the end of *The Generation Game* when all those objects go past – 'Yes, cuddly toy, cuddly toy, tea tray, electric nasal hair remover – good game, good game.' All I now remember is yellow silk wallpaper and bronze statues and the lady in the wash-room saying, 'Why on earth did he send you in here – I've just put flowers in the other one.' I wanted to comb my hair, but on seeing that the comb I'd brought was a joke one with integral tits and bum, I decided to use my hands instead, thus landing myself with moussed hands for the rest of the luncheon hour.

Another beaming footman escorted me into the Reception Room, part of the Royal Guest Suite, he informed me, adding that he'd enjoyed *Wonderful Town* much more than the original version. Why do I never expect people to lead normal lives in public places? I gaze at two floor-length Canalettos and a magnificent portrait of Queen Charlotte, who looks remarkably like the Queen. Whatever else, I suspect that these are not Athena repros. The carpet is embroidered silk in russety shades like the bright autumn light shining through the long windows. The sofas are fat and traditional, the fireplace marble. Glasses? Shall I wear them or not? I decide not and put them in Jack's jacket pocket, which is somehow miraculously made to disappear, so that's more or less the last visual picture I'll be giving you. The rest will be tastes, smells and sounds.

The eight guests had a certain Agatha Christie Chapter 1 feel about them. One judge, two knights, one headmistress, one art curator, one newsreader (Trevor McDonald), one actress and one bishop – well, reverend. All agreed on one thing. Our reaction to the invitation: 'Why me?' According to the Press Secretary, everybody asked that same question. At this point we lined up formally around the room to be introduced to HM, all glancing towards the open doors, anticipating her entrance. Instead, around the corner came two corgis. I held back on my 'bob' fearing it might be misinterpreted by them.

Seconds later around the corner came the Queen, reassuringly familiar and unnervingly different. She spoke firstly with Mrs Brigstock, the headmistress of St Paul's, whilst I mentally rehearsed my knees into doing what my brain instructed. No fear of repeating what she said to me, as I've blanked it out. The only thing I remember is talking about *Wonderful Town* and bemoaning the thinness of the audience in the pre-Christmas period. Then, for some reason I'll never quite understand – probably my fatal and chronic need to entertain – I told her that the musical *Chess* had been cancelled on Saturday night, giving us rather a decent overflow of Swedes in the house. When asked why it had been cancelled I heard myself say in a somewhat Su Pollardish way, 'Well, the drummer was stuck in traffic in the Finchley Road.' Her Majesty expressed some surprise at there not being another drummer who could have been recruited, at which I chuckled, 'Well, you'd think so, wouldn't you, with Ronnie Scott's just round the corner.' I don't know if she thought I was speaking in code, or whether she had the remotest idea that Ronnie Scott's is a jazz club, but she passed on quite quickly to the next guest, leaving me royally flushed and kicking myself.

It is strange how unnatural one feels in such a situation. I remembered standing next to Wayne Sleep and Su Pollard in the line-up at the Royal Variety Performance earlier that year, awaiting the Royal couple's walkabout round the circle of performers. I'd said jokingly to Su, 'Now, when Her Majesty arrives just move your mouth about and I'll throw my voice, 'cos you're bound to put your foot in it.' When Su was actually confronted by the Queen she immediately burst out with, 'Oooh, Yer Majesty, wharra luvly booquet! Wharrarethy, lilies? Oooh, can I 'ave a sniff?' and so saying stuck her spiky head straight into the Royal posy. I didn't speak at all after that.

Luncheon was served in the 1832 Room (each room in the Palace is dated, so to speak), and was a deliciously light, refreshing menu of watercress soup, salmon en croûte and lemon mousse, served on china I hardly dared touch. The only problem was that each course was offered on a silver salver from which one served oneself with two spoons. Having been brought up in a house where meals were put on the plate in toto, it took me years to get used to taking veg from a casserole dish in front of me, let alone from a silver salver in mid-air somewhere by my left ear. (Mental note: read and learn the social etiquette book you got for a wedding present before next visit!)

As it was, I somehow contrived to get the salmon on

my plate whilst leaving the croûte hooked over the edge of the serving dish and dangling dangerously from platter to plate. (I had a similar job with the mousse. Thank God it wasn't jelly.) Things were going well as I chatted to Sir Edwin Nixon, head of IBM, on my left, about osteopathy, until the Queen's Assistant Press Secretary asked me a question on my right. It so happened that I had a boiled potato on my fork on its way to my mouth, and as I turned my head to speak to him I realised, with a sinking heart, that my potato had left my utensil and was in mid-air, sailing neatly across the room to land on the priceless Abyssinian carpet, which was no doubt the hand-knotted life's work of four hundred blind and underprivileged monks from a silent order in Nepal. Royal flush No. 2. I sat there willing a comatose corgo to eat it, but no. Far too well trained for that – or on a low carbohydrate diet. Who knows? At the end of the meal we all returned to the Reception Room for coffee. As the Queen rose the two dogs leaped attentively to their feet, causing me to remark how very well trained they were. Her Majesty opened one hand to reveal a couple of crushed biscuits, which was all the explanation needed for their obedience. Nice touch.

Before you could say 'It'll all end in tears' the lunch was over, and we were on our way. Final glances around the décor, thanks and coats from the cloaks, and I was outside pretending the old Jag with the sweatshirted driver belonged to someone else. Everything was so beautifully stage-managed – boy, I'd love some stage-managers I've worked with to train at Buck House. Smooth as soapstone, unobtrusive, effiency itself. 'Ee – it were a right good "do".'

On the way home I thought, 'Shall I pop in on a friend and let it all hang out a bit?' but decided against it. I felt rather exhausted and fancied half an hour's rest before going on to the theatre. Back home, and having been charged £22 for a £12 return trip for reasons best known to the driver, I found the house for once deserted. Jack at a meeting, Mother's Help gone for the kids, no builders, no repair men. No one to brag to at all. I tried to ring my friend Lizzie. Out. Julia? Out. Astrid? On an answering machine: 'Hello, it's me. I've been to the Palace for lunch. It was lovely . . . I've just got in . . . everyone's out . . . that's all really . . . Talk to you soon. Bye.'

The Art of Being Well Hung

WELL, IT'S HAPPENED at last – as many of you always thought it would. I'm being hung. Sometime later this year. In Hull. I don't really think I deserve it, but somebody obviously does, so I have to bow my head gracelessly and accept my fate. Immortalised in oil, the nearest I'll ever get to feeling like a fishball.

The summons came from the Ferens Art Gallery in Hull, which I oft frequented as a child, and even more oft as a teenager. Every Tuesday morning, actually. Because of 'A' level History of Art – nothing whatever to do with the art lecturer being a young Dutchman with fair hair and a lopsided smile. Not that I noticed his lop a lot, nor did the rest of my friends from Newland High School for Girls. No, it was Rembrandt and Rubens we were keen to hear about. And Goya – oh, boya! We were just fascinated! The fact that we all washed our hair on Monday nights and rinsed it in vinegar for extra shine was, well, just coincidence. Like arriving wearing our berets hanging off the backs of our heads with a single hair grip and bringing along two-inch heels in a plain brown wrapper to slip on before entering the lecture room. God, we must have been alluring! All hanging on his every word and all racking our brains for the most feeble of questions to ask him after the lecture was over. 'Excuse me, sir .I was just wondering whether you felt that the neo-pointillism of Seurat was er, well – er – well, rebellion against the post-impressionist abstraction of – er – thingy – you know, the one we did last week?' How could he resist us? God knows, but he did.

Ten years later I took Jack to the Ferens to show him my favourite picture. Called 'The Card Player', it's by Meredith Frampton, and shows a Thirties-style lady, skin sculptured like alabaster, playing patience at a round, green table. It's photographic enough to be real, yet graphically surreal, really. He liked it as much as I do, so I then took him to William Wilberforce House, the Transport Museum, and The Land of Green Ginger (the tiniest street in England).

Then I took him home. Home to where my mother was having 'An Evening'. When he was confronted by ten married couples, of which all the men seemed to him identical in appearance, and all of whom asked him, individually, which road he'd taken from Manchester to Hull. Some of them, in fact, didn't ask this question, but since he'd failed to catch exactly what they *had* said, owing to the egg-covered bridge rolls which were going in at the same time the question was coming out, he said, 'Oh, the Manchester-Hull road,' anyway.

At home in those days, people had one picture. It was either Tretchikoff's Green Lady, Bernard Buffet's pointed spires, or, as in our case, a little Jewish tailor sitting cross-legged on a table. Jack had quite a collection in his Manchester flat, or so he said when he asked me up to see them. Honestly, it's etched in my memory. 'Are those Lowrys . . . Lowrys?' I gasped. 'Er . . . I did bid for one once at an auction,' said Jack ruefully. It was in the early Sixties. He'd fallen in love with a Lowry at Sotheby's. He had £400 savings and he rang the Bank Manager and a pal to see if he could raise the other £600 he thought he'd need. At the sale, he sat dry-mouthed until the picture came up. 'Lot 31, L.S. Lowry – Industrial Landscape.' He sat forward in his chair. 'I shall start the bidding at fifteen hundred pounds, thank you sir, I hear two thousand, yes, three thousand, yes. I have four, that's five. I have seven thousand' . . . all the way up to £28,000 (which in those days would have been rather a lot of half-hour sit-com scripts).

Jack's cousin Alex was here recently from Israel. Many years ago he taught a life drawing class in Salford. Occasionally, the head teacher would bring a familiar elderly man into Alex's classroom and say, 'You don't mind if Mr Lowry sits in and watches, do you?' Alex was so embarrassed he used studiously to ignore him and get on with the rudiments of drawing hands. His theory now is that Lowry's whole routine of 'I just draw what I see. When I want to draw a cat, I just draw a dog and chop its ears off' was a sophisticated cover for a man who was as capable of classical realism as the next genius, but knew darn well it wouldn't put butter on his parkin. Still, 'I taught Lowry to draw hands' could be the sort of title to put beluga on Alex's bagel.

There is, of course, an English artist who is famous for painting 'the famous'. Unlike Hockney, however, nothing of the sitter comes through and everything of the artist himself. His gimmick is to send an incredibly flattering letter to a celebrity, informing him or her that society is full of dreary, mundane people, which is why he or she is special, part of an élite who should therefore be recorded for posterity. He then invites them to lunch at his house, where he spends a couple of hours capturing their éliteness. It's cleverer than you think because inevitably the celebrity buys his own painting in spite of the fact that it makes him look like Edvard Munch's 'Scream' executed in tomato soup and pigeon poo. Jack was so appalled by his letter that he sent back a carefully worded refusal pointing out the inherent snobbery in it. A year later he received an identical letter with the same request. Honestly – fresh as paint!

It's a couple of years now since I met the artist Humphrey Ocean. It was on a Capital Radio Show called *Thank God It's Friday.* He'd painted the poet Philip Larkin in Hull, and more recently, Paul McCartney for the National Portrait Gallery. The paintings were unique and wonderful. So was Humphrey. 'I'm going to meet this man again,' I thought hopefully, with the kind of insight with which I'm totally unassociated. So when the Ferens Art Gallery rang and asked me to sit for a painting, I felt pretty smug on learning that it was Humphrey who'd been canvassed into doing the oily deed.

It was an unusual experience for me. Sitting still, I mean. Twice a week for several hours. I kept wanting to get up and feed him. It seemed odd having someone in the house all those hours without giving him salmon patties and oven chips. Mind you, I'm like that with most manual worker 'chappies'. Many's the lunch for thirteen that's suddenly sprung into being on a particularly artisan-strewn day. You know the sort of thing: 'Hello, missus, my colleague and I are a bit on the thirsty side. Have you got such a thing as a bottle of Sancerre '78, nothing special?'

Sitting still made me think. Mostly about painting. When this portrait is finished, scholars may argue about the almost mystically curious look in my eyes. Is it perchance the therapeutic nature of Comedy in European Drama, 1576-1931, which causes me to gaze so astigmatically into my parlour wall, or perhaps the wistful recollection of the range of depth-plumbing roles which have slipped through my thespian grasp? Or is it the fact that Les and Brian, self-styled painters and decorators, otherwise known as 'The Hideous Brothers', are painting Château Rosenthal front and back? They finished sanding down some days ago, and are now patiently drumming their undercoated fingers on the windowsill, silently beseeching me to choose, finally, *please*, between Sandtex 'Smoke', Dulux 'Flapjack' and Berger 'Beaver Fur'. Tomorrow is the deadline. I have seventeen paint charts, three in the car, one in each handbag and eight or nine by the bed. Right now, half the front windowsill is country cream, the other half is sort of motorway-signpost green. The house looks as though the Department of Municipal Parks and Gardens is contemplating a take-over bid.

Tomorrow morning I may cut off my ear. For now though, I'll just cut off these words. Humphrey's on his way round again and I want to fix my face. After all, as Max Beerbohm Tree would have it, 'Most women are not so young as they are painted.'

Morose by Any Other Name

I WONDER IF it's too late to change my name. To Floribunda Blythe-Windowlene. The third. And while I'm
at it I could give my house one of those enamelled
nameplates like people do, combining owners'
Christian names. Like MirMar or ShirlJay or RonCelia.
Ours could be called MoJak. Particularly in view of the
balding brickwork.

I know hardly anyone who likes their own name. I
wanted to change mine the minute I got my first part.
Then I arbitrarily signed the contract Maureen
Lipman, and in the absence of an ink rubber and not
wanting to scrape a hole in the contract with a razor
blade, I was stuck with the rather Cohen-and-Kelly-ish
nomenclature you've come to know and mis-spell. As
far as the paying public is concerned, I'm still 'Whatsit
. . . Muriel Lipton . . . The one related to them tea
people and didn't you love her mother in *Agony*?'

As a child, I fancied myself as a Vicky or a Nicky –
something leaderish and lacrosse-like. It was the era of
Janets and Susans, Sheilas and Paulines – our names
stamping us 'baby boomers' as surely as our keeping
crayons in Ostermilk tins. Mothers were all Freda and
Ruby and Jean and Lily, with the exception of my own
whose name is Zelma – or, as she's been introduced all
her life, often by her nearest and dearest, Thelma,

Zelda or Vilma. She was so nonplussed by my birth
that it was left to Uncle Louis to think of a name – and
Maureen O'Hara was very big that week at the Hull
Odeon. Maybe I should have acted as Maureen
O'Lipman. How much wiser to give your child a
constant and classic name which doesn't turn her into
a mother-in-law joke the minute she's old enough to
start reading those 'Drooping Bustline? Try New
Miracle Rock-tit Cream' adverts. All the little trendy
Mauds and Lydias and Jaspers will turn into perfect
apple-cheeked grandparents. But what of Great-Aunt
Tracey, Grandma Krystal, Step-Uncle Darren?

I've always been fascinated by names. My *Pan Books
of Girls' Names* (pink) and *Boys' Names* (you guessed it)
are so well-thumbed that you could, with careful
forensic investigation, discover exactly what I ate for
each meal during both pregnancies. To start you off –
it's almost certainly spinach between Deirdre and
Dawn, custard over Chloe, and a generous spattering
of rollmop on Esmond and Everard. We casually told
my parents that, should our first-born be a boy, we
would call him Mark Spencer, enabling my mother to
return him if she didn't think he fitted. Our second
suggestion was Christian Ham which, we felt,
combined with Rosenthal, would give my father food
for thought.

Amy was always our first choice for a girl. She was
my favourite character in *Little Women*, slept with a peg
on her nose and suffered from terminal selfishness.
Revelation! Other people had faults like mine! Amy, I
thought, was a wildly original choice. So did every
mother-to-be that year. There are three in Amy's class
of twenty-four. Amy F., Amy D. and my own Amy R.
When Jack went to Hampstead Town Hall to register
her birth, I left the choice of 'Amy Samantha' (after
Jack's late father, Sam) or 'Samantha Amy' to him. He

came back looking sheepish. Ewe-ish. Jewish, even.

'What did you put, Amy Sam or Samantha Amy?' I
asked.

He blushed like a man marooned. 'Er . . . Amy
Samantha *Mumble* Rosenthal.' 'Amy Samantha *what*
Rosenthal?' I whispered piercingly. 'Amy Samantha
. . . ' hand over his mouth ' . . . *Burble* Rosenthal.'

Finally I managed to extract the name by gentle
coercion – like threatening to throw a four-week-old
baby girl at him. In a sudden fit of ethnic aberration, he
had decided to 'sling in a Rachel, just in case'. Yes,
you may well ask! In case of what? So there it was.
And is. Thank God he didn't decide to sling it in
between the Amy and the Samantha, because she
would never have lived down her initials at school.
Perhaps he was remembering his own near escape.
His father had wanted to call him Abraham Moses
Rosenthal. How's that for a nice WASP handlebar?
Short of adding Shylock, he couldn't have piled it on
more. His mother, convinced she was having a girl,
had settled for Jacqueline, so Jack had to settle for half
of it. All he wanted was to be called George – after
George Formby who had the same teeth.

I once followed a large, pram-pushing lady down the
street because I was desperate to know the name of her
child. He was a toddler and he was on the run. She
was giving wobbly chase while screaming 'Tar . . ! Tar
. . . ! *Will* you come back here!' to his departing back.
'If I've told you once, Tar, I've told you a hundred . . .
Tar . . . ! Will you come back here,' etc. I was trans-
fixed (which isn't easy when you're running). Could
this little fellow really be a Muswell Hill Tarquin? Ten
or eleven waddles later all was revealed. 'This is the
last time I'll tell you, Tarzan, if you don't come back,
I'll . . . ' I hope to hell he grows up nice and butch.

We've been ever so helpful over the years with the

naming of friends' babies. Somewhere in the world is a young man of about nineteen who has me and only me to blame for the fact that he has to go through life as a Dorian. I'd just been to see a production of *The Picture of Dorian Gray* when his mother produced him and there it was. Somewhere in his attic he may have a yellow crumbling photograph of the aged Thespian I am becoming and I hope it keeps him young and frisky because he deserves to be.

Soon our dear friends the Kings will hatch forth with a little prince. I've so far suggested Joseph, in the hope that I could announce 'This is Mr and Mrs King and you must be Jo King?' and, since his mother is of Norwegian ancestry, Bjorn Toby King, which has a certain ring of authenticity about it, don't you think? So far my suggestions have totally underwhelmed the parents-to-be. Their mothers-in-laws' first names are Winnifred and Peggy, so Amy, who follows in her mother's footsteps even uphill, suggested Winnipeg. Since we know it's a boy, this handlebar could prove a challenge.

The naming of plays and books can be similarly flummoxing. The sub-title for this book was going to be *And Other Slightly Bluish Material* – until the photograph came out green, which somehow didn't have the same double intent. And wee are the small hours we've spent thinking up new titles for Jack's plays, when the producer has suddenly phoned to say we must have a new title by the following morning or the *TV Times* won't allow us in. How do you rename a play called *P'Tang Yang Kipperbang*? 'Nobody can pronounce it, let alone spell it,' moaned the P.R. man. 'Even after people have seen it they're still calling it *Kipper-Whatsit-Thing*.'

We compiled a list. We had eighty alternative titles, many of them obscure lines from the play or dull references to a schoolboy's life. At one point in the play Duckworth, the young anti-hero, treads on a pregnant spider and hundreds of little spiders run out from it. Jack got hooked into *Spider's Belly, In the Belly of the Spider, Spider's Last Stand* and *Spider's Birthday*, which led to more and more 'insect-asides', all telling you less about the play than *P'Tang Yang Kipperbang* which was at least intriguing to those members of the public who were not serious entymologists. After weeks of head banging the crew begged David Puttnam to leave the title as it was. They loved it. Thus the play was called *P'Tang Yang Kipperbang* by the media and 'That Jack Rosenthal play with the daft title' by everyone else. (In America, it was called *Kipperbang* – much more comprehensible, don't you agree?)

When I receive a script which says on the front, 'We would like you to consider the part of Zyntha', my heart plummets. Somebody somewhere, has spent more time on the name than on the script. Similarly, the ones that say, 'Esther, late forties. Reuben's long-suffering wife. Has been handsome but now drawn with cares.' You show me a Jewish play – I'll phone in the stereotype.

Nowadays no bodice-ripper worth its salt is without characters whose names are as outlandish and far-fetched as the plot itself. Would the *Colby/Dynasty* faction be as riveting if Fallon, Bliss, Caress and Sable were Phyllis, Joy, Pat and Skunk? If you are sitting out there with your pen poised for posterity, you could do worse than take three women – let us call them Ecstasy, Acrilan and Embolism – all step-sisters born to the same woman, the fiery, unpredictable multi-millionairess, Flagella Foreplay III, and three different fathers from the far corners of the world. The poor boiled sweet-maker's son from Cheadle Hulme, Busby Chickenshit; the mystical, one-eyed Indian guru,

Banwee Poon, formerly Solly Kaplan of Brighton Beach; and the bruised and embittered Russian poet and miniaturist, Pulya Bulgeintytesoff. The tale unfolds around the dinner table in the Foreplay mansion at Foreplaysville. Nobody eats. Enter a sinister Irish butler, Yeats O'Pillbox . . .

OK, sister. Take it away – it's all yours. Maybe a little acknowledgement and a tiny share of the publisher's royalties? Nothing special – it's up to you. Oh, and perhaps a small part in the TV mini-series – something telling towards the end of the last reel. How's about a shrouded Cornish clairvoyant, Sian Tellwyouagen, who wears a simple black lace gown by Balmain, which the actress gets to keep? Sister – pick up the pen and write and make us both a very happy woman. One who's rich enough to hire Marvin Mitchelson to sue someone for Wallymoney.

Finally, name joke coming up. Three burglars are apprehended. 'Don't give your real names,' whispers the leader. When asked *his* name, he glances down the street and says, 'Mark, sir. Mark Spencer.' Accordingly when asked, the second burglar looks in the other direction and says, 'John, sir. John Lewis.' The third man, when asked, scratches his head, glances right and left and says, 'Ken.' The policeman looks up. 'Ken what?' he demands. 'Ken Tucky Fried Chicken,' replies the burglar.

Oh. A friend of mine who works near Oxford Street informs me that the shops have decided the festive season is upon us. I should therefore like to wish a Cool Yule, as we used to say in the Sixties, to all readers, but especially to all those called Robin, Holly, Noel and Klaus, and more especially to all those macho South American and Spanish footballer readers whose parents did the Hampstead Town Hall trick and 'slung in a Jesu Maria'.

She Was Only the Grocer's Daughter, but She Taught Sir Geoffrey Howe

'IF YOU ASK me, they're all the same. I wouldn't vote for any of them.' No, not some wheezing old soul gawping into camera on *That's Life*, but I, your *Guardian*-reading author, from her husband's Honda. The time: 1983. The place: outside Labour Party HQ. The occasion: Labour's attempt to counter the extra-ordinary American-style Tory rally which had just Saatchied its way on to our screens. Foot's last stand.

I'd watched with thyroid eyes and unhinged jaw as celebrity after celebrity had mounted the banner-strewn platform to sing choruses of 'Hello, Maggie' to the tune of *Hello Dolly*. I'd witnessed Kenny Everett in Goliath-sized plastic hands shout rallying cries of 'Let's bomb Russia!', and, somehow, through clenched eyelashes, I'd seen She Who Must Be Obeyed, surrounded by Brylcreemed acolytes (ah, where are they now?), telling us that inflation was down (along with the country's morale), that the NHS was in safe hands (it was just the nurses and patients who weren't), and that this would be a great year for the small businessman (the Japanese?).

The whole package was as smooth and sickening as the commercial it was, and when the Opposition asked me to take part in *their* TV rally, I leaped out of my socialist armchair and agreed. However, as it became obvious that all the packaging in the world and Camden Town would never contain the spirit of passionate, dear, erudite Michael Foot – not without the ribbon falling off and bits of duffel poking through, anyway – I had second, third and even Fifth Amendment thoughts.

'Don't go in,' said Jack, as I sat hunched in the front seat. 'Not if you don't believe in what you're supporting.'

'I won't,' I said. He started the engine. I opened the passenger door and said, 'I'll go – but I won't stay.' The politics of compromise.

Inside, I found myself in a very different set-up from the one I'd envisaged. For a start, aside from Mr Foot in a smart suit which somehow still appeared to have toggles, there were only five – ahem – celebrities. There was Melvyn Bragg, ministering for the Arts, Colin Welland, he of the Oscar and the gas commercial, Joss Ackland in a large hat, Larry Adler with his tiny organ in his hand . . . and me, Left-Wing Lizzie. With two kids at private school.

Suddenly, a camera whirred into action and so, simultaneously, did Mr Adler, who began to play *The Red Flag* on his instrument. Everyone – all five of us – joined in with frenzied bonhomie and, in my case, faint heart, since the only words I knew were 'The working class can kiss my arse, I've got the foreman's job at last'. Then we all shook hands, slapped each other's backs, nodded vehemently in the direction of Mr Foot and went home. To Hampstead, Barnes, Covent Garden and Belgravia, presumably.

Everything daunted, I attended, during the same

campaign, another public meeting, in Brent. There were four speakers, two of whom were Sue Slipman and Maureen Lipman – which gave the evening an air of pantomime, we being the broker's men. Sue spoke superbly. I thought I was doing okay until two of the audience left during my speech, leaving a teenage boy and two mothers – one of whom was mine, whisked from platform 6 at King's Cross to a Labour platform in Brent Town Hall.

My family's politics are hybrid. My mother's younger brother was a Labour councillor for sixteen years, an alderman and Lord Mayor; my father's politics are just right of Attila the Hun's; my brother can argue both sides with equal passion, and my mother votes for the one whose wife wears Jersey Master suits. Actually, my father once stood as a Liberal. I remember vividly the yellow posters in our front-room window. How he managed to assimilate his 'Bring back hanging and flogging, two eyes for an eye and a full set of dentures for a tooth' politics into a Liberal manifesto, I don't know. But there he was, megaphone fitted to his shooting brake, calling out, 'Vote Lipman – and you'll get a free tie with every suit!', or such-like, flanked by my puzzled mother in a new blue hat ('Well, yellow doesn't suit my skin'). He didn't get in, and has continued, as he did previously, to vote Conservative.

I suppose it's him I take after when I get consumed by a passion for politics which I can't quite back up with reasonable argument. I wish I had a Pifco Juice Extractor for every time I've had my shins kicked under other people's dining tables by my husband, whose finely-tuned antennae had detected that his wife's political bias was about to ruin yet another NW3 dinner party, attended largely by people who are 'something in the City'. It's just that, naïvely, I assume other people have the same biases that I do.

All right, I accept we live in a right-wing society which is moving righter. A nation of *Sun* worshippers which turns to Page Three as a matter of *coarse*. A public which turns on *EastEnders* as a sublimation for turning on its heels and refusing to vote Nanny in for another lying-in. Better the devil! But, GIRLS, how can you vote for a woman who takes away your MATERNITY grant? Who has given virtually only one other woman in government a voice for years: *Edwina Currie*? And worse! GIRLS – how can you vote for a woman with such appalling taste in men? No, seriously, would you vote for Emma Bovary? Or Britt Ekland? For a woman who surrounds herself with B-film smoothies who at the drop of a sexual or financial scandal resign or disappear with tales between legs they can't even stand on . . .

Before the 1987 election I vowed not to get involved with any of them. 'Why should I be used?' I asked my Uncle Louis over the phone to Hull. 'I'm an actress not a spokeswoman and I'm not sure enough of my line of argument to set myself up as a pundit.' 'Well, love,' said Lou, 'you must do what you feel – but things are very bad in the North, and we need all the support we can get. The only thing that matters is to get this government out.'

I did get involved finally, and I'm glad I did. Two weeks after the election, on a quick package holiday in Florida, Louis was killed in a freak car crash. He had been a Lord Mayor of Hull and a tireless champion of the underdog in the city for most of his working life. He'll never be replaced in my family's affections. So I'm glad for his sake that I pitched out for the party when asked.

Lord knows he would have laughed if he'd seen where I ended up, though. Canvassing for the Labour

Party in Finchley! Yes, I actually received a call from LPHQ saying that we had a chance to win Finchley. 'It's marginal,' said Mr Mikardo. 'Will you go up there and help?' Help!? I nearly got lynched! By people of my very own and golden religious persuasion. 'What are you doin' 'ere?' screamed one peroxide meshuggenah, in clinging crimplene trousers, wobbling her way into Tesco's. 'You should be ashamed!' she screeched, lurching towards me jabbing a forefinger or two. 'I've paid good money to see you at the Hampstead Theatre Club – I want it back!'

She turned away and waddled off, then thought better of it and re-lurched till her not inconsiderable nose was too near to my equally not inconsiderable nose. Then out came the finger again with its jabbing gestures. 'You know what you are? You're shit!' she shouted in full intellectual argument now. 'You're a little shit! You should be strung up! You – you – ' here she struggled for the right word – 'you – SHIT!'

'Thank you, madam,' I managed to blurt out. 'Can I assume from those remarks that we have your vote?'

My dear emancipated friends, I thought my end had come. She was finally dragged off my throat and headed off into Tesco's by understanding passers-by, only to be instantly replaced by a burly man in a surgical collar who demanded, 'Do you know that the people you're standing wiv are the same neo-communists who are persecuting your people in Russia?' I looked hastily round at the rather mild, bespectacled young lady canvassing on my left and said, 'You mean her?' His head, ballooning out from his collar, went Labour Party red, and I thought he was going to burst all over me. I was sorely tempted to mention the Spanish Civil War but for once I kept quiet and turned instead to a supporter on my right wearing a deer-stalker hat with Walkman earphones over the top of it. He wished, it seemed, to discuss swimming. Why are the most vociferous people, the ones with the most pronounced beliefs, the ones who, let's face it, are for the most part barking mad – why are they the ones who always show up? At meetings, at hustings, on walkabouts – the general public just walk about, the meshugennahs all want your full personal attention whilst they tell you, at length, what a misguided and malicious pratt you are.

How do they stand it? The professional politicians, I mean. All that public and permanent mendacity, month after month. Year after year. Even the sincere ones get quickly tainted. All that image-building and reputation-slaying in the name of democracy, and at the end of it another four years in opposition to the Tory Tyrannosaurus Regina. Still, I shall treasure certain moments from the last election, now I'm over my depression. Will I ever forget Peter Snow bouncing around his 'end-of-term' chart in the shortest trousers and the longest suede boots seen since the days of Ian Dury and the Blockheads? The fact that we'd never seen him standing up before gave his antics a whole new dimension, like Sabrina talking for the first time. Yes, I go back a long way, but then so do you if you understand that reference. I personally was desolate whenever he was off, and rejuvenated when he returned, bounding with enthusiasm and utterly, utterly, wildly WRONG.

Nor will I forget Margaret Hilda discussing her summer hols with Denis in a pre-election broadcast. 'Now, dear, where shall we go after we've got the election over with?' she boomed with rhetorical rhetoric. 'I thought we might go to Cornwall again.' She added, somewhat unnecessarily, I thought, 'because we love it so.' Denis did one of his splendid Animal Farm impersonations, and we cut to her walking round the rose garden holding the hand of a small, golden-haired and deeply suspicious child. 'Don't touch the thorns and don't eat the apple she gives you!' I wanted to yell at the screen. 'Oh these *are* lovely roses, aren't they, Samantha?' Honestly, it made one almost long for the Two Davids and 'It's goodnight from me and goodnight from him'.

Neither shall I forget how close Denis Healey came to giving Anne Diamond a bunch of fives on the subject of his wife's hip operation. Dirty personal journalism is a 'skill' culled from the Americans. Address the politican and his opinions on issues, not his wife, his children, his choice of dog. Bah! Humbug! For a woman in the media to regard another woman as part of her husband's electoral packaging, particularly when that woman is as fine, intelligent and honourable a woman as Edna Healey, is beyond my comprehension. It was obviously beyond Denis's as well because the answer was there for the taking. 'My wife is her own person, with her own opinions, she is not responsible to me or to my party politics. She is not running in this campaign.' Incidentally, I might have been tempted to ask, '*Where* are you having your baby?'

It's a shabby, lawless, scary world we're living in, and we get the politicians we deserve. As I came out of the theatre last night I saw yellow! Row upon row of car clamps gleaming viciously with the light of private enterprise. One man, legally parked at 8.40 in a space designated safe between 8 and 10, had been waiting five hours to face a fine and a faceful of abuse. Someone had a 'Join the Free-Your-Clamp Club for £25 a year' poster. I wondered idly if the Club had not been launched by the same firm which organized the clamps. Full circle: 'I am going to set fire to your leg now. However, I can offer you cheap TCP and Elastoplast if you sign here.'

Rhino Neal: A Love Story

IT WAS I who thought of Rhino Neal, not British Telecom. I was so damn pleased with myself, too. It was rapidly approaching Jack's birthday and he's a Horn-Again Rhinophile. As we speak, there are twenty-two tusks staring into mine, and one – wait for it – stained-glasserous one in the window. I don't know why he loves them so much, any more than he knows why I love Mayor Eastwood so much. I think these little mysteries keep the interest going in a relationship, don't you?

Strangely enough, when Jack's cousin Alex and his wife were over from Israel recently she revealed a tiny, faded photograph of a charging rhino which Alex had given her when they first met. She'd kept it in her wallet for twenty-odd years. Jack had only seen them once in the same number of years and they knew nothing of his fondness for the animal. Must be in their familial genes.

So. We were driving to Rye for Sunday lunch. This being my new way of coping with eight shows a week, i.e. perpetual 'flu, maternal withdrawal symptoms and a lower back that feels as though a rhino has squatted on it. This is widely referred to as having a successful career. My parents and children were crammed in the back (get all your guilt out of the way in one 60-mile drive) where strangely tuneless selections from *Chess* were being warbled in fluting falsettos.

As we passed through the well-known watering hole of Headcorn, I saw out of the eye that wasn't obviously twitching a sign saying 'Antique Fair'. This, to Himself and me, being the equivalent of 'Tulle and Beading Fair' to Barbara Cartland, we U-turned and drove in.

Amy collects antique cats, Adam likes foreign coins, Jack anything old in need of a polish (which probably explains why we're still together), and I just like signing cheques on my day off. Even my father once had a yen to own an antique shop, although once it became clear how many yen it would take to purchase one, he decided to stick to antique tailoring.

Only my mother found the whole exercise quite unnecessary. She wouldn't dream of buying an object which had been used by somebody else, very possibly with unclean habits, *and* at nine times its original price, *plus* wear and tear and no St Michael's label.

Mid-browse we saw it. About a foot long, eight inches high, skin folded and pitted, jaw pugnacious and aphrodisiac pricked up. No, not Baby McEnroe. It was Rhino Neal, the rhinoceros of our dreams. 'Too much money,' said Jack firmly, with a longing he couldn't hide, for a hide he could only long for. 'Nonsense,' quoth I. 'It's fate that's brought us to Headcorn and Neal shall be yours. Egad, I'll haggle for it!'

Now, I bet you all think I'd be dead good at haggling, don't you? A born saleslady. Everybody does. My idea of a good haggle is to say, for example: '£200? Really? Gosh. That seems rather . . . erm . . . would you take . . . er . . . well, you wouldn't? Oh, well, I suppose it *is* quite rare . . . erm . . . would £198 seem . . . oh, it wouldn't? Oh, well, great . . . I'll write out a . . . oh . . . and it's £2 for packaging, I see . . . oh, well, fine! Thank you . . . very much.'

In short, Neal came with us for lunch – vegetarian for him, of course, Rye-nosh-for-us – and behaved impeccably. This is more than can be said for some of the Rosenthal family who became mildly hysterical when the waiter asked us if we would like him to 'run through the sweet trolley'. 'Certainly,' muttered one 40-year-old mother of two who should know better, under her breath, 'and then could you walk through the wall?'

Where is misleading? you may be querying. It's leading, my patient reader, to an incident a couple of weeks later when Neal had his 'coming out' party. After devoted grooming and polishing with Brasso, wire wool, and God and Desmond Morris know what else, Jack announced that Neal was neither bronze *nor* brass, and since he didn't know of what he was made, he was taking him to Sotheby's to find out.

With equal devotion, I packed him up in an airline bag covered in polystyrene pellets left over from a cat-attacked bean bag, and off they went out into North London, man and endangered species. A couple of hours later, the phone rang. A crystal-cut voice asked for Mr Rosenthal, and, on learning he was out, said it was Sotheby's speaking. 'But he's with *you*, isn't he?' I said like a suspicious wife. 'He was, yah,' clipped the voice, 'and he's very kindly loaned us his rhino for the party, but we wanted to ask him if he'd like to come along as a guest.'

'What party?' I asked, knowing my husband's fondness for standing up for hours with a glass attached by a plastic ring to a plate full of puff-pastry in the company of scores of strangers saying 'yah'.

'Well, actually, it's a rhino party.' I was silent. 'Are

you there? Yes, it *is* a coincidence, isn't it? We're launching our new book *The Rhinoceros, from Dürer to Stubbs*, and your husband just happened to walk in with his rhino and it makes a most fabulous centre-piece for the table.'

Not only did he go to the party, but, following my suggestion, as only he would, he went wearing his custard-yellow 'Save the Rhino' T-shirt. This meant, of course, that the doorman refused to let him in. Once inside, he joined the bespoke guests and was approached by the organisers with a view to throwing him out again. However, after some heavy name dropping, he was soon accepted as a mildly amusing eccentric, and with the distinct advantage of having read the book which the party was launching, he became something of an attraction. The odd reporter even sought his views on the emotional and ecological underbelly of his T-shirt.

Since then various members of the media have phoned with requests to photograph this shy creature, 'Rhinoceros-Writeros', in his natural habitat. I keep thinking I can see David Bellamy peering through the overgrowth with his long lens in his hand. In the meantime, nightly missives arrive for me at the theatre offering rhino heirlooms in materials from rattan to rubber.

The dénouement is all Neal's. A Sotheby's lady rang to tell us that he was (sniff) 'mere cold-cast resin by an unknown sculptor' and, like most of my acquisitions, almost worthless. Not so. Neal Desperandum. Mr Rosenthal will shortly be dipping into his small pots of bronze paints and the real art of conservation will commence. Listen, it's a sideline – 'Rhinovations Inc'. Whaddya think?

Shleppilogue

BEFORE I START the countdown to launching this book, publicising *All at No. 20* and setting up for my one-woman show about Joyce Grenfell, I thought I might do a sort of spontaneous vanishing without trace. I shall eventually be discovered by members of *The Disappearing World* team somewhere in the vicinity of the Azores, operating a Desert Island Disco, but how I got there will remain a mystery since one length of Hornsey baths makes my chest creak and I'm terrified of plankton. Still, dawn will find me sans contact lenses, sans cordless phone, sans Access card – sounds awful.

Unable to get customer service for *anything*, not just the important things like, say, the carpentry, I shall develop extraordinary skills with a couple of coconuts, a keg of seaweed and a few dingo bones. The disco's prime attraction will be its Shish and Doner Iguanarama stall, and music will be courtesy of a washed-up Irish skiffle group, The Islanders. That means, on hollow trunk – Oran O'Tang, on reed flute – Keroc O'Dile, and on catgut fiddle – Cock O'Toole. Take it away! (That reminds me, my favourite Irish joke: An Irishman went for a job on a building site and was asked by the foreman to distinguish between a girder and a joist. 'Well, that's easy,' beamed the

applicant. 'Goethe wrote *Faust* and Joyce wrote
Ulysees.')

During my many contemplative hours I shall invent a
way of converting wood bark into petrol, to ensure that
recycled newspaper will become a revolutionary new
means of undercutting the oil market. It will also mean
that people can travel to and from work fuelled by
their own beliefs. All my out-of-work actor friends will
finally find a use for *The Stage*, my parents and
relations will visit each other's houses courtesy of *The
Jewish Chronicle*, except on Saturdays, and the buses
can run for ever on those wretched mail order
catalogues which offer such necessities as 'His and Her
Monogrammed Cheese Parers'.

As I lie back on my palm frond hammock (monogrammed by the same mail order firm, also converts
with a flick of the wrist into an electronic, simulated-
mahogany egg-timer), my entire youth will flash
before my eyes. This is fortunate as I shall need all the
flashing I can get to see me through the night. (I'm
such a *secure* person that I only wedge one chest of
drawers under the door knob when Jack's away, and
only move it once during the night for fear of fire
before replacing it because rape is worse than leaping
through secondary double glazing.)

Who shall I chat with during the quiet season on my
island where the Bong-Tree grows? It may be all right
for Edward Lear but nice Jewish girls don't have
philosophical discussions with piggy-wigs – particularly camp ones with nose rings. Perhaps I will
perform Joyce Grenfell for my fans in the gullery. It
will remind me of the time I cried so much in an
aeroplane over the book *Joyce, by her Friends*, that I had
to visit the loo to mop up the mascara. Once there, I
removed my one-piece jump-suit at the split second
that the loo door opened, revealing much of me to

much of the plane. It will, I feel, be as well to remember such magic moments to counter a glut of perfect sunsets.

I shall, of course, post off bottles full of letters to my loved ones each day, mostly berating them for the amount of money I've spent on their education when they patently don't have the brains and resourcefulness to rescue me. I shall also post the manuscript of my _Power, Passion and Perversion_ novella, delicately etched on the bark of a gum tree, in a separate bottle or perhaps a carafe to my publisher. (Acknowledgements: 'To my friendly island snake for teaching me there's more to life than being a bookworm.')

Finally, whilst standing meditating at the twenty-third palm, I shall be rescued. Probably by Richard Branson on a disposable, waste paper, psychedelic hydrofoil, in which he is attempting to shatter the world's free fall, under water, gift wrapping record.

Once home I shall learn to love my new drapes, which aren't quite the colour I'd expected; to accept that my son will never hear any statement I make unless I say it four times or it contains the word 'cricket'. That my daughter will continue to hate boys, pop music and hair brushes until the day I ban all three from the house, and continue to insist her shoe size is still 12½, although it is obvious to all and sundry that her foot is bunched into a permanently hedgehog-shaped ball. That my mother will continue to tell me how wonderful the cast is of every show she sees without ever acknowledging that I was in it too. That my beloved husband will continue to make that noise when eating toast, and will still say 'What it is, you see, is that . . . ' before telling me what it is. That my agent will continue to ring me at home on the days she's booked me in the studios, and that the milkman will never deliver on Thursdays but to compensate will leave six bottles on Monday. That my Mother's Help will have more phone calls coming in than Scotland Yard, but will never answer the phone, and that in two years' time, when my publisher says 'How about another book?' I'll have totally forgotten how bored, lonely and knackered this one has made me and say, 'Yes – let's have lunch.'

Well, why not? When that first person says, 'Didn't you used to be Miriam Lipton?', it'll be something to fall back on.